"We got u

Boston, an

late tonig ***some serious precipitation here—as much as five inches by the time the storm peters out—which will probably take at least three days. Three days of rain and thunder and lightning and just general foul stuff...."***

When the weather outside proves frightful, weddings can still turn out delightful—with a lot of strenuous effort and frenzied courting on the part of three determined heroes!

Three unforgettable trips down the aisle by

JULE McBRIDE
RUTH JEAN DALE
KATE HOFFMANN

About the Authors

Jule McBride received the *Romantic Times* Reviewer's Choice Award in 1993 for Best First Series Romance, and ever since has continued to pen heartwarming love stories that have met with rave reviews, been nominated for awards and made repeated appearances on romance bestseller lists. A native of West Virginia, she is a two-time Reviewer's Choice nominee for Best American Romance, and has also been nominated for a lifetime achievement award in the category of Love and Laughter. Having produced thirteen novels in four short years, she is definitely a romance star on the rise!

Ruth Jean Dale loves all kinds of romance novels, which is why she writes for Harlequin Superromance, Temptation, Love & Laughter and Harlequin Mills & Boon Romance. She made her first sale to Harlequin in 1988 and today devotes herself full-time to writing, a position which makes her feel as if she's died and gone to heaven! She is also a wife, mother and grandmother who lives in a pine forest in Colorado with one husband, one Siberian husky named Mishka, one Border collie named Reckless, a striped cat named Thom T. and a calico cat named Patches. In a previous life, she was a newspaper reporter and editor in Southern California.

Kate Hoffmann began reading romances in 1979 when she picked up a copy of Kathleen Woodiwiss's *Ashes in the Wind.* It inspired her to try her hand at her own historical romance. But when she gave that up to write a short, humorous contemporary novel, she found her métier. She finished the manuscript in four months, placed first in the 1993 national Harlequin Temptation contest, and quickly found a happy home with that line. This talented award winner has gone on to write eighteen more novels, two of which were featured in the WEDDINGS BY DEWILDE continuity series. A former teacher, Kate has also worked in retailing and advertising. She now devotes herself to writing full-time and resides in Wisconsin.

JULE McBRIDE
RUTH JEAN DALE
KATE HOFFMANN

Bridal Showers

Harlequin Books

TORONTO • NEW YORK • LONDON
AMSTERDAM • PARIS • SYDNEY • HAMBURG
STOCKHOLM • ATHENS • TOKYO • MILAN
MADRID • WARSAW • BUDAPEST • AUCKLAND

HARLEQUIN BOOKS
225 Duncan Mill Road, Don Mills,
Ontario, Canada M3B 3K9

ISBN 0-373-83350-4

BRIDAL SHOWERS

This edition published by arrangement with Harlequin Books S.A.

Printed In U.S.A.

CONTENTS

JACK AND JILLIAN'S WEDDING 9
by Jule McBride

RAINING VIOLETS 125
by Ruth Jean Dale

SHE'S THE ONE! 243
by Kate Hoffmann

JACK AND JILLIAN'S WEDDING

Jule McBride

Chapter One

Friday at midnight,
fifteen hours before the wedding...

JACK SIDWELL CHUCKLED softly, squinting into the gift box he'd just opened. "Wool socks?"

Jillian Williams nodded. Standing beside him on her parents' back deck, she gazed at the man she was to marry at precisely three o'clock tomorrow. He was devilishly handsome, with hair the color of wheat in sunlight and amber, olive-flecked eyes that sparkled with humor and glowed with heat. His lips were fuller than a man's had a right to be, and they'd captured Jillian's mouth with countless kisses—some so tender they'd made her heart ache, others so wicked she'd do anything the man asked. Now she playfully stuffed a wool sock into each of his suit pockets. "In case your feet start getting chilly tomorrow."

"Cold feet? Not a chance."

"Good. Because if you haven't noticed, I am seriously in love with you, Jack. So if you do something nasty like jilt me, I'll die posthaste of a broken heart."

"Right there on the white runner, huh?"

"Yep. And not only would you destroy my every chance at happiness, Amy would be totally ruined. Let's face it, unless my kid sister catches the bouquet, there's not a snowball's chance in hell any man will ever take her."

"At least no sane man," Jack agreed with a throaty rumble of laughter. "Your sister doesn't need a bouquet. She needs an act of God."

Jillian sighed loftily. "So true."

Jack flashed her an easy smile. "So, I'm marrying you for Amy's sake? Since not catching the bouquet could be the last nail in her marital coffin?"

"In her *hope chest,*" Jillian corrected. "And just think. If you don't show tomorrow, those white net bags of birdseed won't be thrown. All those poor little wrens will starve and..." Exhaling a sudden rush of air, Jillian breathlessly said, "Oh, Jack, I can't even joke about this anymore. Please, can you just hold me?"

He drew her close. The hands that parted the front of her sky blue blazer felt warm through her white blouse as they circled her waist. He leaned against the handrail and pressed a gentle kiss to the top of her head.

Nearby, light from the family room shone through sliding glass doors, adding to the soft, romantic glow of the twinkling white stars and pearl moon overhead. Gazing into Jack's eyes, Jillian felt suddenly sure she would burst from sheer excitement. Her heart swelled; her cheeks felt warm from smiling, despite the cool, dewy spring air. They'd had such a wonderful sunset. *Red sky at night, sailor's delight,* she thought.

"Okay?" Jack whispered.

She nodded.

"Don't worry, Jilly. You're doing the right thing. I *am* the most irresistible guy you've ever known, right?"

Feeling steadier, Jillian rested her palms on his lapels. "Discounting Ruffhouse? Absolutely the most gorgeous." Ruffhouse was the Williamses' Yorkshire terrier.

"And here I thought you loved me for my intellect," Jack protested huskily, murmuring the words against her neck, leaving behind a trail of damp, burning kisses.

Jillian smiled. "Hardly."

His answering smile was lazy. "It's almost bedtime."

"I won't sleep a wink."

"Good. So the sandman—" the suggestive wiggle of Jack's eyebrows said that meant him "—should sneak into your bed."

Because the nearby Sidwell estate had been leased while Jack's mother traveled abroad, Jack was staying overnight at the rectory, with Jillian's family. "Are you kidding?" she returned archly. "Tonight? With my Bible-thumping papa on the prowl?"

Jack laughed. "Oh, c'mon. He's a minister, not a farmer. He doesn't even own a shotgun."

Jillian's lips twitched. "No, if we got caught in bed together, you'd merely have the wrath of the Almighty to contend with."

"Oh, is that all?" Jack's amber eyes drifted possessively over her. "Well, as wicked as I intend to get with you, Jilly, I'd deserve every hailstone and lightning bolt."

"I think that's brimstone, Jack." She playfully poked his chest. "But have no fear. Tomorrow night we'll be legal. And in the Virgin Islands. Alone."

"And you'll be at my mercy."

"I can't wait."

As if counting the seconds, Jillian glanced pointedly at the delicate gold wristwatch Jack had given her when she'd named the wedding date. As well as being the more impulsive, creative of the two, she was also the least prompt. Jack said the watch would ensure she reached the altar on time. Now she lightly tapped the face with a French-manicured nail, a hitch of excitement in her voice. "Only fourteen hours and forty-four minutes left, Jack."

"And then you're mine."

The warning was ominous, but the naughty twinkle in his eyes said he had plenty of ideas about how to while away these last remaining hours. Especially when his gaze drifted drowsily over the blue suit she'd worn to the rehearsal dinner. The color was good on her, deepening her blue-gray eyes and making her short, dark red hair vibrant.

His expression became severe. "Aren't you afraid I'll turn into a frog again after tomorrow?"

She frowned. "I guess I'll just have to keep kissing you, so you'll stay a prince." She tilted her head, surveying him.

"Ah, Mrs. Sidwell," he murmured, trying on the name.

"Mr. Sidwell," she murmured back.

His voice was husky. "What are you thinking now?"

"About the night we met."

"The night I fell in love with you?"

"Did you really?"

"Yeah. At first sight."

They'd met exactly thirteen years, five months and three days ago—Jack always kept track. Jillian's father—or rather, the stepfather who'd raised her from infancy—had just been transferred from urban South Boston to Lace Point on Massachusetts Bay. The area boasted sprawling estates, including the Sidwells', that hugged the coast and housed wealthy commuters—to Cambridge and Harvard, to the financial district and publishing offices on Beacon Hill.

Mere miles from the cramped South Boston apartment where she'd previously lived, Lace Point had seemed a whole new world to Jillian, so the last place she'd wanted to go during her first week in town was to a party alone. But, as the daughter of the new minister, she'd been invited to a formal

Christmas dance. Never before had she visited a house so large. The simple white dress that had been so perfect in South Boston was hopelessly provincial compared to the designer clothes worn by the other girls. All the boys had seemed so much older and sophisticated.

Especially Jack. Even back then, he'd moved with his hips, not his shoulders, in a way that was suggestively sinuous and faintly predatory and that announced his sexuality and quiet strength. When their eyes met, Jillian's heart had fluttered. And when she'd realized he was strolling toward her, she'd wanted nothing more than to run. Moments later, her ninth-grade knight was gently coaxing her onto the floor for a slow dance, saying, "Hey, I'm Jack."

Even then, he'd had a warm, rich voice that could do wicked things to a girl. "I'm Jill," she'd managed to answer.

He'd thought she was joking. When she finally convinced him she wasn't, they'd both made silly jokes about walking up hills, pails of water and broken crowns. "Jack and Jill," he'd finally said. "I guess this means we're meant for each other."

And they were. Jillian had felt it that night—deep in bones that melted beneath Jack's touch. As they danced, her gangly teenage limbs had turned graceful and fluid, and under his discerning gaze, the dress that hadn't been quite right suddenly seemed perfect. Before he'd relinquished her, Jillian was already imagining how his lips might feel pressed hard against hers. Not that he'd kissed her. At least not for two more years.

Now she squeezed his shoulders, loving the powerful feel of them, the strength she laid claim to as his future wife. This body, so virile and utterly male, belonged to her.

His voice was as soft as the night breeze. "Nervous?"

She shook her head in denial. "How could I be? We've waited so long, Jack." Too long.

Thirteen years.

Turning in his arms, she looked over the lawn and inhaled deeply. Jack's scent mingled with the mixed-up, pungent smells of the April night—the salty ocean breeze, some green wood burning in a bonfire downwind on the beach, the dark black earth from the woods flanking the rectory. Closer still were scents of flowers and freshly cut grass. A radio inside the house was playing rock and roll oldies. Recently installed floodlights illuminated the wide expanse between the rectory and the church proper, and it was on that lush field of rolling green that the wedding would be held. Already the white reception tent was set up on the lawn; inside, the gathered fabric walls were strung with tiny white lights. Grecian columns topped by potted ferns graced the four corners, and the buffet and cake tables were swathed in gossamer peach fabric.

"It's going to be perfect, Jack."

Threading his fingers through her hair, he ruffled the short strands. "You're worrying."

"I'm not really."

But she was. If only for her mother's sake, she told herself. Barbara Williams had planned this wedding so carefully. The owner of a bed and breakfast was providing rooms for out-of-town guests, and tomorrow, the florist, organist, videographer and photographer would arrive. A four-man ensemble would play at the ceremony, jazz musicians at the reception. On a modest budget, she'd wheeled and dealed to make everything just right, and countless business owners in the congregation had offered services as gifts.

So far, the weather forecast had called for sunny and warm, so rows of chairs for the ceremony had already been arranged. Urns of crisp green ferns would grace the aisle. Soon the white runner would be unfurled.

Jillian suddenly pressed a hand to her heart. Staring into the empty darkness, she could actually see it, exactly as it would be tomorrow: walking down the runner in her white satin sheath, her face covered by the veil from Filene's, her trembling fingers clutching a nosegay of lotus pods, peach roses and pansies. Her bridesmaids—clad in peach, Empire-style dresses—were smiling their encouragement from the end of the runner.

And Jack.

Always Jack. He'd be inwardly fidgeting, she

knew. Calm as a statue, but fighting the urge to fiddle with loose change in his tux pocket.

"Oh, Jack," she suddenly said. "I just hope the cake's okay."

He squeezed her shoulder reassuringly. "It's fine."

She'd designed it herself—a white, four-tiered basket weave cake decorated with mint-colored leaves and delicate peach roses.

"And the tree," she murmured. The only thing still marring the landscape was a diseased elm near the tent.

"Don't worry. It's being removed first thing tomorrow."

"But what if Mom changes her mind and tells them to tear down the tree house? She keeps saying it's an eyesore."

"They won't tear it down, Jilly. I promise."

Backlit by the gray-white oyster moon and nestled in the leafy branches of a stately oak, the old tree house was where Jillian and Jack had first made love. Not that Barbara Williams knew that, of course. Or that to this day, hidden in a knotty crook, was an old Whitman's Chocolates box containing Jillian's childhood treasures, including the blue hair ribbon she'd worn that special night.

Tomorrow really marks the end of my childhood, Jillian thought now. And the end of six months of wedding planning. She and Jack were about to cross the final threshold—from childhood to adulthood.

From single to married life. Suddenly everything seemed heavier, fraught with emotion. All the preparations had been made. Everything was in place. Now all they had to do was take their vows.

Her voice caught. "It'll be the best of all our weddings."

"And to think we almost eloped."

"Wedding one," Jillian said, sighing wistfully.

Jack had been eighteen, and right before he was to leave for Oxford University in England, Jillian had sneaked out her bedroom window to elope with him. Her half sister, Amy, had raised the alarm, and the Lace Point police had pulled Jack and Jillian over. In an all-night Sidwell-Williams sit-down, the young couple had been persuaded to attend college first.

Now Jillian laughed. "Amy's no more wedding friendly than she was at age seven." At seventeen, Jillian's sister was a self-proclaimed women's activist.

Jack frowned. "Is she still referring to me openly as 'the white male oppressor'?"

Jillian nodded. "Let's just hope she doesn't voice her opinions when Daddy asks if anyone objects to our marriage."

"And that she doesn't wear Doc Martens under her bridesmaid gown."

Jillian felt suddenly preoccupied. "I did get her to remove four of her earrings."

"That's a start."

She sighed. "Well, this third time's the charm, Jack."

Neither mentioned wedding number two.

It was to have taken place two years ago. Jillian had almost finished creating the menu when Jack's father was diagnosed with bone cancer. Shortly after his death, Jillian's grandmother had passed on. By then, Jillian had been accepted to culinary school in New York, and Jack had taken a job in the financial district in Boston.

For so long, things had interfered. Parental wishes. Geographical distance. Schooling. Illnesses. Family deaths. But recently, with money left to Jack by his father, they'd combined Jillian's culinary talents with Jack's business sense and opened "Jack and Jill's," a struggling but promising café and pastry shop in Boston's North End. They'd rented a newly renovated walk-up apartment on a nearby street, though they couldn't move in for another two weeks. The place wasn't fancy, not Beacon Hill, but it had plenty of old-world charm—a cobbled courtyard and window boxes blooming with spring daffodils.

"We *have* to get married this time," Jillian said.

"If for no other reason than you're setting more wedding dates than Zsa Zsa Gabor and Liz Taylor combined."

"I just wish..."

As usual, Jack read her mind. "Someone could still walk you down the aisle."

"No. I'm going alone. It's the only thing that feels right."

Harold Williams wasn't Jillian's biological father, but he'd raised her from infancy, and she and Jack wanted him to preside over their ceremony. It had been decided that he'd wait for her, with Jack, at the altar.

Deep down, maybe walking the aisle alone was a sort of protest on Jillian's part—a gesture meant to mark the absence of her other father. After all, foreign news correspondent and photojournalist Nate Ralston had never even offered to become part of Jillian's life. He'd been starting his career when Barbara became pregnant. And while Jillian hated him for caring more about his work than about her and her mother, she still craved some kind of relationship. Didn't Nate Ralston ever think of her? Miss his daughter? His flesh and blood?

As if sensing the turn of her thoughts, Jack buried his lips in her hair again. "Maybe one of these days he'll come around, Jilly. Meantime, so many people love you. Especially me."

"I especially love you, too, Jack."

"And don't worry. Wedding number three will go off without a hitch."

That made her smile. "Without a hitch? I'm not sure that's good for a wedding."

"Oh, we'll get hitched, all right." Gently, he squeezed her shoulders, turning her fully toward him and sliding his palm around the nape of her neck.

"Kiss me, Jack," she whispered.

"I was just about to," he whispered back, right before his lips settled over hers. When his tongue followed, her body went limp, and she leaned into him like a flaming taper—its wick burning at the core, its wax hot and melting. As her tongue warmed against his, whispered phrases flitted through her mind. *Lawfully wedded husband. Married in the eyes of God. Until death do us part.*

You could say you loved a man, Jillian thought. You could love him with your body, lying naked in his arms until the wee hours, talking in whispers and sharing all your secrets. A million times your heart could flutter at the mere sight of him. Day after day you could run toward him like a schoolgirl, with love making your steps light, as if you could never reach him fast enough.

But somehow only marriage made it all real. *Tomorrow Jack and I will finally be married.*

His kiss had stolen her breath, and as she leaned back in his embrace, she smiled and tapped the watch face again. All around them everything was so still, so quiet. "Fourteen hours and twenty minutes."

His voice was husky. "Nothing can stop us now, Jilly."

"Absolutely nothing," she returned.

But just as Jack's lips grazed hers again, a loud clap sounded. Startled, Jillian wrenched in his arms just as a jagged electrical bolt sizzled overhead. Low rumbling thunder grumbled through the heavens. And then dark ominous clouds rolled across a sky that had been clear only moments before.

She tilted her head, suddenly cognizant of the DJ on the radio inside. "Remember that schmaltzy old song called 'Singing in the Rain'?" he was saying. "Well, nobody's going to be singing in *this* rain. I've been handed a weather advisory that's enough to make a grown man cry. A nor'easter's hitting Boston late tonight, and we're in for at least three days of rain, thunder and lightning. Well, a man can take only so much bad news, so let's hear some Elvis!"

"Heartbreak Hotel" began to play.

"Not another freak nor'easter," Jillian whispered in shock.

Jack shook his head. "No, not on the night before our wed—"

But he didn't even finish. Because the sky opened. And a hard rain began to fall.

Chapter Two

Saturday morning, nine o'clock,
six hours before the wedding...

"JILLIAN?" Jack pounded on the bedroom door. "Are you in the bedroom or the bathroom? And what are you doing in there?"

Oh, nothing unusual, Jack. Just sitting on the closed lid of the toilet in my wedding gown. She glanced around. Three doors led from the bathroom—one to her bedroom on the right, another to Amy's room on the left. Jillian faced the third, leading to the upstairs hallway. All three doors were locked.

Still she'd found no privacy.

Poor Ruffhouse was in the bathtub, hiding behind the shower curtain with his tail between his legs, terrified of the raging storm. Jack was shouting. And Amy was on the other side of the door to the right, sprawled across Jillian's bed.

It wasn't exactly how Jillian had imagined the glorious morning of the big event.

Even worse, the full-length bathroom mirror was a constant reminder that she'd gained a pound or two since yesterday, when she'd last tried on her gown. A gown that now pinched around the waist.

"Jilly?" Jack shouted. "Are you *sure* you're all right?"

"Just fine," she called. But she felt faintly nauseated. And it was far more than prewedding jitters. A small wooden stick seesawed precariously on the lip of the sink, and the double line in the window panel on it indicated a positive pregnancy result. Just how reliable were these home pregnancy tests, anyway?

"I'm pregnant," she murmured. *On our wedding day.* "And Jack and I are usually so careful." As she recalled a particularly sexy, heated moment that had been an exception to the rule, everything inside her fluttered.

A baby, she thought. Just as joy bubbled in her throat, so light and frothy she thought she'd burst, she had to fight down a wave of queasiness. Was it really morning sickness or just sheer nerves?

"C'mon, we've got to pick up my mother at the airport."

"Jillian's in the bathroom, Jack," Amy shouted.

"Well, what's she doing in there?"

"Probably watching her future life flash before her eyes," Amy returned. "You know, the usual. Dishes. Laundry. Serving beer and pretzels on poker nights. Being passed over for Monday night football. Pretending not to notice when your hairline recedes. Being old and gray and trying to remember when she first started getting high-waisted cotton panties in her Christmas stocking rather than those sexy nighties from Victoria's Secret. Dirty diapers.''

Jillian gasped. *Dirty diapers!*

Had Amy guessed? Jillian's quick inhalation reminded her that the gown was too tight. As happy as she was about the baby, panic made her heart pound. *Great. I'm going to walk down the aisle in a dress that fits like a latex glove.* If there *was* an aisle. Outside, thunder crashed ominously.

Jack was getting testy. ''Jillian?''

''Jack, honey,'' Barbara Williams called now, ''I really don't think you two should go anywhere in this storm. Not even to pick up your mother. Can't she get a cab?''

Her query was met by silence.

No doubt *that* had made Jack livid. He was very protective of his mother.

Just thinking of Miranda Sidwell made Jillian doubly nervous. Miranda, with her year-round suntan, silver-white bob and wardrobe of navy and cardinal red, was the quintessential Lace Point matron. From the age of forty, when her only son was born, she'd presided over every aspect of his life, however minute—at least until Jillian had named the wedding date.

Then Miranda had abruptly leased the Sidwell estate, promptly packed her bags and left town. Miranda was well versed in Emily Post, which meant she knew hosting the rehearsal dinner was her responsibility, but she hadn't bothered. Jillian guessed it was her way of saying that Jillian wasn't good enough for Jack. As if Miranda hadn't implied that at every opportunity for the past thirteen years.

Oh, maybe Jillian hadn't studied at Oxford University, like Jack. Or gone to fancy summer camps, like the more advantaged kids in Lace Point. But Jillian's father was a minister, and she was respectable. Well, more or less. Her trembling fingers cupped her curving belly, and she tried not to imagine her father's reaction if he ever guessed she'd been pregnant when she took her vows.

"Why couldn't Miranda be a little more thoughtful?" Jillian muttered. Why couldn't she have flown home before the eleventh hour? And how could she expect the bride and groom to pick her up at the airport in a storm, just hours before the wedding?

If there was a wedding. The tempest outside really didn't bode well. Another thunderous crack sounded, and Jillian ducked instinctively while Ruffhouse dived for the edge of the shower curtain again. More angry crashes followed, sounding like dishes being flung down from heaven. Jillian stared bleakly through the dark square of window behind her; it was marbled with clouds. Rain slashed the panes and gurgled in the drainage gutters.

Jack's exasperated shout came over the howling wind. "Please, Jillian, couldn't you hurry?"

Why wouldn't he quit yelling? Seeing as she was locked in the bathroom, didn't he suspect she was totally on edge? "I'm coming, Jack!" *Coming apart at the seams, anyway.* Literally. She studied where the wedding gown hugged her waist. Yesterday, she could swear, it had still fit perfectly.

Jack's tone carried a warning. "Don't start yelling at me."

"I'm not yelling," she yelled.

Feeling overwhelmed, Jillian carefully buried the home pregnancy test indicator and box in the waste basket. For good measure, she plucked tissues from a holder on the back of the toilet, then artfully arranged them in the waste can, hiding the test box. *That should do it.* All she needed was for Amy to find out she was pregnant before she could tell Jack.

But what was she going to say?

Jack could be so rigid and controlled. He was a planner. According to him, this pregnancy wasn't scheduled for two more years. Jack wanted to forge their joint identity as a married couple first, put their café in the black and save a down payment for a house. Although he'd never understood Jillian's adamant refusal to accept financial help from his family, he'd finally agreed that they'd be entirely self-supporting, even if it meant sometimes doing without.

She groaned. Amy *was* right. Her future life was flashing before her very eyes. For example, she knew that when her pregnancy was announced, Miranda Sidwell would undoubtedly offer to buy them a house.

"Nothing special, mind you," Jillian's mother-in-law would say, "but I picked out a nice four-bedroom brick, with a fenced-in yard. Jillian," she'd continue, pumping out the guilt, "are you really going to refuse this meager gift and make your poor child, my only grandchild, suffer? Will that little baby—not to mention my deprived son—have to live in a cramped apartment just because of your juvenile pride?"

Yes. And Jillian didn't intend to accept all the expensive furniture, baby clothes and toys that would follow, either. Of course, that would prompt a blowout fight with Jack. Even though he'd promised they'd be self-supporting, he'd want to let Miranda help. But Miranda's gifts, even the smaller ones, might come with strings. And Jillian wasn't about to be jerked around like a marionette for the rest of her life. Besides which, her own parents would feel bad because they couldn't help out the kids in Miranda's high style.

Jillian suddenly blinked. She hadn't even told Jack about the baby and she was already anticipating *Miranda's* reaction!

She forced herself to stand. Catching a glimpse of herself in the mirror, she found unexpected tears pressing her eyelids. Boy, she'd been off base. She'd thought her missed periods were due to the bustle of planning the wedding. "Buck up," she murmured, coaching herself, "the gown isn't *that* tight."

But it was.

She plopped down on the toilet lid again. Why was she even worrying about the snug dress, when she'd just discovered she and Jack were having a baby? *Because gaining two pounds is far less intimidating than motherhood,* she thought anxiously as she clasped her hands in her lap with exaggerated calm.

Ruffhouse peered at her with concern, his paws resting on the lip of the bathtub. Small, white plastic barrettes shaped like wedding bows clipped his long bangs away from soft, liquid brown eyes. The doggie wedding barrettes were another of Barbara Williams's thoughtful touches.

"Well, both of us really do want babies," Jillian whispered. "So what if this one's coming two years earlier than Jack expected? Right, Ruffhouse?"

For the first time since the storm began, the terrified terrier barked agreeably, then he thumped his tail against the floor of the tub, as if in encouragement.

Rising, Jillian inhaled deeply—at least until the gown's tightness cut off her breath. Well, she and Jack could easily weather an unexpected pregnancy. Opening the door, she strode into her bedroom.

Amy glanced up from the bed. Dressed in threadbare jeans and a sweatshirt, she was twirling her long red hair around an index finger and popping gum. "Hey, sis," she said between purple bubbles, "I put some blue nail polish in your top drawer."

How could Amy lounge around so casually when all hell had broken loose this morning? *Well, that's the trouble with pulling together a first-class wedding on a shoestring budget,* Jillian thought now. *Shoestrings can unravel.* "Blue nail polish?"

"Yeah, you've got to wear something blue. Remember?"

Jillian barely heard. Oh, she and Jack had known each other a long time, she was thinking, but they'd so rarely mentioned children. In exactly two years, the first was to have appeared in the magical, balanced equation of Jack and Jillian's lives. Now Jillian even remembered saying, "Our kids? Oh, Jack, don't worry. They'll be real cute and make everybody happy."

How flip, she thought. How glib! What about reality? What if she and Jack disagreed on specifics—such as schooling, day care, finances? *Which we will.* Wasn't that the real reason neither ever broached the subject?

"Earth frequencies to Jillian," said Amy. "Please tune in."

Jillian stared down at her hands. "Uh, thanks for the blue nail polish, Amy, but I already got a French manicure."

Amy rolled her eyes. "I know. The blue's for your toenails."

"Fine." Something old was a pair of heirloom earrings. New was a necklace from Jack. Borrowed was a pair of her mother's gloves. Blue had been a pending issue for days.

As Jillian turned toward the closet, she caught another glimpse of herself in a vanity mirror. At least she'd fit in with her wedding party, she thought dryly. She and Jack were the last holdouts of the old gang. They'd waited so long to get married that three of Jillian's five bridesmaids were pregnant. And not with first babies. It was why Empire-style, high-waisted gowns had been chosen.

Of course, one bridesmaid *was* divorced.

That thought made everything slide off-kilter again. Divorce was definitely the last thing Jillian wanted to contemplate this morning.

"Jillian, did an ambulance just drop you off or what?"

She stared blankly at her sister. "Hmm?"

"I said, where's the wreck? You've been standing there for five minutes like a trauma victim, and I still don't hear any sirens."

"Oh."

"You know, you don't have to go through with this, sis."

Jillian lifted a hand. "Don't even start, Amy."

"Well, marriage *is* a mere construct of patriarchal hegemony," declared Amy. "Since it's economically based, it's historically residual. Today's woman *can* fulfill her own needs...."

Jillian had no idea what Amy was talking about. Sighing, she stared out the window. The diseased elm that was to have been removed this morning had fallen and crushed the lovely white reception tent, while last night's gale-force winds had blown away the chairs arranged for the ceremony. Right now Jillian's brother—who'd arrived home from college with his hair dyed bright straw yellow—was chasing chairs in the rain with his school buddies.

"No wonder weddings only happen once in a lifetime," Jillian murmured over Amy's diatribe. "What a mess."

Jack pounded harder on the door. "Jillian, c'mon."

"I'm sorry. I'm coming, Jack."

"Look..." He was losing his patience. "Are you decent?"

"Yeah."

He flung open the door.

Jillian just about fainted. "How could you, Jack!" she exclaimed nervously. "I'm in my wedding dress, and all we need this morning is more bad luck!"

As testy as he was, his eyes softened at the sight of her. "How could seeing you be bad luck when you look so gorgeous?"

He looked so sexy in his bone slacks and chambray button down that he almost had her. Maybe her nerves would have calmed if he hadn't continued. "Now, I'm really sorry I opened the door, Jilly. But we've *got* to go. My mother..."

I can't believe you just saw me in my gown—and

all you can talk about is your mother. Before Jillian could respond, her own mom bustled down the hallway, toward the stairs.

"Jillian, Jack's not supposed to see you in that dress!" she admonished playfully.

"I know," Jillian snapped.

What's wrong with me? Even her mother's cheerful demeanor, usually such a comfort, was now unnerving her. Seeing the water damage this morning, the unsinkable Barbara Williams had simply grinned and said, "Well, the show must go on!"

As if Jillian and Jack were singing a Broadway musical today instead of exchanging sacred vows.

"Rain's great luck on a wedding day!" her father had said.

"But it's not supposed to rain," Jillian had protested. "I'm supposed to walk down the aisle, not row up on a raft! And how was I to know I should have chosen orange dresses for the bridesmaids—to match their life preservers?"

Everybody said she was overreacting. Jillian had no idea why. This was her *wedding,* for heaven's sake.

Now Jack blew out a long-suffering sigh. "I repeat, I'm sorry I saw you in the gown, Jilly. And you *are* absolutely beautiful."

"A little more bad luck can't possibly hurt at this point," she conceded.

Her mother's head popped around from the stairwell. "Don't worry about a thing, you two. If the jazz ensemble can't get here in the storm, Brian's offered to play at the reception."

Over my dead body. Jillian loved her brother, but his sophomoric delusions of grandeur included thinking he was Jimi Hendrix reincarnated. He wasn't. "Mother," Jillian said shakily. "Brian plays electric guitar. And badly."

"I know, dear, but I'm doing the best I can. The landscapers said they can't move the elm in the rain, but Major Phillips does think he might have another tent...."

The retired war veteran was a member of the congregation. Jillian's heart sank. "You mean, like a camouflage *military* tent, Mom?"

Her mother looked only faintly concerned. "Oh, I know it won't really do, but it was nice of him to offer. Don't you think? Anyway, I just want you to quit worrying. Your bridesmaids will arrive soon—and I know the sun will come out. It simply can't rain on your big day."

Right. Jillian stared through the window at the angry storm, then her eyes pleaded with Jack's. Why wouldn't he help convince her mother to work on alternate plans? "I don't want to be negative, Jack," Jillian whispered, "just realistic."

Jack shrugged helplessly.

As her mother vanished downstairs, Jillian raised her voice. "Mom," she ventured weakly, "if Sumner Tunnel isn't reopened, the cake won't get here. The ferns inside the tent are unsalvageable, and the photographer is at home, pumping out his flooding basement. Uh, maybe we should move the wedding inside the church...."

Barbara reappeared, quickly pulling a bobby pin from a messy red bun, then stabbing it back in. Deep apology shone in eyes that were a lighter blue than Jillian's. Her mother's glance was so full of love, devotion and maternal self-sacrifice that it made Jillian's heart ache. Soon she'd be looking at her own child in that same way, she thought.

"Honey," her mother said, "I didn't want to have to tell you, but Reverend Peterson has a funeral in the church at three today."

Jillian's jaw dropped. Her father shared parish responsibilities with the other minister. "Excuse me?"

Barbara, who was long used to living with the joys and tribulations of a whole congregation, sighed as only a minister's wife could. Births and deaths were always the order of the day in the rectory, in spite of anyone's personal plans. "There was a mistake in scheduling."

"The church is being used for a funeral at the exact hour of our wedding?" Jillian clarified.

"I'm sorry, honey. The coffin's already been delivered. But the sun *will* come out. I promise."

As if her mom could control the very weather. When she was gone, with Amy following, Jillian murmured to Jack, "I think everybody's gone whacko this morning."

"You think *I'm* crazy?"

"Jack, we can't drive in this." The winds had died, but the rain was coming down in sheets.

"You know," he said, "I think you could make a little more effort when it comes to my mother."

Granted, Jillian hadn't exactly become the daughter his mother had never had. But it wasn't her fault. "Sorry," she managed to say, trying to tell herself her mother was right. The sun would come out. Besides, Jack was a great driver, so the trip to the airport would be safe. "Just give me one more minute, Jack. I'll change."

He nodded. "I love you, even if you're always late, Jilly."

She decided not to point out that he was hustling her along twenty minutes ahead of schedule. "Love you, too, Jack."

She shut her bedroom door, feeling as if she'd forgotten something extremely important. "Something about being ahead of schedule..."

The baby!

She swiftly reopened the door. Jack groaned, giving his watch a quick, pointed glance Jillian found particularly annoying.

"If we don't get going," he warned, "we won't get back before three."

Oh, she wanted to say innocently, *is something happening at three?* Instead she found herself saying, "Can I have just one more second of your precious time before I change to meet your mother, Jack?''

''That's about all we have. A second.''

Great. She now had one measly second to tell her future husband about the single most important thing in their lives.

Jack looked thoroughly exasperated. ''Please,'' he said, ''could you give it to me in a nutshell?''

''Fine,'' said Jillian. ''Here's the nut. I'm pregnant.''

Jack didn't exactly look overjoyed.

So, while his jaw was still dropping, Jillian simply shut the bedroom door.

Chapter Three

Five hours before the wedding...

PREGNANT?

Jack still couldn't believe it. It must have been after the rehearsal dinner they'd catered for the Stuarts. He and Jillian had become so excited about their own upcoming wedding that, in the heat of the moment... He swerved, narrowly missing a tree branch that had blown across the road. Not that hitting it would have caused any damage. He was creeping along at all of two miles an hour. Hunching closer to the windshield of the prize Mustang he'd refurbished himself, Jack flexed his hands on the steering wheel and peered hard into the rain. Because the storm was interfering with radio reception, the only sound was the wipers, and listening to the unnerving *tha-thump,* Jack was almost relieved each time crashing thunder intervened. Or when Jillian heaved an exaggerated sigh, as she did now.

He fought the urge to say, "What?" Because if he did, Jillian would have some snippy response. And then they might start fighting. Again.

He didn't look at her, either. Because every

time he did, his anger dissipated. God, she was beautiful. With moist, healthy skin. A high, broad forehead and wide-set, blue-gray eyes fringed with inky eyelashes. Her short, dark-red hair was cut above her ears, but fuller on top—a riot of short finger curls. He'd never seen a neck more slender or bones more delicate. Which was why he didn't look. He had every right to be mad.

"Jack, are you ignoring me?"

He didn't so much as glance at her. He didn't have to. He knew exactly what she was doing—hunching grumpily in the passenger seat in a sexy short skirt and bright yellow rain slicker, her long arms and legs angrily crossed.

"I *was* going to tell you about the baby."

"When? On our honeymoon?"

"When?" she echoed. "I told you immediately. And you can't get much faster than immediately, Jack."

Without looking, he could feel the trademark Jillian stare. Turning toward him, she'd dipped her chin so that it nearly touched her chest, sharply raised the perfect half-moons of her eyebrows, defiantly crossed every appendage and then puckered her kissable, pink-glossed mouth. That her voice hadn't carried the faintest hint of apology only further stirred Jack's temper.

"Jack, I told you the very *second* I took that test this morning."

Right. But apparently, she'd suspected she was

pregnant for nearly two months. Which meant he'd missed the first two months of fatherhood. *Forget it. It's our wedding day, and I refuse to ruin it by arguing.* "I'm not even gracing that with a response, Jilly." Jack trained his gaze through the windshield.

So did Jillian. Which was ridiculous, since there wasn't a thing out there to look at. Barbara had been right. Jack never should have brought Jillian out in this storm. He'd been so angry, he'd driven a full twenty minutes before he'd realized how bad the weather really was.

The damp air was thick and dense with eerie fog. It was midmorning, but as dark as twilight; early spring, but as cold as September. The roads were deserted. At least Jack thought so. *Hoped* so. Because he could barely see ten feet in front of the car. He was pretty sure that anyone with common sense was staying indoors. Through the gray water that sluiced down the windshield, he could barely make out the arbor of tree boughs that arched overhead, further blocking the light. Occasionally, lightning flashed and the world beyond the windshield would flare for an instant, granting a quick impression of trees and roadway.

As Jack switched on the headlights, Jillian rested her hand against the dashboard and turned to him. "Jack," she said, "I don't know why you're so angry."

He sighed, trying to tell himself it didn't matter.

In the thirteen years they'd known each other, they'd fought more rounds than heavyweight champs. *But it's our wedding day.* What had happened to last night, when everything seemed so perfect—the calm before the storm?

"Jilly..." He fought to keep the hurt from his voice. "You didn't go to a store this morning. So last night, when we were out on the deck, you'd already brought the test home. And you said you've missed your period twice. So that means you suspected—"

"I just wanted to be sure, okay? As soon as I knew, I shared it with you."

His voice was deceptively soft. "But this..." He struggled for words. "This isn't yours to share with me, Jillian. It's *ours.* Both of ours. This baby's mine, just the way it's yours." The baby was the two of them, joined. One... Jack wasn't sure he was even making sense. Hell, he didn't know exactly what he was trying to say. But how could she have withheld such a thing?

"Funny," she said after a long moment. "Judging from the look on your face when I told you, *sharing* was the last thing on your mind."

His lips parted in protest. "What—"

"Jack, you looked terrified. Maybe I didn't tell you last night because I was afraid of your reaction."

Well, he *was* terrified. What responsible man in his right mind wouldn't be? He thought back to a half hour ago. He'd been intent on getting to the airport. Ever since his father had died, he'd worried about his mother; she hadn't been herself. It was her responsibility to host the rehearsal dinner, and Jack had even assumed she'd offer to help pay for the wedding, especially since she'd served up a lengthy guest list. And she was financially far better off than the Williamses.

Instead, she'd simply vanished, hopping on a plane to Europe—a fact the Williamses had been kind enough not to mention. But his mother was better than well-bred, from old Beacon Hill money, and she loved hosting parties. So Jack couldn't figure it out....

He'd been mulling it over when Jillian's announcement had catapulted him onto a whole new track. In a second flat, Jack was thinking about the rising cost of college tuition and real estate. And how he was going to strong-arm Jillian into accepting some cold, hard Sidwell cash, which his mother would willingly bestow on them. Surely Jillian would let his mother help financially now, since a baby was on the way....

"You may not have liked my reaction, Jilly, but I don't think it's wrong for someone to consider the practical implications."

"Implications?" she said, as if sensing he was going to broach the subject of money. "This isn't a business prospectus, Jack, it's our baby."

A long silence fell.

"And Jack," she finally continued, "practical is one thing. But when you found out we were pregnant, you didn't even kiss me."

He winced. He hadn't, had he? Oh, damn. "Oh, Jilly." It certainly wasn't from lack of loving her. He really could be practical to a fault. Just as he turned from the windshield toward her, she lifted a hand, palm out.

"Save it. For once, you're a little late."

He felt terrible. But he sure wished she wasn't starting to get so sanctimonious. He flexed his hands on the steering wheel again, then closed tight fists around it. "You *did* slam your bedroom door in my face."

"I shut it quietly."

"I guess that's a matter of opinion."

Why couldn't she understand that even now his mind was spinning? He was wishing so many things: that he was better prepared for fatherhood. That his father, now dead, had lived to see his first grandchild. That his mother would embrace this occasion—both the wedding and now the baby—in some way other than packing her bags and leaving town....

"Sorry, Jilly. I've got so much on my mind."

"You know," she said, "I've got lots on mine, too."

Of course she did. He bit back a frustrated sigh. How could they fight like this on their wedding day? And on the day they'd found out she was pregnant? Sure, the weight of responsibility was the first thing he'd felt when Jillian had told him. But then he'd felt a bone-deep sense of completion, that their lives were coming full circle. He just wasn't the effusive type.

At least try, Jack. "We're both under pressure, Jilly. It's a big day. Lots of expectations." *And one of them was that we're supposed to share everything in our lives. So why didn't you tell me about our baby before now? I would have loved to wait for the test results with you.*

She sighed. "I don't want to fight."

He almost smiled. "We always fight."

Their personal styles were simply too different. Even without a watch, Jack's precise internal clock kept him punctual, while she always ran late. While she threw caution to the wind, he was the one who showed up wearing a life jacket and waved from shore, holding a compass. *Shoot,* he thought, staring into the abysmal rain. Even in this mess, Jillian had run for the car with nothing more than her cute, bright yellow slicker for protection. He, of course, had run behind her—thrusting out an open umbrella, protecting her glorious head of waving red hair while he got drenched to the bone.

Even their upbringings had been night and day. He thought of the dark, cool rooms in his family's home, of the precise arrangements of antique furniture and gilt-framed pictures and of the sedate relationship between his conservative, older parents.

By contrast, Jillian's parents had been children of the sixties. Jilly's mother had been overseas in the Peace Corps when she'd conceived out of wedlock, and she'd been prepared to raise Jilly alone. Then she'd met Harold Williams, who was working as a missionary. Contrary to the Sidwells, they kept a cheerfully untidy house, full of rambunctious kids, stray pets, loud music and laughter.

Jack loved both that house and his own. And he needed both, just as he needed Jilly and their baby. Call it old-fashioned, but if Jack wasn't jumping with obvious joy, it was only because he so desperately wanted to be a good father and provider. And deep down, Jilly knew it.

"Look," he said. "I know you're scared. You've got the jitters. So do I. But I'm still mad that you didn't tell me. I don't want to fight, because I want things to be perfect for us today. But if there's one place I don't intend to ever be excluded from, it's your life, Jilly."

There. He'd said his piece. He shifted his gaze back to the windshield. "That's the way it has to be," he added. "You and me together. Everything shared. That's what we're doing today. That's what our wedding is all about." When he glanced at her again, her eyes had turned achingly vulnerable, suddenly brimming with tears. He damned himself for pushing. He hated it when he hurt her, hated it on the rare occasions their fights made her cry.

Her lower lip quivered. "I just wish you'd looked happier."

Her eyes. The thought was senseless, had nothing to do with the conversation. But her eyes were such a smoky, misty blue, so expressive. And yet Jillian's temperament could be as fiery as her red hair. She was all extremes—melting in his arms one minute, turning as hard as cold steel the next. His tone gentled. "I guess the news was just sudden."

"Sudden! Jack, we've been dating for thirteen years!"

He winced. "You've got a point there."

But he'd hardly expected to hear such news today. When he'd found out, they should have been... He shrugged. "I feel like we should have been alone in a restaurant, or walking on the beach." *At sunset. With the gulls crying out and the salt breeze lifting your hair, Jilly.* It suddenly seemed as if he and Jillian hadn't taken a romantic stroll for a very long time. He imagined walking in the sand, molding his hand on her belly. As soon as this storm passed, the baby would bring him and Jilly together in so many new ways....

In the cool interior of the car, the windows were fogging, so he cracked his window an inch.

Colder air circulated, clearing the glass, splashing in rain, bringing a damp chill that seemed to settle in Jack's lungs.

"Jack, we've been engaged for so long...." Jillian began.

Her voice was so frighteningly solemn that real fear gripped him. He knew where this was heading. He tried to keep his voice even, but it sounded low and gravelly to his ears. "Which means a baby is the next logical step." Unable to take his eyes from the waterlogged windshield for long, he hazarded a quick glance in her direction.

"Jack," she said in a rush, "we always avoid this topic. And we need to talk—"

"We've talked about everything under the sun," he countered, fighting exasperation. "And that's just for starters." People could talk themselves blue in the face, but observation told more. Already he and Jilly knew each other better than some married couples, certainly most newlyweds.

She blew out a peeved sigh. "You're in complete denial."

"Denial?"

She stared at him. "So, we'll compromise? Raise the baby in the apartment in Boston? Not move to the suburbs—"

"The suburbs are safer."

"And you're going to be against public schooling." It wasn't a question. It was a statement of fact.

"Private schools are better."

"I knew you'd say that." The steely quality of her voice almost relieved him. At least it was the old Jilly talking. "I went to public schools, Jack."

He wasn't touching that with a ten-foot pole.

"And I'm not moving to the suburbs," she added. "I mean, we just rented our place in Boston. We've both wanted to live in Boston for years."

His lips parted in protest. "But with a baby..."

"No doubt you'll have a heart attack when I strap the baby on my bike and ride to day care?"

He merely gaped at her.

"A lot of mothers do it, Jack."

"Day care?" he finally repeated, as if he'd never heard the term.

"Well, I can't stay home full-time. We just opened the café."

"Why can't we get a nanny?"

"We can't afford a nanny."

Jack's lips compressed into a thin line. "Well, we *could*, if you'd simply give in and let my mother help us out. I know she'll want to—"

Jillian threw her hands in the air. "Jack, we've been over this a thousand times!"

"And you never see reason."

"And *you* never back down." She heaved a loud sigh. "Look, maybe we should postpone the wedding, at least long enough to come to some consensus about these issues. We absolutely cannot raise a baby together if we're fighting each other every step of the way.''

For a second, everything inside Jack seized up. He felt as if his heart had quit beating; his muscles tensed, freezing. *I'll just pretend I didn't hear that.*

''I'm not saying we shouldn't get married,'' she said quickly. ''But we've been together so long. Let's face it, if we'd eloped, our kids would be in junior high now. And this storm... I mean, every time we try to get married, something bad happens. Maybe that's why it's raining. Maybe it's to stop us from...''

Taking our vows.

The words hung ominously in the damp, foggy air.

His tone was careful. ''Don't even pursue this line of thought, Jillian. I've already apologized. And I'm only going to do it once more. I am damn sorry I didn't respond in the right way, the way you needed, when you told me about the baby.''

''It's not about that!'' she said explosively. ''It's just that...well, you're always so...so—''

''Controlling?'' he suggested with deceptive calm.

The preoccupied nod of her head further tweaked his temper. ''This is the biggest thing in our lives Jack...and I—I know you're probably upset that the timing's off. But this isn't one of your cars. It's our baby."

"I want our baby," he said flatly.

"I know you do. But for once—and I mean it this time, Jack—you've *got* to start making some compromises. I just wish you'd be a little less...less..." She winced. "Controlling."

"Fine time to mention it," he returned. "Just five hours before our wedding. Besides which, I *am* willing to make compromises. I just don't see why taking a little cash from my family is such a large—"

"There you go again! You swore we'd be self-supporting—"

"But things are different now and—"

"Jack! Look out!"

Just as he saw the tree across the road, Jillian's hand slammed down on the dashboard again. Jack wrenched the wheel left, but they were hydroplaning. The car veered sideways, the tree looming larger the closer they came. He felt a moment's sheer terror for Jilly and the baby she was carrying, and he madly pumped the brake. Not a second too soon, he got traction. Pulling out, Jack guided the Mustang to the road's shoulder and brought it to an abrupt, shuddering halt.

Then he stared at the tree. Or what was left of it. Lightning had splintered the trunk. Long, tapering, clawlike roots had been wrenched from deep in the loamy soil. It reminded him of his and

Jilly's relationship. Were years of growth about to be pulled out, uprooted from the foundation? Was she seriously contemplating not marrying him today? *Oh, that's crazy, Jack. Don't be foolish. This is merely an inconsequential spat about child care.*

"Oh, no," Jillian whispered, as if she'd just now registered their near-death experience.

Ever the rational one, he said, "Maybe it's just as well. I was about to pull over, anyway."

Shocked, she was still gaping at the tree. "Why's that?"

"To kiss you or strangle you," he admitted. "I'm not sure which." Turning in the seat, he continued, "I have no idea how we're going to move this tree, or get my mother from the airport now, or make it back to your house in time for the wed—"

"The wedding's been rained out."

He ignored her. "For the wedding at three o'clock," he said, plowing on. "But I do want to know one thing."

Looking dazed, Jillian turned toward him slowly. "Hmm?"

He'd had it. "Just what's gotten into you this morning?"

She didn't bother to ask what he meant. Instead, his wonderful Jilly merely blinked her beautiful foggy eyes rapidly. She shot him a confused glance that was heartbreaking in its sincerity. "Oh, I just don't know, Jack," she said in a rush. "But I keep having so many bizarre thoughts today. All morning they've buzzed around in my head like bees."

"Thoughts like what?"

She shrugged. Her eyes darted around—a little wildly, he decided. He tried to tell himself that her crazy allusion to calling off the wedding was nothing more than jitters. A bad case. He reminded himself that where structure made him comfortable, it could make Jilly feel positively trapped. A big traditional wedding certainly counted as structure.

"C'mon, Jilly," he repeated carefully. "What thoughts?"

"Oh, I don't know," she murmured vaguely. "Like thirteen's an unlucky number. And that we've known each other exactly thirteen years." Getting to the core of the matter, she rushed on. "Oh, Jack, don't you understand? It's totally irresponsible to start a family if we can't reach the simplest consensus about how to raise our child. And this time I'm not backing down or making all the compromises. If we don't hash this out before three o'clock today, our baby's going to be tugged every which way but loose. I don't want him or her to hear us fighting and—"

"That's it," Jack muttered. "I've had it." Taking his foot off the brake, he slammed the car into Park and let the engine idle. Swiftly reaching across the seat, he unbuckled Jillian's seat belt, grasped her shoulders and pulled her against his chest. He quickly glanced around. Still no other cars on the road. Good.

Her voice was breathless. "Jack, what are you doing?"

His hands raked roughly through her hair. As he felt the silken strands spill through his fingers, something inside him gave. He was feeling testy, but just one touch always ignited sparks of need between them. His voice was low, but with a dangerous edge. "You mean you don't know what I'm doing, Jilly?" he taunted seductively. "I mean, how could that be? A controlling tight-ass like me is probably so predictable...."

She stared up from his chest, her foggy eyes wide with concern, and she squirmed uncertainly against him. "Really, Jack. What *are* you doing?"

"I'm going to make you remember why you're marrying me today," he growled.

And then his lips crushed down on hers.

THE SECOND JACK'S searing mouth closed over hers she was lost. "Jack," she whispered feebly.

"What?" he murmured huskily between kisses.

She didn't know what to say, how to explain. She'd seen his face when she'd said she was pregnant. Oh, she knew he didn't take kindly to changing horses in midstream. But his gut-level response scared her. Just once, she'd wanted to see Jack throw caution to the wind. To grin and whoop and holler. Instead, she'd watched the wheels turn; he'd been thinking about home ownership, Christmas clubs and mutual fund investments.

And now he actually expected her to take the Sidwell money.

Even worse, their ideas about family life had always been completely at odds.

She decided to approach the issue from another angle. "Jack..." She tried to edge away, but his teeth caught her lower lip—nipping, pulling her back. She managed to say, "When I told you about the baby...I was thinking about my mom."

Jack drew back a fraction. "Your mom?"

She nodded. His close proximity was making it hard for her to think. It often did. His breath was warm against her cheek as he nuzzled her skin. His clothing—slacks, chambray shirt and windbreaker—felt damp against her, and the sweet, earthy smell of spring rain was mixing with his stronger, masculine scent, arousing her.

She rushed on, her lips a mere inch from his. "I thought of how my father might have looked when my mother told him she was pregnant, Jack." Not that Jack would walk away, as Nate Ralston had. But all those years ago, had Nate Ralston looked at Jillian's mother with eyes that registered duty, concern, responsibility? Hadn't there been any wonder? Any joy? Any desperate longing for his baby? For Jillian?

Now, Jack's eyes sparked to life with flinty anger that brought out the flecks of green in the amber irises. His silken lips were close enough to move on her skin, his voice unusually restrained. "I'm not your father."

"I know that, Jack, but—"

"No buts!" His gruff words were swallowed in a kiss meant to sweep away all her arguments, yet it roused both her temper and her desire.

"I'm trying to talk, Jack." Not make love.

"Talk about what, Jilly?" His mouth brushed hers. "About how you want me to compromise myself?"

"Make compromises," she corrected.

"Hmm. And about the way I always control myself?"

Right. He wasn't showing an ounce of control. Shifting his weight, he pulled her closer and then his mouth delivered a practiced, thorough plundering that left her ravenous for the taste of him.

"Oh, Jilly," he taunted mercilessly between kisses. "I think I'm losing control now. Why, I don't have the faintest idea what I'm doing!"

He knew good and well what he was doing. With another kiss—this one as hard and relentless as the driving rain—he was stirring excitement inside her. Whisking it into a frenzy, he kept on, until tempestuous fire swirled in the belly where she carried the life they'd created. Until she could no longer tell where the storm outside ended and the one inside her began. Jack was the lightning rod and she was the ground. And each time his sizzling lips locked over hers, he channeled zigzagging, white-hot volts from her head to her toes. All her nerves and sinews were energized, and her blood was charged, running with a live current.

"Jack," she whimpered.

His thunderous groan of pleasure was sudden—a rumble in his chest, two ragged words against her mouth. "Oh, Jilly."

They could fight forever. But here in the closed confines of the sports car, with the storm raging around them, there was no use denying chemistry. One touch, and Jillian's need for this man had always been too great to resist. She became aware of her breasts—how they'd softened, crushed as they were against the bunched muscles of his chest. How they tingled, longing for his hands and mouth. She became aware of his heartbeat, as steady as the rain. Aware of the kisses that he dropped on her neck in a torrent.

Leaning back, he grasped the ends of her yellow slicker. Unpopping the string of snaps, he shoved the jacket back from her shoulders, deftly opened her blouse, released the front catch of her bra and gave her breasts firm squeezes. She knew she could live through eternity and never feel such pressing insistence in another man's touch. Or hear such heartfelt invitation in another man's panting breath. Jack gave a greedy, thoroughly masculine gasp as his hands stroked the soft mounds of her flesh, and as he coaxed her nipples to pebbled peaks, his fingers seemed to flicker even lower still, vibrating against her darkest, most secret places.

"This is one reason why you love me, Jilly. Remember?"

Even as he built the need inside her, stoking heat in the belly that held their child, Jillian swallowed hard, glancing around. "But Jack, we could get in trouble...."

It was a token protest. Beyond the fogged windshield, the world was flooded, just the way she was, and as dewy moisture gathered, heavy and sweet between her legs, the water outside gushed, rushing in rivulets at the road's shoulder, sluicing over the car. Inside, Jack's mouth delivered tumultuous kisses to her breasts, cresting over the stiff turgid tips, then flowing as warm and salty wet as lapping waves. When he lifted his gaze, it was all smoldering fire and amber, a liquid warm honey that evoked her hunger. He was so hot for her. He always was. Their steamy bodies had warmed the car. And Jillian's mind was now as foggy as the windows.

"Remember—" his soft utterance was a tantalizing rasp against her cheek "—when I worked at the gas station?"

She wanted to say she couldn't remember a blessed thing right now—not when her skin was so prickly with anticipation. Or when her hands were inching along the tensed, hard muscles of his thighs.

But of course she remembered. Jack loved exotic cars. So, back in high school, he'd worked for a station that serviced them. After she got her license, she'd often driven around for hours, using up gas until she had an excuse for Jack to fill the tank again. Lord, she would have driven to China if it had meant exchanging two more words with him.

"And remember the first time we made love, Jilly?"

The fits and starts of her breathing made her voice jagged. "How can you expect me to think right now?"

"Remember?" he urged.

That night they'd driven down the beach, the wind singing in their hair. Hers, long then, was hopelessly tangled, and she'd tied it back with a powder blue ribbon. Later, Jack had chased her across the rectory lawn, and she'd clambered up the ladder attached to the trunk of the old oak. In the tree house, she'd breathlessly spun around, only to be caught in Jack's arms just as his mouth descended. He'd loved her on the hardwood floor—and yet it had been softer than any feather bed, scented with autumn leaves, starlit sawdust and the musky perfume of their young bodies.

Then and now, Jack's glorious kisses brought a sense of weightlessness. Then and now, his lips carried an undeniable heat. Always, desire as necessary as her own lifeblood spiraled through Jillian as she felt his need, the powerful erection that now, so heavy and potent and strong, pressed against her belly.

Just as she released a strangled moan, Jack's lips claimed hers again, so thoroughly she thought she'd drown. Against her kiss-swollen mouth, he murmured, "And remember visiting me in England, Jilly?"

There'd been rough weather, just like today, with turbulent winds and slashing rain. Coming from the airport, they'd gotten drenched, and in an old Victorian hotel, Jack had swiftly lifted her skirt and stripped off her wet stockings. Wordlessly, with a fire crackling in the hearth, they'd fallen on the floor—and each other.

Now her voice was as low and smoldering as the hot, dry ashes left after that fire. Emotion swelled her heart. "Oh, Jack, we missed each other so much."

"You've been so far away from me this morning, Jilly." Jack's throaty breath stirred her hair. "Don't you miss me?"

"I miss you," she whispered senselessly.

His words were barely audible. ''C'mon, sweetheart. Get on top of me.''

His bold hands were beneath her skirt now. Shifting his shoulders in the tight confines of the car, he managed to find the waistband of her tights, and pulled them down over her knees, taking the lace scrap of her panties with them. Her breath hitched as a finger dipped, probing her readiness. Then there was only harsher breath, a needy gasp, the flap of his belt and the rake of his zipper. Lightning suddenly flashed in tandem with the frenzy.

And then both his hands cupped her bottom in a tender caress. Ever so gently, he coaxed her closer, until she straddled his lap.

''Oh, Jilly,'' he moaned as she poised above him. His hand molded to the curve of her belly, as if feeling their baby. ''Jilly, my Jilly.''

Her inner thighs quivered with strain as he guided her hips, urging her down. And down. The sheath of her closed around him, enveloping him as he pushed inside, and then everything in her turned to water. A mindless sob was shaken loose from her lips when he'd completely filled her. Another as he filled her again. And again.

When his mouth finally caught hers—roughly, wetly—and his tongue thrust deep in a lasting kiss that would drive her over the edge, she was buffeted by so many sensations, so many emotions. The rain was all gone, doused by Jack's hard fire.

She was crying out now, hugging his neck and hovering with him at the precipice, steadied only by the clutching of his damp hands on her hips.

"Jilly!" With a final gasp he pulled her down and arched his hips, burying himself with a last greedy thrust. His release came in a warm jet that shattered her like glass, and his kiss caught every sharp cry of her pleasure. Then he drew back and whispered, "Remember?"

"Yes," she sobbed out. "I remember."

And she did.

She remembered every wonderful moment. Thirteen whole years of love and longing with this man.

But was what they shared enough to sustain and support another life? A child about whose care they would so vehemently disagree?

And with a stable life for their child at stake, was she so very wrong to have doubts on her wedding day?

Chapter Four

Four hours before the wedding...

JILLIAN'S LOW, HUSKY HUM teased his ears. "You're so great in bed, tiger."

Jack raised a lazy eyebrow. "We're in a car, Jilly."

"Well, we could have been in a bed," she returned, smiling as his hands explored the gentle curve of her belly. "Or in a jungle. I mean, one kiss and you always make me forget our exact location."

"Funny," he said. "Because I always know where you are."

"Oh? Where's that?"

"Where you belong. With me."

Feeling sure the storm had passed, Jack relaxed against the driver's door, drawing Jillian closer against his chest. Lightning and thunder had ceased for the moment, and shutting his eyes, Jack listened to the rain—just impatient fingers drumming the car roof, reminding him they were running late. For once, he didn't care. No more than he cared about their unresolved arguments. Surely everything would work out now....

Cuddled this way, on the deserted, tree-lined road,

he felt as if he and Jillian could have been wrapped in each other's arms in a cozy cabin with a tin roof. At least until she sat up, rearranged her clothes and shrugged back into her slicker. "Well, I guess we'd better see about moving that tree."

Moaning in protest, Jack grasped for her hand, but she didn't even wait. The next thing he knew, the Mustang door swung open, cool air rushed in and Jilly was charging toward the tree. She didn't even bother to find the umbrella or pull up her slicker hood. It was almost as if she'd suddenly wanted to escape from him. *Me. The man she's marrying this afternoon. The man whose baby she's having.*

"If I don't get out there, she's going to move that tree with her bare hands," he muttered. And she could injure herself or the baby. Grabbing the umbrella—a large golf one—from the back seat, he swung open his door. His foot didn't touch terra firma; it sank deep into a puddle. Oozing mud and frigid water chilled him to his ankle. Letting loose a string of expletives, he plunged into the driving rain, his eyes fixed on Jillian's back. In the oversize slicker, she looked like the Morton Salt girl. With her hands on her hips, she was scrutinizing the tree, and as he neared, he could hear rain pinging against her jacket. Her hair was soaked.

What had gotten into her? "Jilly?"

The storm had returned full force, and thunder crashed, drowning out her name. When he saw her face in the eerie morning darkness, his heart wrenched. He thrust the umbrella stem beneath his chin, and slid his hands around her waist. Her rain slicker soaked his slacks and jacket, but he couldn't have cared less. She looked miserable. Her delicate shoulders drooped like drenched flowers.

Didn't she share his feelings at all? Hell, wedding or no, he could have stayed snuggled in the Mustang for the rest of the day. They'd just found out they were having a baby, and he wanted to sit quietly alone with her, holding her.

His voice was muted by the rain pounding on the umbrella. "Please, Jilly. Talk to me. What's going on here?"

Warring emotions crossed her features—confusion, apology, regret. She looked as if she couldn't find the words. "Jack," she said, as if she shouldn't need to explain it, "we have a lot more talking to do about the baby."

He sighed, pushing wet, curling tendrils of hair from her forehead. How was he going to get her to accept Miranda's financial help? Wouldn't Jilly agree to have a nanny, at least? He strongly felt their child should be cared for at home. But was he really too uncompromising? "First we've got to get out of the rain," he said. "C'mon, hold the umbrella while I rig up something to get this tree off the road."

Looking vaguely relieved, she clutched her slender fingers around the umbrella handle as if around the hand of a long-lost friend. Within moments, with her help, Jack had backed the Mustang to the tree and tied a rope between a branch and the car trunk. Even though Jillian was doing her level best with the umbrella, the wind was howling again and they both got soaked. Nevertheless, using the car for horsepower, they were able to drag the tree into a ditch.

For a second, when they were on their way again, Jack wanted to just keep driving. To hide out in some cozy New England bed and breakfast, where they could celebrate the coming of their child, where he could dry her with a brisk warm towel and order a room-service picnic to share in bed. He settled for reaching across the seat and stroking a thumb down her cheek. "You sure you're okay?"

She nodded. "Yeah."

He knew better. He busied himself: adjusting the wipers and headlights. Cranking up the heat, so they wouldn't freeze. Pointing to a towel in the back seat, so she could dry her hair. She dried his, too, as he drove. Not that it helped much. And his slacks were so wet they sucked at his skin. He kept waiting for her to broach the subject of the baby again, but she didn't.

Near the airport, traffic got heavier, and Jack crouched, peering harder through a windshield that was awash with gray, sluicing rain. Headlights—his own and others—shone faintly as the murky glimmers in the unnatural midday dark. Jack spun the radio dial but found only static. *It's just as well,* he thought, glancing to one side as they crossed a bridge. Below, on a flooded road, a car was stalled, and the water eddying around it reached the back bumper. Jack needed to concentrate on driving.

Still, when the windshield fogged, he reached in front of Jillian and with his index finger scribbled "I love you" on the glass.

That got a smile out of her.

Finally, she said, "Jack, do you really still love me? I mean, *really?* The way you did back in high school?"

What in the world was going through her mind? After the way they'd just made love, how could she even ask? He couldn't completely keep the anger—manifested as an ironic twinge—from his voice. "Jilly, I hate to say this, but I feel like I woke up to a whole new fiancée this morning." His Jilly was feisty, free spirited and never doubted his love.

She raced on. "I'm just worried. I mean, I want to believe you'll make compromises, but you often don't. You have to trust me more when I make decisions about raising our child. If you can't, that means we don't really have what it takes—"

"Have what it takes?" he repeated. "This is our *marriage,* Jillian. Not a commercial for the army." He half expected her to say something now about being the best they could be. Dammit, instead of kissing at the altar, maybe they'd wind up giving each other a brave smile and a thumbs-up. As if they were going to war, not to the Virgin Islands on a honeymoon.

She was now shaking her head, preoccupied. "You were so right, Jack. I *should* have told you about the baby sooner. I was keeping a secret. And...if we really couldn't live without each other, why did we wait thirteen years to get married?"

Get married? He was beginning to think he'd kill her first. His hands closed in tight fists over the steering wheel. "Jillian, we were kids when we met," he said levelly. "Pardon me if I didn't propose in junior high school."

"Oh, Jack, I didn't mean that. And I love you. I could never love anyone else. Or anyone more..."

It took everything he had, but he didn't panic. This was inevitable. Just the jitters. Just predictable fallout, since the explosion of wedding plans had nearly obliterated his and Jillian's romantic life for six solid months. The café they jointly ran had kept them busy, too, with hiring new staff and organizing special promotions. And now they were pregnant—and had no cohesive plan for raising a baby. Great. He took a deep breath. "You love me...but what?"

"But are we really in love? I mean *in love?*"

This time when Jilly said "in love," she punched the air to emphasize the intensity of the emotion they should feel, as if she were a boxer warming up for a fight. Jack really couldn't believe it. His voice was tight. "Of course we're in love."

"So, you *will* compromise? We'll stay in the city, I'll continue working and we'll take the baby to day care?"

"That's not a compromise," he replied. "That's you getting your own way."

She didn't say anything, which was just as well. One more word and they'd be arguing again about accepting money from his mother. Guilt suddenly rushed in on Jack. Talk about keeping secrets. Hell, he'd lied to Jilly all along. She thought the start-up capital for their café came from an inheritance. But Jack's mother controlled the money left by his father, and so, right before she'd left town, she'd offered to write Jack a check, so he could start the business. He'd sworn his mother to secrecy—and then lied to Jilly about the source of the gift.

It was wrong. Really deceitful. But dammit, it had been the only way to fulfill Jilly's life dream of owning the café. Besides, being able to help them had done his mother's heart good. And in two years, the café would be in the black, and he and Jillian would have a solid financial base from which to support their family.

A family that was apparently coming a little sooner than expected. *But you promised Jillian you'd be self-supporting, didn't you, Jack?* a small voice inside him chided.

"Jilly," he said aloud, his tone gentling. "We'll work everything out."

"Before three today?" The worst thing was the pain in her expression. She was obviously trying to do the right thing. "Jack, we've waited thirteen years. Shouldn't we wait maybe just a couple more days, until we've ironed out these very last kinks?"

"Kinks?" he managed to say. "Now you're talking about the raising of our child as if he's a wrinkled shirt."

"She," said Jillian. "It could be a she."

"*He* is the most commonly used pronoun when gender is in question," Jack returned tightly.

"Well, regardless of the sex, you won't be happy until our baby's dressed in a navy, prep-school blazer and being carted around the suburbs in an off-road vehicle."

She was right, of course. "It's safer than bumping along cracked city sidewalks, wearing open-toed Birkenstocks, with a baby strapped to the handlebars of a bicycle."

Jillian rapidly blinked back tears. "You make it sound so terrible," she said miserably.

"Not terrible. Just unsafe."

She swallowed hard. "Even dual air bags can be dangerous, Jack."

He would have pulled over again, hoping to kiss her into submission, but they'd reached the airport's ground transportation area. "Look," he muttered, even as his eyes started scanning the crowd. "If you insist on calling off our wedding, fine. Feel free to make the announcement at your convenience. But I promise you one thing, Jilly. I won't make it easy."

The tears now swam in her eyes. "Jack, I just want to make sure—"

"If thirteen years hasn't made you sure, nothing will." *And after thirteen years,* he thought, *there's no way in hell I'm losing you. Certainly not my child.* Nor was he going to make all the concessions. Just then his eyes landed on his mother, and in spite of the tension in the car, he felt some semblance of relief. Given the crazy way his mother had left town, he'd half expected her not to show. He said, "Just do me one favor."

"What?"

He rolled down his window and waved. In the sea of disheveled travelers, only Miranda Sidwell seemed to have a life vest. She looked utterly poised in a smartly belted raincoat, and her silver-white bobbed hair didn't so much as lift in the stormy winds.

"While my mother's in the car," Jack said, "could you at least *pretend* we're getting married?"

"While she's in the car," Jillian agreed contritely.

The words gave Jack little comfort.

Chapter Five

Three hours before the wedding...

JILLIAN GLANCED AROUND the room, at her mother, Miranda, Jack and Amy, then loudly cleared her throat. "I have an announcement to make." She'd kept her promise and kept mum in the car. But now this had to be done. Oh, it was awful. In fact, the whole damnable day was, what with the rain and the ruined flower arrangements and fighting with Jack about the baby...

Quit obsessing, Jillian! Just stop the wedding until you and Jack can reach some consensus about how to raise this child! She clapped her hands briskly, like a schoolmarm. "Please. It's important!"

But it was no use. All hell—or, more specifically, hail—had broken loose. Poor little Ruffhouse, terrified of the frozen pellets tapping the windowpanes, was yowling to beat the band. Literally, since all the members of her brother's music band were clomping through the Williamses' family room, carrying sound equipment.

Jillian's mother was chattering away, giving Jack's mother the wedding update. Sumner Tunnel was reopened, so the wedding cake would arrive from Jack and Jill's café in Boston. The landscapers were outside, trying to remove the fallen elm and save the white tent without getting themselves electrocuted. Quite unfortunately, a coffin was still resting in the center aisle of the church, but on the upside, all the bridesmaids and groomsmen were accounted for.

Jillian half expected her mother to punctuate the end of her brightly delivered speech with a cheerleader's "Hooray!" Instead, she confidentially informed Miranda that, according to one highly reputable weatherman, the storm was about to break up, which meant the coffin didn't really matter, since they'd still be holding the wedding outside.

The overhead lights flickered.

"Obviously, the weatherman in question is in the wrong career," Jillian whispered. She imagined mailing him a copy of the job-hunting guide *What Color Is My Parachute?* And then Jillian felt suddenly trapped and wished she *had* a parachute. Especially when she caught Jack glaring at her from across the room.

"Well," her mother was saying, "maybe Jack should go ahead and run you home, Miranda. I'm sure you'll want to get ready for this afternoon...."

Jack stepped forward. "We've got a small problem."

"Just one?" Jillian said. She drew in a deep, fortifying breath and braced herself.

"Mother's still renting out our house," Jack said. "And there's no room left at the bed and breakfast. She tried to get a room near the airport—or anywhere in Boston. But because of all the delayed travelers, there were no hotel vacancies...."

This was the worst. Did this mean Miranda Sidwell was bunking down with Jillian's parents? It didn't even make any sense. Jillian had been told Miranda rented to friends of friends. Surely they'd let her stay in her own home for a few days.

Jillian's temper flared. Why hadn't Jack mentioned this in the car? Darn it, her mother was the most gracious woman on earth, but she'd worked hard on this wedding. And Miranda, who'd offered absolutely no help whatsoever, had some nerve, imposing at the last minute.

Jillian suddenly realized that her usually composed supermom was looking positively frazzled. Her thick, lush red hair was tumbling messily from its bun and stress was accentuating the tiny wrinkles around her kind blue eyes. "Why don't we put Miranda in my room, Mom?" Jillian quickly suggested.

Her mother shot her a grateful glance.

And Miranda at least had the grace to look apologetic. "It would be wonderful if I could use the room," she said. "Just for tonight, of course, since Jack and Jillian will be leaving for their honeymoon...."

"Well, now that you mention that honeymoon," Jillian began. Her eyes flitted to Jack. "I'm not sure we *should* go to the Virgin Islands tonight. You see, Jack and I have been avoiding some very important issues. I mean, uh, I thought we had a couple of years to talk them through, but now..." She could hardly say she was pregnant. "Well, I'm thinking we should just postpone the wedding."

Once again, something went wrong—either a crack of thunder drowned out her voice, or everyone thought she was making a bad joke, or they simply ignored her. She raised her voice a few decibels. "Will someone please listen to me?"

Barbara, looking thoroughly preoccupied, turned slowly away from Jack's mother. "Did you just say something, honey?"

Say something? Jillian had nearly been screaming. "I said Jack and I aren't getting married!"

The lights flickered again—and went out.

In the sudden, abrupt silence, Miranda squealed and then murmured, "Oh dear, that thing that just touched my leg was a dog. At least I hope it was a dog."

Ruffhouse barked reassurance.

Then Barbara said, "Jack and Jillian, could you please help me find flashlights? I keep two in a kitchen drawer in case the electricity fails. And I do believe I have some candles."

Hadn't anyone heard what she'd said? Was this just another instance of everyone's complete denial about the rained-out wedding? Jillian gave up and fumbled after her mother, just as Amy's voice boomed from the darkness, over another crash of thunder. "Where's Daddy?"

"He's practicing the wedding ceremony, honey," Barbara called. As she began striking matches, thin, yellow-white flames glimmered from strategic perches on the TV and mantel, weakly illuminating the room.

Her father was practicing the ceremony, Jillian thought, feeling touched. Harold Williams had performed the wedding ceremony for countless couples and he could recite it by heart. And yet today he was nervous.

Not as nervous as I am. Darn it, she simply couldn't go through with it. Not as things stood. Too many times, she'd been flighty and impulsive. She'd *had* to open the café, even though Jack's careful fiscal calculations had clearly proven a restaurant-bar would have been more profitable. She was the one who'd insisted on their botched elopement years ago. Oh, Jack had pretended it was his idea, so he'd take most of the heat, but he'd wanted to wait, to make sure they finished college.

Now the tables were turned. Jack wanted to plow ahead, without coming to an agreement about how they were going to parent the baby. And she knew Jack. If she didn't take a firm stand right now, she'd be a full-time mother in Lace Point next year, driving a Land Rover, compliments of Miranda Sidwell. Jack, of course, would be in the city all day, single-handedly running the business that had been Jillian's life dream.

Darn it, she wanted her child raised in a freer, more open environment—with the diversity and stimulation of Boston. *So whatever you do, don't back down this time, Jillian.*

She glanced around. Miranda's designer garment bag was draped over the couch back. Nestled in a corner of the couch, Miranda looked so calm that she could have been ordering a highball at the Lace Point country club. Ruffhouse wiggled forward on his belly, poked his nose from his hiding spot beneath the couch, then settled his head on his paws, next to Miranda's navy pumps. For an instant, Jillian's eyes riveted on the wedding bow barrettes clipping back the terrier's bangs.

"There," Jillian's mother said, lighting a final candle.

Just as Barbara's satisfied eyes swept the room, Jillian's father appeared. Short and well muscled, he was bald on top, gray at the temples and dressed almost from head to toe in black.

"Thank the good Lord you made it safely back from the airport before the power outage!" he exclaimed, tugging at his white clerical collar and collapsing worriedly into his La-Z-Boy. "Your mother and I were getting worried. And we still need to find another white tent, since the landscapers aren't sure they can move that elm—"

"It's *really* of no concern," Jillian said, having

never felt so exasperated. "The announcement I am about to make will solve everything."

That got their attention.

Jillian almost wished it hadn't. Jack's amber eyes bored into her as he moved toward the couch and Miranda. Sensing bad news, Amy sidled next to their mother. Jillian cleared her throat again. "Well, Jack and I have talked about this—"

"Oh no." Jack shook his head. "I did *not* talk about this." He stared around the room. "This was entirely Jillian's idea."

Everyone was watching her intently. "Well, it's just that...well, you know..."

"No dear," Miranda finally said. "We *don't* know."

"Well, with something so all-important as marriage..." Jillian began to pace, rubbing her hands together the way her father did when he was sermonizing and searching for words that would be exactly right. "It's very important not to make a mistake, right?" She flashed a quick, weak smile in the ghostly, candlelit darkness. It would be so much easier if she could say she was pregnant and that she and Jack had extremely different views about child care.

"Oh, I know..." She tried again in a chiding tone, turning gracefully and throwing her hands up in a gesture of mock despair. "I'm a proverbial p.k. And as a preacher's kid, I *am* bound to take marriage—" *and motherhood,* she added silently

"—more seriously than most. I mean, let's face it, no one in the whole history of our family, throughout eternity," she clarified pointedly, "has ever made a mistake and had to divorce." Her voice rose sharply in pitch, and with a perkiness she didn't begin to feel, she looked encouragingly around the room. "Marriage *is* for a lifetime, right, Dad?" She punched the air for emphasis. "'A complete and total commitment,' isn't that what you and Mom always say? And it seems to involve some compromises that Jack and I haven't yet made, so I was just thinking..."

She stopped and grinned nervously.

Everyone stared back. No one smiled. There was dead silence.

"That waiting another day or week or year wouldn't really matter," she continued quickly. "Now would it?"

There was another appalled silence, finally broken by a crack of thunder.

Jillian's mother's voice wavered like the candle flames. "Excuse me, honey? A minute ago, I really thought you were joking. Did I miss something here?"

Sudden tears stung Jillian's eyes. Her nose burned and she had to fight to keep from breaking down. It was no use to try to put a positive spin on this. "I'm so sorry, Mom," she said in a rush. "And Jack. But I'm just so confused. We can't get married when I feel this way."

Miranda Sidwell's haughty voice rang out. "Then I highly suggest that you simply feel some other way!"

Barbara suddenly gasped. "Oh, Jillian!"

Jillian's temper flared. "Look, I'm trying desperately to be responsible—to myself, to Jack." *To our unborn child.* "And," she added weakly, "there *is* a storm, anyway."

"In more than one sense of the word," remarked Miranda.

Jillian's voice caught. "Something bad always happens when Jack and I try to get married. Like this storm. I mean, it could be a sign, right, Daddy?"

Thunder crashed as if to make her point.

Yet another long, terrible silence fell.

And then Reverend Williams, now perching on the edge of the La-Z-Boy, bellowed, "Jillian, this storm is not—I repeat, *not*—a sign from God."

After that, everybody spoke at once. Cans of worms opened left and right. Jack was pleading. Miranda was taking her son's side, telling Jillian she was letting her nerves get the best of her. "After all these years," Miranda said, "all these sacrifices—"

"Sacrifices?" Jillian gasped, suddenly seating herself in a straight-back chair. Miranda hadn't sacrificed even a day of her fancy European vacation. Well, the Williamses might not have the Sidwell fortune, but they had class. Her mother hadn't shirked *her* responsibilities. Before Jillian stop herself, she snapped, "Oh, Miranda, you never thought I was good enough for Jack, anyway."

"Good enough?" said Miranda. "You mean rich enough?"

Jillian scowled and nodded.

And then the strangest thing happened. Miranda burst out laughing. Had Jack's mother gone crazy? "You think I think you're after Jack for his money?" she asked.

Jillian didn't get a chance to answer. Jack said, "That's enough, Jillian. Mother." His gaze swept the room. "The storm has nothing to do with this. Would everyone here like to know the real reason—after thirteen years of a steady relationship—Jillian has just decided not to marry me today?"

Curious assents sounded around the room.

And Jack replied, "Because she's pregnant."

WHY HADN'T JACK KEPT his mouth shut? The man he'd thought of as his father-in-law for most of his life—at least until moments ago—was madly clawing at his clerical collar and choking, while his wife raced to his side and pounded him on the back. No doubt it had never once occurred to Harold Williams that Jack and Jillian had ever gone further than a good-night kiss. And now Jack, like a fool, had just informed Harold that his sweet little girl: a) had very definitely gone past first base b) wasn't, in fact, even a virgin anymore. And c) was now going to have a baby out of wedlock, since she'd just called off her wedding to Jack.

"Look," Jack said. "I'm *really* sorry, Harold."

Somehow the words didn't seem quite adequate.

With a wheezing intake of breath, the minister gasped, "Did you say *pregnant?*"

Jack winced. "Uh, yes, sir."

In response, Jillian's father shut his eyes—either getting himself under control or praying, Jack didn't know which.

Ripping off his clerical collar, Harold opened his eyes again. "You two...!" he said. "This is very definitely *not* the time to call off a wedding."

"My feelings exactly." Jack shot Jillian a glance of censure. Her crazy announcement had made his blood boil. Often he took the blame for her impulsiveness. But damned if he'd let her family think he'd had second thoughts today. He didn't care how vulnerable her blue eyes looked in the candlelight or how the flames flickered in her red hair, making it glimmer with gold. Or how her translucent skin glowed, looking as softly moist as water. Did she really think he didn't mean to make *any* compromises when it came to the baby?

"So, you want the baby, Jack?" Harold asked, as Amy slipped from the room, presumably to find her brother.

Never taking his eyes from Jillian's, Jack said, "More than life." Even as he said it, hurt welled within him. Why couldn't she at least try to see his point of view? How could she consider not marrying him, even for an instant? Especially now. Hell, suddenly even Harold's question infuriated Jack. "It's my baby," he said through gritted teeth. "Of course I want it. What kind of man do you think I am, anyway, Harold?"

"The kind that's been sleeping with my daughter," Harold said retorted.

Miranda's tone was stiff. "Harold Williams, it takes two to tango. And my son always accepts his responsibilities."

Responsibilities. Jack loved his mother for standing up for him, but he wished she hadn't said it that way. As if what he felt for his child wasn't love and joy alone. But then, Sidwells were big on duty and responsibility. Not to mention the acquisition of wealth. He sighed. "Let's just sit down. Maybe you all can help Jilly and I come to some joint agreement about how we're going to raise this baby. That's the real problem."

"You'll stay in Lace Point, of course," said Miranda.

"But Miranda, they just got an apartment in Boston," protested Barbara.

Jack sighed. The in-laws weren't going to agree any more than he and Jillian were. He glanced around and realized he was the only person standing. Just as he started to take a seat, Jillian's brother, Brian, arrived.

"What's going on here?" he demanded. He

rushed headlong into the room—bare-chested, wearing only his tux pants and gaping at Jack as if he'd never seen him before. "Amy says Jillian's pregnant, Jack."

Why was Brian addressing him, not Jilly? "She is, Brian."

Brian's blue eyes bugged out under his straw yellow bangs. "And Amy says you're not going to marry her now."

Did Brian think he had called off the wedding because of the baby? "Brian, that's not exactly—"

But Jack didn't get to finish. Brian's arm arched wildly through the darkness. As his fist made contact, there was a sick sound of splitting flesh. Then Jack's eye exploded with pain. He thought he heard Brian say, "Don't ever touch my sister again."

And then everything went black.

Chapter Six

Two hours before the wedding...

MIRANDA CIRCLED a dining room chair, lifting a silver-white lock of hair from her forehead with a peach-painted fingernail. "For someone raised in a family that preaches nonviolence," she said, "that boy can sure deliver a wallop. Hold still, Jack."

"Ouch." He winced as his mother held a compress against his puffy, purple left eye. The lights had flickered back on and the lightning and hail had ceased, but rain was still falling.

Brian appeared in the doorway, his mop of straw yellow hair combed back and his penitent face so solemn it was almost comical. "I'm really sorry, Jack. I completely misunderstood."

Jack nodded. It was the fifth time Brian had apologized.

"I guess I should have punched my sister," Brian continued dryly. "But then, she's a woman. And pregnant. It never occurred to me that *she* was the one who was calling off the wedding."

"Well, she did." She'd barely even stuck around long enough to see if her hot-tempered fireball of a brother had killed Jack. Damn, but Brian sure packed a punch. Jack had been tempted to wrestle him to the floor and give as good as he'd got, but by the time he'd regained consciousness, Brian was begging for forgiveness. Not to mention his life.

Jack's mother chuckled as Brian left. "Don't worry, Jack. You and Jillian will come to terms with this. After all, how could she not marry the father of her baby?"

Taking the compress from his mother, Jack held it against his eye. "Easy. Just say 'I don't.'"

Miranda's usually strident voice softened. "But she loves you, Jack. She always has." She smiled. "And a baby..."

The swelling in Jack's heart mirrored the emotion in his mother's voice. Was it a boy or a girl? he wondered. Either way, it would be wonderful. How could it be otherwise? He and Jilly always did such good work together—whether they were making love or managing their café.

But she called off the wedding.

He tried not to think about it. Especially since she was right. When it came to the baby, he did want his own way. *But so does Jillian, Jack. And she deserves to make the decisions, too.* Glancing up, he decided he'd never seen his mother's brown eyes look softer than now, when they were lit by the prospect of a grandchild. His heart squeezed tightly. Did Jilly realize how much happiness they were bringing into the world, not just for themselves, but for everyone?

"Why don't you let me borrow the keys to your car while you go try to talk to her?" Miranda murmured. "I'll drive to the house. Surely they'll let me in long enough to get the cradle from the attic...."

Let me in? His mother said it as if she hadn't rented to friends of friends, but to strangers. Jack frowned. Why had she leased the house, anyway? In the past, she'd often left for extended periods without doing so.

"The Sidwell cradle," she repeated with a sigh. "Do you think Jillian will like it?"

"Yes." That his mother had thought of it touched him. Handed down from generation to generation, the antique, carved mahogany cradle had rocked every Sidwell child. Twice a year, always anticipating her son's firstborn, Miranda took it from the attic and polished it. "Why don't you make it a gift from you, Mom?" Jack said gently, wishing Jillian and his mother were closer.

"All right."

That was a concession. After all, the rift between the two women wasn't entirely Jillian's fault. Miranda had hoped—assumed, really—that Jack would marry into an old, prestigious Beacon Hill family, and Jillian had picked up on those feelings. Still, over the years, Miranda had accepted Jillian. Now, if Miranda would make more gestures of kindness toward Jillian...and if only Jillian could let go of her pride...

Not that it mattered, Jack reminded himself.

Jillian had called off the wedding. Apparently, last night *he* should have given *her* the wool socks. Not that he wanted to back down, either. He sighed. Accepting a monthly allowance from his mother could mean so much for the baby....

His mother murmured, "And that cake..."

His swollen slit of an eye darted toward the huge white baker's boxes that had just been delivered from the café, and he got another reminder of how gorgeous the wedding would have been. That fool cake bespoke all the reasons he loved Jillian. Her impulsiveness drove him mad, but she definitely possessed creative genius. And that he loved. Oh, she would modestly say, "The cake? It's nothing. Just a big old white thing with some peach-colored flowers on it."

But she'd spent months designing it. Sumptuous stacked tiers were arranged in an interlocking-wedding-ring pattern and iced in a basket weave. As if popping from a huge, layered basket, peach-icing roses mingled with pansies and spilling cascades of bluebells.

"It's the most gorgeous thing I've ever seen," Jack's mother had pronounced when she'd first seen it.

Not that she'd tell Jillian. And even if she did, it would hardly propel Jillian down the aisle.

How could Jillian doubt their love? Jack wondered. Or their ability to reach some consensus about the baby? That hurt him like a wound that refused to heal.

Hell, maybe he should tell her that Miranda had given them the money for the café. After all, this morning he'd faulted Jillian for not telling him about the baby sooner—when *he* was keeping secrets himself.

Yes, he owed Jilly the truth. And so much more, he suddenly realized. He usually got his way. She'd wanted to keep her maiden name, but he'd insisted she become Mrs. Jack Sidwell. And his damnable financial prospectus for the bar-restaurant had nearly destroyed her confidence in the café—to the point that she'd almost been willing to give up her dream. If he persisted, Jack knew their baby would grow up in the suburbs and attend private schools, too. *Oh, dammit, Jack. Face it. You railroad her into doing what you want.*

No wonder Jillian had decided to dot all the i's before she said "I do." If Jack was honest, he'd have to admit she did have reason to doubt he'd give an inch. A cool tentacle of fear snaked through him. Never once in all these years had he been confronted with the possibility of losing Jillian. But when it came to the baby, he knew she meant to stand firm.

This time, he'd have to back down. Which he could. The thought of living without her was more than he could take. *Oh, Jilly,* he thought, *I'll make any compromise, if only you'll marry me.* Trouble was, because he'd never compromised before, she had no reason to believe him now. The thought made his heart hammer. No wonder she'd called off their wedding.

"I really don't want to speak ill of her, Jack," his mother suddenly whispered, looking out the window. "But I think she's lost her mind."

Rising quickly to his feet, Jack held the compress against his eye and strode to where his mother was staring anxiously out a window. "What's gotten into her?" he murmured, barely able to believe his remaining good eye. It was Jillian. She was clad only in her skirt and blouse. And she was running barefoot through the rain.

"OH, JILLIAN!" her mother exclaimed with a soft laugh. "What on earth?"

"Please, Mother," Jillian said simply.

Looking not the least bit perturbed, the unsinkable Barbara Williams held her arms wide, stretching out a big, thick woolly towel. She wrapped it tightly around her daughter, clothes and all.

"Now, what were you doing out there?"

Jillian didn't have a clue.

After Brian decked Jack, she'd simply run out the door.

The next thing she knew, she'd kicked off her shoes and slipped off her tights. In spite of the cool spring air, she'd started running barefoot across the grass, the wet green blades tickling her feet, the mud oozing between her toes, the cold rain pelting her skin and dropping into her open mouth.

For a few blessed minutes, everything—the wedding, fighting with Jack, the coming responsibilities of motherhood—simply vanished. She'd barely even noticed the determined landscapers—four guys in rain-splattered jeans with chainsaws—who'd stopped working to gape at her, or the indefatigable florists, who were clutching their raincoats closed and setting up salvaged flowers.

Maybe it had been Jillian's own little bachelorette party—one last rush of freedom, a moment of being completely herself before she became a wife and mother.

Maybe.

Of course, now she was wrapped in a towel and her mother's arms, shivering and dripping water on the floor like a naughty kid.

Her mother merely plopped a kiss on Jillian's nose and with an understanding smile said, "Nothing like a good run in the rain, now is there?"

Jillian's tears mingled with the droplets on her face, and she suddenly hoped she could be half as good a mother as her own. "Did you ever think about not marrying Daddy?"

Her mother grinned. "Oh," she teased, "I still think about it every single night, when his darn snoring keeps me awake."

Jillian smiled. Her father's snores could wake the dead.

Her mother gave her another quick, reassuring hug, then her loving eyes settled on Jillian's face. "Honey, every woman worries about losing herself when she gets married. But Jack's going to enhance your life, just as he always has. Whatever your ideas about raising the baby, just stick to your guns. He'll come around. He loves you. Now, why don't you go on up and hop into a nice, hot shower?"

Even though she had absolutely no intention of marrying Jack today, Jillian managed a nod.

As she headed toward the stairs, she knew she'd never wanted anything more than Jack—and the child she could feel growing inside her. Just thinking of the baby filled her mind with wonderful images: cradling the child close in the soft morning light, packing a sandwich into one of those adorable little lunch boxes. But she couldn't give up her work or move out of the city. Those were dreams, too, just like having a family with Jack. Oh, her love for Jack was so strong it stretched her heart to breaking; it was so full she felt she'd burst. She couldn't bear to hurt him. But she'd made so many concessions over the years. She'd waited for Jack, and she was giving up her name. She'd had to fight to open the café. Maybe she'd never really forgive him for that.

And so she'd run through the rain like a lunatic, thinking that Jillian Williams was someone she'd come to like immensely over the years. What if Mrs. Jack Sidwell wasn't the same woman? What if she didn't even have a say-so when it came to rearing her own child? "What am I going to do?" she murmured.

Just as she reached her bedroom door, she ran into a male chest. Not the concave, bony chest that belonged to her brother. Or the roly-poly barrel chest that was distinctively her dad's. Or Jack's sexy, muscular bunched pecs.

"Who are you?" she managed to gasp, clutching the towel around her as she stepped back a pace and glanced up.

"Your father."

Oh, no. Not now. Jillian could merely stare. Her heart seemed to quit beating altogether, and her throat seized up, shutting with a quick spasm.

He looked uncertain. His eyes said, *Have you heard of me?* "I'm Nate Ralston."

He was about fifty. In the flesh, he looked every inch the tall, rangy, handsome traveler who trotted the globe, covering newsworthy danger spots. For so long, Jillian had dreamed about this moment, and yet unexpected fury now welled within her. How could he show up on her wedding day? Today was about her and Jack, not him. Oh, maybe she should have expected this of a man who'd abandoned her and her mother. It seemed so selfish. He could have at least called to warn her.

He was watching her carefully.

She opened her mouth, but nothing came out. There had been so much she'd wanted to say to him over the years. *How could you abandon me? How could a career count more than me? Don't you know how hard it was for me as you rose to prominence? To see you on TV news shows, to know we were flesh and blood, and yet never to receive so much as a birthday card from you?*

"My father?" Jillian blinked back the fresh tears that welled in her eyes. She clutched the towel, still shivering and dripping on the carpet. "I don't know why you chose to show up today of all days, but let's get one thing straight. I already *have* a father."

Nate Ralston didn't look particularly surprised by her reaction. "I know you have a father. He was...helping to settle me with your brother's friends, in the guest room. I'll leave if you want me to, Jillian."

Just hearing this man say her name was breaking her heart. Nevertheless, if she had one more decision to make right now, she thought she'd scream. "Look, uh, Nate. I guess I'll call you Nate instead of Mr. Ralston. Right now I have to decide what to do about my wedding." The mere thought of returning all those gifts made her blood run cold. "I'm pregnant," she found herself adding in a rush, "and my fiancé and I don't exactly agree on how to handle family life." She edged toward her bedroom door and the hot comfort of the shower. "So, please. I really can't be expected to make any decisions for *you.*"

His craggy, sculpted face showed no emotion, but the man's voice suddenly dropped to a strangled whisper. "Then I'll be here, Jillian."

Chapter Seven

One hour before the wedding...

TIME WAS RUNNING OUT.

Brian said Nate Ralston had arrived and that Jillian wasn't exactly thrilled. Not that Jack had time to worry about Nate. Or about his own mother, who had come home from a vacation that should have energized her but had left her looking unexpectedly frail. Right now, only an hour remained to convince Jilly to walk down the aisle. Jack took a deep breath and knocked on her bedroom door. "Jilly?"

The door swung open. Fresh from the shower, she smelled of soap and flowers. As his gaze settled on the soft blue eyes he'd hoped to wake to every morning of his life, he realized they were as red and swollen as the one of his that Brian had pummeled. She'd been crying.

Reaching up, she grazed a fingertip across his temple. "Brian did a real number on you."

Jack nodded, his eye hurting like the devil. "Forget it. I just dropped by to say I love you."

She puffed out her cheeks and exhaled a sigh that didn't give Jack any more comfort than her outfit.

In shorts and a T-shirt, she looked ready for a sporting event, not a wedding.

Her voice was creaky from crying. "I love you, too."

"That's a start. Jilly, I just...want to say a few things."

She nodded, stepping back. Even the sight of her room made Jack's heart ache. Pillows were bunched in the middle of the wrinkled bedspread, where she'd apparently been weeping. Clothes were strewn on the floor, and shoes were jumbled in the bottom of the closet. Just as soon as she messed a place up, he knew, she'd launch an all-out cleaning campaign. A digital bedside radio was now coming in without static, and the DJ was delivering a droning account of freeway accidents and flooded roads.

Jack didn't hear a damn thing about the sun coming out.

"C'mere...." He pulled Jilly against his chest. "It's hard becoming an us," he said softly. "But I'm not giving up." How could a relationship that had weathered thirteen perfect years possibly end in a mere fifteen hours?

Jillian's arms snaked around his neck and tightened. "Thanks for saying that, Jack."

He nuzzled his lips into her sweet-smelling hair, still damp from the shower. "I know we can work out our differences about how to raise the baby. And you know, you're not the only one who's kept secrets...." How she tensed in his embrace gave him pause, but he was determined to give the same honesty he expected from her.

She lifted her chin, her eyes narrowing. "What did you do, Jack?"

It hurt to say it, but he had to. "I...I lied about where I got the money for the café."

It was obviously the last thing she'd expected him to say. She merely stared at him, then tried to step back a pace. In response, he drew her closer, his hands locking around her waist. "Please—" His voice caught, and with his sudden sharp intake of breath, he drew in her heavenly scent. "Don't move away from me." *Never move away from me, Jilly.* "My dad didn't leave me any money when he died," he said, forcing himself to continue. "He left it to my mother. Right before she went away, she offered me the start-up capital. I knew you'd never accept, but I also knew opening the café was your life dream. So I asked my mother to pretend the money came from an inheritance."

Jack had known Jillian for years. Most times, he could read her forward, backward and sideways. But right now he didn't have a clue as to what she was thinking. He prayed he'd just done more than give her yet another reason not to marry him. "Jilly?"

"You went back on your promise to me? That's what you came in here to say?"

Suddenly, the anger he'd felt this morning came rushing back. "No." His voice became fierce. "I want to say I'll die if you don't marry me. I'm begging you. Damn it, Jilly. Let's make it work. Total honesty between us, from here on out."

Their eyes met and held. She swallowed around a lump in her throat. When she spoke, hurt laced through her words. "I always *have* been honest. How could you take money from your mother like that without telling me, Jack?"

"I'm telling you now. Even if I can't believe I've chosen this particular moment."

"Why did you?"

His amber eyes burned into hers. "Because I don't have a choice when it comes to you. I won't hold back anymore. This might make things worse between us, but if we get married today—something I'm seriously beginning to doubt—I want it to be because we're ready to share everything. I don't want any secrets between us. Or lies."

A hint of tears made her eyes glisten; their glassiness reminded him of the smooth surface of a still blue lake. "I didn't really hold back, Jack," she said tremulously. "Well, not for long. I mean, I thought my missed periods were due to stress. And I wanted to be sure. I know how...certain you like to be about everything."

Right then, he hated himself. She had so much heart. So much honesty. And she was right. He wouldn't have slept or eaten until they'd gotten a decisive test result. "Oh, Jilly. All I want is for you to be happy. I want you to keep your maiden name, if you want. And I'm sorry I gave you such a hard time about the café. We *will* make money, you know."

"We would have made more if we'd followed your financial prospectus for the bar-restaurant."

His voice was gentle. "But the café is your dream. From a financial perspective, I just felt we needed to know the odds. What I really think is that there's only one thing that could stop it from being a success."

There was a hitch in her voice. "What?"

"Having to close it because we're not together. The business needs us both."

"You're still avoiding the real issue, Jack."

He shook his head. "We'll raise the baby any way you want. You can make all the decisions, straight down the line. I promise."

"You've said that before, though. You promised we'd be self-supporting, but now that I'm pregnant, you want to accept money from your mom again." Jillian's voice rose. "And even before I was pregnant, you went behind my back and took money from her. Money that radically changed our lives. Jack, you lied to me! Don't you see why I can't marry you? Don't you see that sometimes love isn't enough. I don't want to be indebted to your mother."

His heart squeezed tightly. Was he really going to lose Jillian? "We're not indebted. Besides, this time I mean it, Jilly. I'll make any concession necessary. I—" His voice broke. "I can't lose you."

Suddenly, Jillian tilted her head and her eyes widened. As she turned slowly toward the radio, Jack realized she was reacting to something other than what he'd said.

He arched an eyebrow, and just as quickly, winced in pain. His left eye was now swollen all the way shut. "Jilly?"

She cocked her head toward the radio. "Did you hear that?"

He listened.

"...Makeshift shelters all over the city. Christ's Church in Boston has now opened its doors to the stranded travelers. Since the airport closed last night, countless people have been sleeping on lobby seats, on the floor...."

Jack stared at Jillian. "If the airport's been closed since last night, what was my mother doing there?"

Jillian's expression was grim. "Since I apparently need to thank her for a rather large financial gift—a gift that has a lot to do with why we shouldn't marry—I guess we could go find out."

"MIRANDA?"

Jillian paused in the doorway of Amy's room, with Jack beside her, his warmth pressing against the length of her side. As they'd come down the hallway, she'd still felt livid about his confession. And she was still reeling from the appearance of her own father. She wanted to talk to Jack about Nate's arrival, but now was hardly the time. Her mother, of course, would accept any houseguest—even Nate Ralston—with absolute grace. And Harold Williams was hardly the kind of man to feel threatened....

Jillian shook her head to clear it and watched Miranda, who was fluffing the pillows on the bed. Her toiletries, most of which were stamped with expensive designer logos, were arranged neatly on the dresser.

"Mother?" Jack said.

Miranda turned, quickly swiping at her cheeks in a way that made Jillian's breath catch. Had Miranda been crying? The very idea was jarring. Miranda was like Jack, always so...controlled. Even now, in spite of her red-rimmed eyes, her navy traveling suit was crisp and not a silver-white hair was out of place.

Her voice was strangely soft, almost apologetic. "Your mother already put me in here, Jillian, so I could freshen up."

Jillian hazarded a glance at Jack. But with his mother in the room, he'd turned one-hundred-percent pure Sidwell. And Sidwells didn't discuss emotions among themselves. Fortunately, Jillian wasn't a Sidwell yet, and probably never would be now. "Miranda, have you been crying?"

Miranda shook her head in denial.

"Mother," Jack said cautiously, "according to the radio, the airport hasn't been open since last night."

At that, Miranda's eyes darted toward the door,

as if Jack and Jillian were blocking her escape. When she blinked, a tear slid down her cheek. With sudden, shocking certainty, Jillian realized this woman had probably never cried in front of another human being in her life.

Beside her, Jack seemed frozen solid.

He didn't even move when Miranda's erectly held shoulders suddenly caved in. Gingerly seating herself on the edge of the bed, she clasped her hands tightly in her lap, looking defeated. Even as she bit her lower lip to keep it from trembling, another tear fell.

Jillian stepped forward, stopping short of the bed, since Miranda wasn't exactly the huggable type. Still, Jillian's mind was running wild—and guilt coursed through her. Had Jack's mother left town because she feared Jillian was taking away her only son? "Please..." Jillian peered into Miranda's eyes. "What's wrong?"

When she didn't answer, Jillian squinted imploringly over her shoulder at Jack. She'd never seen him look so shaken. He was coming from the bathroom, tissue box in hand. He set it gently on the bed, next to his mother.

His voice was strained. "Mother, can you please tell us what's wrong?"

Drawing a tissue from the box, Miranda dabbed at her cheeks. "I—I just don't know..." Her watery, brown-eyed gaze raised, just as a heart-wrenching sob escaped her lips. "Oh, dear, Jack," she murmured.

Jack looked positively terrified. "What?"

"Jack," she said, "your father didn't leave any money."

"As in no money at all?" Jillian couldn't help but say, barely able to comprehend the thought. The Sidwells were among the wealthiest people in Lace Point.

Jack collapsed into a bedside chair. "What do you mean, no money?"

Miranda was too overwrought to respond. Regally, she tried to hold back the dry sobs that were now shaking her shoulders, but it was no use. They escaped with the tears that slid from beneath her delicate sandy eyelashes. "Your father...lost money in stocks in the eighties, you know. And then he made some poor real estate investments. There *is* some money, but it's tied up in various ventures. And so—very privately, of course—I've been trying to sell the house—"

"Sell the house?" Jillian echoed. Not the Sidwell mansion! It had been the country seat of the Boston Sidwells all the way back to the Revolutionary War.

"My Lord," said Jack.

"I couldn't find a buyer immediately...."

Of course not, thought Jillian. The Sidwell estate wasn't exactly a starter home. It was the sort of place philanthropists bequeathed to historical societies. No doubt such a place would be on the market awhile....

Miranda continued with a start, as if just now realizing that unburdening herself could be a relief. "I'm so sorry, Jillian. I wanted to help with the wedding. Believe me..." Miranda's perfectly manicured hands shook and she pressed them against her chest, as if trying to staunch an aching wound in her heart. "I couldn't be more embarrassed. I had hoped to involve myself with every little detail, right down to the last birdseed bag."

Miranda had wanted to help? Jillian's nose burned with unshed tears, and she rested a hand on one of Jack's powerful shoulders. Without him, she was fairly certain she'd keel over. This was definitely a side of Miranda she'd never seen. Still, things didn't quite add up. If Miranda was too financially strapped to help with the wedding, how could she afford a fancy six-month stay in Europe? "So why did you go abroad?"

Jack's tone was sharp. "Yes, tell us everything."

Another smattering of tears leaked from Miranda's eyes. "Well," she began tentatively, "I got the idea to lease the house with the staff included—the cook, gardener and housekeeper—which made it attractive to a wealthy New York financier...."

Jack's lips parted in protest. "But I thought the people in the house were *friends,* Mother."

Miranda shook her head. "Well, not exac—"

Jack's gasp cut her off. "Is that where you got

the money for the café? Was it the rent from the house?''

Had Miranda rented the estate to raise capital for the café, and then gone to live somewhere less expensive? Jillian was so stunned she couldn't move. Her heart hammered, and her suspicions made her feel positively sick. ''You didn't go to Europe at all, did you? Miranda, where have you been staying?''

''Oh, don't worry—'' Miranda dabbed a tissue-wrapped finger into the corner of an eye ''—I'll be right back home before you can say boo.''

Everything from her quivering lips to the tears splashing down her papery cheeks said she believed otherwise. Jillian's eyes scanned the room, then she quickly crossed to the dresser, snagging a plastic, logo-stamped key chain.

She gasped. ''The One-Two Hostel in Boston?''

There was nothing wrong with the hostel, of course. With its ultracheap weekly rates, it was perfect for student tourists. Some of Jillian's out-of-town friends had stayed there. But it was noisy, and tenants usually lived out of backpacks. The rooms, though clean, had small iron cots, no radios or televisions, and carried the scent of pesticides.

It was no place for Miranda Sidwell.

Jillian's voice was weak. ''Please. Tell me you haven't been staying there for six months.''

Miranda crossed her arms and drew up her shoulders defensively, embarrassment tinging her cheeks rose. "Not that I care what the girls at the club would think."

The girls. Jillian would wager not a one of those "girls" at the Lace Point Country Club was under sixty-five. And Miranda Sidwell cared with her every breath. For years, her social life had revolved around that fool club.

"Let me get this straight." Jillian still couldn't believe it. "The rent from your house is the money we used to open Jack and Jill's?"

"The tenants paid quite a lot in advance," Miranda admitted.

Jillian could merely stare. "And you've really been staying at the One-Two Hostel?"

Miranda smiled bravely through her tears. "Oh, Jillian, I'd live the rest of my life in that awful place if it would give you two just a glimmer of my happiness. Jack, I loved your father so much." Miranda's eyes shifted and grew unfocused, becoming distant and yet bright, as if lit with inner fire. She clutched a tissue-filled hand to her heart. "Ah, we were so young. Rich. And we had the whole world. Oh, we didn't agree on everything, no more than you two apparently agree on how to raise your baby. But you know what? Not a bit of that mattered. Because the thing we cared most about was being together...."

She glanced from Jack to Jillian, then continued. "The faintest hint of the love my husband and I shared could carry you both through a lifetime. Still,

I wanted you to have a financial leg up—the café for Jillian, a basis for earning money in the future, for the kids." Her voice was suddenly laced with steel. "After all I've done, you can't call off the wedding! And if you don't get married, what will become of the café?"

A sob threatened to escape Jillian's lips, so she clapped a hand over her mouth. Even though Miranda was recently widowed, she'd leased the Sidwell estate, and the house that held all the memories of the husband she'd loved. Unable to explain it to her friends at the country club, she'd been living alone in Boston—cut off from everyone, including her only son.

She'd done it all so Jillian could have her café. And now Jillian had called off the wedding, making Miranda's sacrifices pointless.

"Oh, Miranda..." With a sudden gasp, Jillian dropped onto the bed, instinctively gathering the woman into her arms. "Yours is the most wonderful gift in the world. I can't believe it. All these years...oh, I completely misjudged you."

"And so did I."

It was Barbara Williams. She was standing in the doorway, wiping tears from her eyes. Coming forward, she embraced Miranda, too.

Stunned, Jillian listened as her mother took charge. "Now, Miranda, first thing tomorrow morning, Harold and I will drive right down to Boston and get the rest of your things from the hostel.

Whether Jack and Jillian get married or not, you're staying right here with us!"

"But I simply couldn't—"

Barbara wasn't taking no for an answer. "We'll tell your friends you got tired of Europe. And that, like a fool, you'd leased the house. And so I convinced you to stay on after the wedding."

The catch of hope in Miranda's voice said more than a thousand words about the sacrifice she'd made. "Why, maybe we *could* say that—"

"Of course we could," said Barbara pragmatically. "Now, c'mon."

As Barbara marshaled Miranda from the room, Jack rose and grasped Jillian's shoulders from behind. She started to turn, but her eyes fell on the Sidwell cradle, sitting beside the door. She'd first seen it years ago, when she and Jack were in the Sidwells' attic. Now she saw that a tag was attached that read, "To my dearest daughter-in-law."

"I can't believe your mother," Jillian whispered. As guilty as she felt, she knew that was no reason for changing her mind and marrying Jack today. She started to say more, but something in Jack's expression stopped her. His one good eye was fierce with amber fire and as hard as an agate. She could feel the chesty rumble of his voice vibrating through his shirt as she craned her neck to look up at him.

"Jilly," he said, "we're supposed to get married in forty-five minutes."

The words made her heart pound dangerously

hard against her ribs. She tried to turn and fully face him, but he kept pressing her shoulders, forcing her attention toward the window. "Look," he said simply, his voice nearly a command.

Outside, people were running every which way in the rain, stacking chairs under a lean-to to keep them dry until the last minute. Pots of ferns marked where the aisle would be, and a bright array of rain-splashed flowers peeked from a latticework archway. The elm was gone. The four men, who'd given up on staying dry, were squinting through the rain, their wet hair plastered down. They were still trying to resurrect the ruined white tent.

"Do you see that, Jilly?"

She'd never seen such an exercise in futility in her life. "They're all crazy," she whispered. But it touched her. Somehow, deep down, it touched her. She felt the weight of Jack's hands on her shoulders, imparting their quiet strength.

"They're not crazy, Jilly. What you're looking at is faith. Against all the odds and most of the predictions, everybody out there knows the sun's coming out. And that's what marriages are based on. Pure blind faith. Your parents have it. Like my mother said, my parents had it. And before today, you and I had it." His hands tightened on her shoulders. "You've got to believe we'll work out our differences about the baby. There's no time left to hammer out all the details—to cross the i's and dot the t's. But you've got to believe in me, to believe that I'll give you what you need. You've got to take it on blind faith."

Jack's words became so incredibly, gently soft that she barely heard them. "So good luck, my love. Good luck, my sweet Jilly."

"Good luck?" she whispered.

"In having your faith in me restored," he whispered back.

She was still staring into the rain, watching it pour down on the floral archway beneath which she and Jack were to take their vows, when Jack's strong hands left her shoulders. The warmth of his body withdrew from behind her. His voice ceased.

Suddenly, her breath catching, Jillian whirled around—so fast, she could have been turned by the wrenching of her own heart. "Jack?" she whispered.

But he was gone.

Chapter Eight

A minute before the wedding...

LOOK OUT HERE, JILLIAN.

Jack gazed nervously from his position next to the floral arbor, all the way up the long white runner to Jillian's bedroom window. She was still up there, he was sure of it. Not that he was moving. He'd wait for her right here all day and all night. In rain or shine...

But, of course, the sun *had* come out.

Gloriously. All at once, in a bright white burst that appeared as mysteriously as the storm. Suddenly, the drizzle simply dried up like so many impulsively shed tears, and the clouds rolled up like a thick, gray carpet. High in the sky, the sun was now sending down steady, warm beams that caught all the remaining raindrops and made magical prisms on grass blades and flowers.

The tent was raised. The elm was gone. The cake was assembled. The jazz ensemble, photographer and videographer had arrived. Of course, it might be the only ceremony in Lace Point history where the groom's eye was swollen shut. Or where ushers handed guests paper towels so they could ensure their chairs were dry. Nevertheless, the guests were here, and hats and best dresses were fluttering like flowers in the breeze, which wafted perfume through the spring air. Four musicians, seated unobtrusively to the side, had replaced the four landscapers. And at a podium behind the floral arch, Harold Williams was waiting, utterly composed in his vestments.

Look out the window, Jilly. Was she even there? Jack wondered. Couldn't she see how perfectly things had turned out?

Maybe not.

The bridesmaids weren't inspiring much confidence. Oh, they were smiling, but like all the groomsmen, they were lifetime friends of both Jack and Jillian's. Beneath their smiles, they looked downright stricken. Jack searched their faces. Was Jilly coming? No, she'd told the bridesmaids to simply go on. She'd said she'd be right behind them. Jack would bet his life on it.

Especially when Amy walked down the aisle. As the maid of honor, she was transformed, looking more like a grown woman than a teenager, more statuesque than pretty. Her professed objection to weddings seemed to have vanished. But Jack could tell she was fighting not to turn around. No doubt she wanted to run back and get Jilly.

Damn. Jack wished someone were giving Jillian away; that, at least, would have insured her being here. *So much for getting her that watch, so she'd be on time.*

Amy took up her place, not five feet from Jack, her eyes bugging out with distress.

The music stopped. Another song began, announcing the arrival of the bride. Everyone turned, waiting for Jillian to appear.

And Jack's heart wrenched. Because there was a missed beat. And another.

And then the musicians began playing something else.

JILLIAN'S THUMB and index finger squeezed the face of her delicate gold watch. No matter how hard she tried, she couldn't stop the palsied shaking of her hands. *It's twenty past three!*

"I can't believe I'm just standing here," she whispered. She was poised in front of the vanity in her bedroom, unable to move. *What did I come back here for?* She wracked her brain. *Hurry up! Remember! Everybody is waiting!*

But she couldn't.

Through the window, she could see that everything was going exactly as planned. How it happened, she'd never know, but it was sunny and warm, and the bridesmaids and groomsmen were all in their places. Jack was waiting, too, staring up at her window from the other end of that incredibly long-looking white runner. There were so many people down there!

She'd run back for something blue.

Now she remembered. If she could just put a dab of Amy's blue nail polish on her big toe, even through her stockings...

But she was frozen solid. Again. Had she really decided to marry Jack? Was she truly ready to take this leap of faith, to have the baby, not even knowing what compromises she might have to make?

"May I show you something?"

Startled, she gasped and whirled around. The speaker was Nate Ralston. Her biological father. In spite of her distress, Jillian almost laughed. Funny, she thought. All her life, she'd waited for some sign that this man cared about her. But today, with all the excitement, she'd completely forgotten about him. Well, almost.

And now he wanted to show her something? When she was twenty minutes late for her own wedding? She blew out a shaky sigh. "You sure pick your moments."

He merely strode into the room, a large book wedged under his arm, a camera hanging from his shoulder by a thick black strap.

She shook her head. "I can't believe you're not even wearing a suit."

He shrugged apologetically. "The airport here was closed, and I'd already checked luggage. I wound up renting a car out of Pittsburgh."

That gave her pause. Had this man ditched his

plane ticket and driven all the way up the coast for her wedding?

She scrutinized him, as if seeing him for the first time. His face, although remarkably handsome, was strewn with lines—crow's-feet at his eyes, deep grooves by his mouth. But she recognized her own blue eyes. His, like hers, were grayer, foggier than her mother's. *He's really your father, Jillian.* Her heart suddenly ached. For so long, she'd wanted love from this man she didn't even know....

Jillian told herself not to hope. "It's a little late for a father-of-the-bride talk, don't you think?"

His voice was deep, serious. "I hope not, Jillian."

And with that, he hauled the book under his arm onto the top of her vanity; his bronzed hand splayed on the cover and his gaze caught hers.

"I want you to know..." He swallowed audibly and a tick started at his jaw.

She watched him warily. "What?"

"That all those years ago, when Barbara..." He cleared his throat uncomfortably. "When your mom told me she was pregnant, I was selfish."

No joke. Jillian's heart hammered, and she held up her hand. "I'm not sure I need to hear this right now," she managed to say. "I'm pregnant myself and am supposed to be getting married. I need a chance to think. I need—"

"To hear this." His firm voice reminded her

that he had an important career, one where he was used to giving orders. "I admit I was weak, Jillian. I was a coward and I ran. I got everything I thought I wanted in life, too—a huge career. All I can say now is that it was easier for me to chase headlines, to care about the whole world, than it was for me to care about a baby."

He was lonely, she realized with a start. Her voice gentled. "It's all right."

"No. Not really. Oh, I told myself I stayed away all those years for your sake. That having two fathers might confuse you, and that I wanted you to think of Harold as your father, which you do. I told myself you'd be too young to care about seeing me. And then too old to do more than resent my sudden reappearance. So I convinced myself it was better for us not to have a relationship."

And all those years, while she'd been growing, Nate Ralston had missed it all. There was such regret in his voice. Her own caught. "Maybe we can now," she said.

"I'd like that."

The words were simple. But the emotion behind them was unmistakable. For a moment, their eyes met and held, and a world of forgiveness flowed between them. A slight smile lifted the corners of his lips. And in it—how funny!—Jillian could actually see her very own smile.

"I've overheard enough to realize you're arguing with Jack about how to raise your baby. But marry him anyway. Don't deprive him of what I've lost." Nate swallowed hard. "I—I came today because I got a very special invitation."

"You did?"

He nodded. "And I came because I wanted to see firsthand the kind of love that's already lasted thirteen years. I figure that's the kind I gave up when I left your mother."

"Thirteen years?" Jillian echoed. "How did you know Jack and I have been together that long? You don't know anything about me."

"But I do."

Nate opened the book and began turning the pages. "I've taken pictures all my life, Jillian. It's what I do. But these mean more to me than any of them."

Jillian could merely stare down in shock. Her whole life was represented here—surrounded by neatly placed photo corners and careful captions: Graduation. The Prom. Cutting the Ribbon at Her and Jack's Café.

Had Nate Ralston followed her all these years in silence, photographing her?

He turned to the final page. There were four photo corners in place, awaiting a final picture. Beneath the blank square, Nate had already written, "Jack and Jillian's Wedding."

Nate's voice was soft. "Please, Jillian. Let me

take the first picture of you two as man and wife. After all these years, I owe Jack."

Her heart thudded. "Jack?"

Nate nodded. "He's written me letters since he met you, telling me about how wonderful you are, Jillian. Even though I never answered him, he kept sending the pictures. And, of course, he sent the invitation to your wedding."

Jillian's eyes blurred. All these years, Jack had been trying to give her biological father back to her. It was so totally unexpected. And so predictably Jack. "My Jack sent you pictures of me? Letters about me growing up?"

"Yes," Nate said. "Your Jack."

And he *was* her Jack. Her eyes flew to the window. Far off, next to the floral archway, he was waiting. All at once the storm that had raged within her all day ceased—and a gentle calm descended. How could she have doubted, even for an instant, the transcendent power of the love they shared? And how could she doubt now that the man who'd written her father all these years could deny her anything she needed concerning their own child. Surely their love could sustain them and the family they were meant to share.

Suddenly, she wanted to run to his arms. She'd do anything it took to keep her, him and their baby together. Nothing could stop her.

Impulsively, she turned toward Nate, her eyes swimming with tears. "Want to give me away?"

His blue eyes softened. ''Never again,'' he whispered.

She smiled. ''Let me rephrase that. Nate, would you like to walk me down the aisle?''

He looked shocked, but he didn't say no. He glanced down at his rumpled khaki shorts and safari shirt. ''Like this?''

She nodded. ''Just like that. Camera and all.''

It was how she wanted Jack to see her—marching with the father he'd returned to her, toward the father who would wed her to the man she loved.

Nate Ralston's voice was rock steady. ''Jillian, it would be the greatest honor of my life.''

Just as she took his arm, she gasped. ''Something blue!''

When she opened the drawer, her heart nearly stopped when she realized the nail polish was gone. But in its place was the old Whitman's Chocolates box from the tree house. With trembling fingers, Jillian lifted the lid. And sure enough, there it was. The blue ribbon, now faded, that Jack had taken from her hair all those years ago, the night they'd first made love.

''Jack,'' she whispered, threading the ribbon through her gloved fingers, then clutching her bouquet. There was just no stopping the man. *My husband.*

She glanced through the window a final time and realized there was a rainbow. Her eyes traversed the arched ribbon of blue and red and yellow.

And landed on Jack.

Always Jack. Her man at the end of the rainbow.

HAROLD WILLIAM'S deep voice carried over the rows of chairs. "Do you, Jillian, take Jack to be your lawfully wedded husband? For rich or for poor? In sickness and in health?"

"I do."

Jack's hand shot to his heart. For an instant, he completely lost his breath. Only now did he realize how hopelessly nervous he'd been all day. Over and over, he'd told himself that this was their third attempt at a wedding, and that the third time was the charm. But maybe he hadn't really believed it until now. "You do?"

Jillian, who looked more radiant than he'd ever seen her, squinted at him through her veil as if he'd lost his mind. "I do, Jack," she whispered in a hushed tone.

"You do?" he said again. "Even though we haven't hashed out all the details about the ba—" He cut himself off, realizing they had a large audience.

She looked scandalized, as if this was a fine time for *him* to fall apart. Under her breath, she said, "Yes, Jack, I do."

Jack suddenly wished not quite so many people

were watching. And listening. So far, things had gone perfectly, in spite of the late start. And Jack thought he'd handled the last fifteen hours pretty well. He hadn't even lost control when Jillian called off the wedding. Not even the bad news about the Sidwell finances had shaken him overmuch, since he was thoroughly prepared to put his own Sidwell business acumen to use and rebuild the family fortunes. Which he would. Besides, one problem was solved. He and Jillian couldn't fight over the Sidwell fortune, since there wasn't one....

Oh, yes, he'd been in control all day, not so much as blinking when he'd found out he was going to be a father, or when Nate Ralston walked Jillian down the aisle wearing short pants. Or when his own mother had switched to the bride's side, just so she could cling to Barbara and cry. While the two women drowned in their own rainstorm of tears, Jack felt as if he'd been watching his extended family being born.

But he hadn't broken down.

Now he loudly said, "Please. Just give me a minute."

And then, while the crowd started to whisper and chuckle, Jack put his hands on his hips and started pacing.

Jillian's eyes were sparkling beneath the thin white veil, which, without ceremony, she now lifted, just to get a better look at him. "Jack? Are you all right?"

"Am I all right?" He gazed deeply into her eyes. "Jilly, I'm ecstatic. Joyous. I could leap over mountains. Run faster than a gazelle." And suddenly, completely unable to stop himself, he stepped forward, wrapped his arms tightly around his bride, lifted the veil all the way over her head, and with a deep, hard kiss on her lips, tried to impart all the joy and relief in his soul.

Only when he drew away did he realize that Jillian was grinning, her eyes glittering with tears. "Oh, Jack," she said. "All my life, I've wanted to see you lose control like that."

She looked so terribly pleased that Jack silently vowed to lose control a lot more often.

"Daddy," she said, turning to the podium, "can't I just put on the ring now?"

Harold Williams's lips twitched with good humor. "It's a bit out of order, but somehow I don't think God will mind."

And moments later, in a jumbled ending that switched prayer-book paragraphs faster than musical chairs, Jack and Jillian were legally married.

"By virtue of the authority vested in me, I pronounce you husband and wife," Harold said. "You may kiss the bride." After a second, he added, "Again."

"Nothing can stop us now, Jilly," Jack whispered.

''Nothing,'' she whispered back.

And nothing could. Not even the low rumble of thunder that groaned through the finicky heavens. Or the sizzling lightning bolt that now flashed in the sky. Or the rain that was about to fall again.

Jack ignored it all and merely captured Jillian's lips with his own, making a warm, living force flow between them. Joy in life always came between the storms. Sometimes its light was faint. Sometimes just a mere glimmer. But the storms were always there. And so he and Jillian would shelter each other. And their family. And search the dark clouds for all the soft, silver linings.

And wait together for these glorious warm rushes of joy, these amazing moments when the sun burst through the clouds and shone—as strong and eternal as the love they were meant to share.

RAINING VIOLETS

Ruth Jean Dale

Chapter One

THE WAY SHE SAW IT, Carrie Duncan had two choices: she could marry Hank Brady as planned or she could kill him.

Assuming he ever showed up, of course. With every passing minute, killing him gained favor.

Wearing her beautiful white satin wedding gown again, and clutching a bouquet of blue and white violets again, Carrie stood at a lace-draped window in the bedroom of her boss's Boston town house looking out on a January snowstorm and trying not to come undone. So Hank was late for his own wedding. So what else was new?

Her own father had been late for his engagement party, so she'd been told. Her mother had married him anyway. As a result, Carrie had grown up with a world-class workaholic as a dad. Hadn't she learned anything?

The Reverend Wills, a family friend, waited in Josie Jones's picture-perfect living room to do the honors—scheduled to begin 27 minutes ago, in case anyone besides the bride-to-maybe-be was counting. The few guests willing and able to brave a snowstorm that meteorologists predicted would paralyze all of New England also waited.

Among those guests was Minerva Duncan, Carrie's little, white-haired grandmother, who now entered the bedroom. With her bright blue eyes and cheery disposition, she could easily have been mistaken for Mrs. Claus. Despite the weather, she'd come all the way from her winter condo in Florida to see her granddaughter marry a man who had charmed Granny from day one. Her face, normally placid and pleasant, was creased with lines of concern.

"Relax, dear," she suggested. "He's not *that* late."

Carrie groaned and turned back to the window. From here she could barely see the street outside for the falling snow. "If he stands me up again," she announced grimly, "he's a dead man."

"But, dear, he never stood you up before."

"What do you call that debacle in December?"

"That was something quite different." Granny sat down on the edge of a brocade-covered chair. "And to his credit, he did call that morning and say there was a problem before you actually got to the church."

"But the bottom line is we didn't get married. If you don't consider that being stood up, I don't know what you'd call it."

Granny folded her hands demurely in her lap, her expression sanctimonious. Hank was so much like Carrie's father—charming and single-minded and ambitious—that Minerva was inclined to forgive him anything, simply because he reminded her of her son. "It wasn't his fault that he got caught in the worst traffic jam in the history of Massachusetts," she replied, arguing Hank's case.

"It was his fault he decided to stay to cover the story for that rag he works for," Carrie countered.

Granny didn't like Hank's newspaper, the *Boston World.* As far as she was concerned, journalism began and ended with the *Globe,* and the *World* was nothing but an upstart. But for Hank, she'd always been willing to make an exception. "He's a reporter," she stated. "It was his job."

"Yes," Carrie agreed tartly, "and it was my job to go to the church and tell all those people they'd made the trip for nothing. Now it looks as though I may get to do that all over again. *Aargh!*"

"We don't know that. You must be patient, Caroline dear."

Granny always counseled patience. She'd said the same thing to her daughter-in-law, Carrie's mother. Remembering her father's lack of consideration for his wife and daughter, Carrie had a hard time seeing where patience had ever gotten either of them. Both her parents were dead now, but in her family, patience had been strictly one-sided. Over and over again, Carrie'd wondered why her mother had put up with the situation. *She* certainly never would!

Granny went on. "I just hope Hank's all right. He could be—" her blue eyes widened "—dead in a ditch somewhere."

Carrie turned abruptly, yards of white satin billowing around her. ''Please don't start that. I'm sure it's simply a case of something more—more *interesting* coming along to distract him. He couldn't be hurt...could he?''

Granny rolled her eyes. ''Light dawns over Marblehead!'' she declared. ''I don't mean to frighten you, dear, but with weather this bad, anything could happen. You might want to give the boy the benefit of the doubt until you know for sure.''

''My God, you're right.'' Carrie felt nauseated. Yes, he'd embarrassed her in December, but that was in the past. Whatever was keeping him now had to be something beyond his control—of course it was.

A light tapping on the door announced Josie's entrance. Carrie's best friend was also her boss and owner of three Josie's Posies shops in Boston, one of which Carrie managed. In her red matron-of-honor dress, the blond and elegant Josie looked even more sophisticated than usual.

''How are you holding up?'' she asked Carrie.

''Not terribly well.''

''I'm sure there's a logical explanation. If it's any comfort, Sean's not here, either.''

''Really?'' Carrie perked up. Sean Kelly was Hank's best man, so they must be someplace together. And since Sean was a policeman, they couldn't be in any trouble.

Could they?

"The guys Hank invited from the newspaper aren't here yet, either."

Carrie frowned. "What do you suppose *that* means?"

Josie shrugged. "Beats me. I'm not sure anyone who was at the bachelor party last night is here. Maybe they're all down with hangovers...I'm kidding!" she added, seeing Carrie was in no mood for joking. "I'm sure there's a perfectly logical explanation."

Josie's attempt to lighten the situation failed miserably. *How can this be happening to me?* Carrie wondered, sitting on the edge of the bed. She slumped dejectedly. She loved Hank, she truly did, and when he'd proposed to her she'd accepted with alacrity. But now she wondered if they were ever going to make it to the altar—at the same time, anyway.

She heard Josie say, "Mrs. Duncan, maybe you could go back down there and try to keep everyone calm? The natives are starting to get a little restless."

And Granny's reply: "Of course, if Caroline doesn't need me."

"You go on, Granny," Carrie said without looking up. The last thing she needed was Granny alternately scolding and frightening her. "I'm fine."

"If you're sure. Just remember, dear, no matter how dreary it looks now, it'll soon be raining violets."

Raining violets—Granny's way of saying that everything would come out all right in the end. Raining poison ivy was more like it.

With a little detour to plant a light kiss on Carrie's bowed head, Granny left the room. Josie sat down on the bed and put an arm around Carrie, giving her a comforting squeeze.

"Stiff upper lip, pal. Everything's going to be fine."

"Will you put that in writing?"

"You're about to marry the writer. Me, I'm all talk and no—"

A scuffle of feet sounded in the hallway and the door flew open. Hank Brady, twenty-nine-year-old, drop-dead-gorgeous ace newspaper reporter on the fast track to fame and fortune, stood there. His smile was dazzling; *he* was dazzling in his tuxedo and white shirt. Black haired and blue eyed, he looked perfectly self-confident, if a bit harried.

Behind him, his sister Amanda, manager of Josie's Posies number one, exclaimed, "Hank, I told you it's bad luck to see the bride before the wedding! Carrie, I tried to stop him but he wouldn't—"

Stepping inside the room, he closed the door in her face. "Josie, honey, would you mind givin' us a few minutes alone?" His sweet Texas drawl flowed around Carrie like honey. It had been one of many things that had attracted her to him when he'd relocated from Texas a couple of years ago to work for the *Boston World*.

Josie glanced at the bride-to-be, read her correctly and rose from the bed. "Okay, but we're more than a half hour behind schedule. I'd suggest you two hustle your buns before that bunch out there turns into an ugly mob."

"We'll do that," Hank promised, his gaze never straying from Carrie's face. He waited until the door closed behind Josie before stepping forward with arms outstretched.

Carrie surged from the bed and went to him as if going home. "Oh, Hank," she murmured, lifting her face for his kiss.

Familiarity had not lessened the power of his touch. When his lips parted over hers, she felt the tremors all the way down to her toes. Clinging to him, she closed her eyes and gave herself up to the myriad sensations he always roused in her.

Aided, no doubt, by the fact that they hadn't slept together since the disaster in December. Furiously she'd announced that he wouldn't be welcome in her bed again until they were married. He'd accepted her ultimatum without grace and only after trying his charming best to persuade her of her folly.

She'd stood fast, although it hadn't been easy for either of them. Now, wrapped in his arms on their wedding day and feeling the heat rising between them, she gave thanks that the drought was nearly over.

He lifted his head and smiled down at her, his

beautiful blue eyes filled with passion. "I love you," he said.

"I love you, too."

They kissed again. He tried to slide his knee between hers, but yards and yards of satin barred his advance. He groaned.

"I can't wait to get this thing off you," he muttered, his hand clenching a fistful of the glistening material.

She caught her breath at the desire in his voice. "Me, too."

"Think we got time for a quicky?"

Her laughter helped diffuse any lingering tension. "You've got a one-track mind."

"All us Texans do," he said ruefully. "Can't help it, sweetheart."

She ran her fingers through his thick dark hair, afraid to ask but knowing that she must. "What happened, Hank? Why are you so late? I've been going out of my mind. After the last time—"

"Now, don't go there." His tone was lightly admonishing. "You forgave me for that, remember? And didn't we agree we wouldn't talk about it ever again?" He brushed light kisses across her cheek, distracting but not diverting her.

"Yes, but—"

"It wasn't my fault this time, Carrie darlin'. Honest, it wasn't." He nibbled at her ear.

She wanted desperately to believe him, but something made her press onward. "But still, I—"

"Do you have any idea how gorgeous you are? As my ol' granddaddy used to say, you're 'purty as a pitcher.'"

"They say all brides are beautiful." She arched back against his arm and he nuzzled her throat. "I still want to know—"

"You're not all brides. You're *my* bride."

The pride in his voice thrilled her. So did the press of his lips on the swell of her breast above the sweetheart neckline of her gown. "Was it...the storm that delayed you?"

"It's snowin' to beat the band, all right."

"Then that's the reason you're late."

"Not...entirely." He cupped her breast with one hand, over the lace and satin and pearls.

She felt it as if he'd touched bare skin. "What...else?"

"Well..." He lifted her breast, making a plump target for his lips. "We..."

"W-we?" She could barely stand.

"Sean, the fellows, you know. Uh...we were enjoyin' the traditional prewedding basketball game when—"

"Basketball game?" She blinked and tried to pull away from his busy mouth, but couldn't quite find the strength.

"I needed to work off a little tension, darlin', nothin' sinister about it. Shootin' a few hoops always makes me feel better."

Her blood pressure must have soared twenty

points. "Are you telling me that while I was here going out of my mind, you were—"

"No, no, that's not how it was at all. We were just winding down when Jim Archer showed up. You remember Jim."

"Your editor?" Hank kept kissing and nibbling his way across the landscape of her bosom, but the effect was no longer quite as potent.

"That's right. Jim had some really great news—can't wait to tell you—"

A pounding on the door to the bedroom interrupted Hank and he changed directions without a hitch.

"—But maybe we'd better get this show on the road before our guests turn ugly."

"Your *editor* caused you to be late?"

"That's what happened, all right." He stood her on her feet before straightening his tie, settling his coat across his shoulders, smoothing his trousers. "Sure, Jim had a hand in it. But when you hear what he had to say, you won't even care if I was a few little ol' minutes late."

"A few minutes." She repeated his words, trying to clear her head. She was having a hard time calming down enough to refute him, because she couldn't believe what she was hearing.

"Carrie!" Josie pounded on the door. "Can we start now? People are getting anxious. They're afraid they'll be snowed in!"

Hank leaped in with a glance at Carrie. "Tell 'em

to start that wedding march, Josie, 'cause we are on our way!'' Touching his fingertips to his lips, he pressed the kiss on Carrie's cheek. ''See you at the altar, sweetheart. Just a few more minutes and you'll be Mrs. Hank Brady.''

Whistling a jaunty tune, he strode to the door, opened it and disappeared into the hall. Josie gave him a confused glance and then hurried inside.

''What were you two—'' She stopped short. ''Don't answer that. You don't have a speck of lipstick left and you're falling out of your dress.'' She hurried to the makeup table and retrieved Carrie's lipstick. ''Put this on and I'll get the veil.''

Numbly Carrie colored her lips and stood unmoving while her friend placed the garland of white violets on her head, then spread the gossamer veil in graceful folds.

And all the while she was thinking, *He was playing* basketball? *He was talking to his* editor?

Josie stepped in front of the bride and peered into her face. ''Are you all right?''

''Of course I'm all right,'' Carrie said automatically.

''Are you ready to go?''

The strains of the ''Wedding March,'' played enthusiastically by Josie's teenaged niece, reached them. Carrie's heart clenched into a knot of terror. She licked her lips. ''I'm not sure. I...'' Breath failed her. Was she her mother, after all?

Josie waited. She looked as if she, too, was holding her breath. The two women stared at each other for an eternity.

Finally Josie spoke. "In that case...it's time for you to give me your engagement ring so the man of your dreams can slip that wedding band into place. I promise to guard it with my life."

Carrie tugged the ring from her finger. "I almost forgot," she whispered, offering it with a hand that trembled.

"You've got a lot on your mind. Oh, Carrie..."

Amanda Brady, Hank's pretty twenty-something sister, bustled into the room. "Are y'all comin' or not?" She made it sound like a joke, not a choice. "That poor little thing at the piano is gettin' desperate and the guests are gettin' surly."

Carrie took a deep breath. "I'm coming," she said in a voice barely above a hoarse whisper. Of course she was. You couldn't get people out for a wedding on a day like this and then disappoint them.

Especially not a second time.

JOSIE WAS A GENIUS when it came to flowers, and she'd outdone herself for the wedding. Moving slowly down the curving staircase in time to the music, Carrie looked into the living room with a kind of detached admiration.

It wasn't as if this even *felt* like her own wedding. Still in a curious state of separation, she moved automatically and without thought. The long veil seemed to enfold her, wrap her in anonymity. She was grateful that it did.

The guests sat on white folding chairs rented for the occasion. The aisle ran down the middle, defined by ribbons and bows and white violets, with two enormous cascades of violets and greenery at each end. More ribbons and bows draped the ceiling and walls.

Everyone turned to see the bride make her entrance. As she passed the first of the two cascades, the audience rose as one.

Carrie, like most little girls, had dreamed of the day she would be a bride. In her imagination, she'd walk with exquisite grace to the side of her bridegroom, usually a rock star or Hollywood's man of the moment.

But that wasn't Brad Pitt waiting for her, it was Hank Brady—a man who played *basketball* on his wedding day. A man who left her to wait and wonder, and then expected to escape his just desserts with a few hasty kisses and a lame excuse about his *work*.

He smiled.

She didn't. But he probably couldn't see her expression very well through the veil.

The music from Josie's piano quivered to a halt. The Reverend Wills gave the bride an encouraging smile and cleared his throat. "Dearly beloved, we are gathered here today..."

Carrie and Hank had finally settled on a traditional ceremony, minus the "obey" part. Hank, being a writer, had naturally wanted them to compose their own vows, but Carrie was too much a traditionalist for that. She had held out for a classic wedding ceremony and she was about to get it.

If there could be anything classic about a man who'd stand up his intended, not once but twice. She closed her eyes and tried to concentrate on the words wafting past. Thinking about Hank's lame excuses wasn't doing her a bit of good. She was working up a full head of steam, all right.

She glanced at Hank out of the corner of her eye. He looked so composed, so self-confident. The hand that held hers did not tremble; it was warm and dry and masterful.

What was she doing, marrying a man who would treat her as her father had treated her mother? Carrie would never hold first place in his heart, but even so, she had to go through with it. She could do absolutely nothing but what was expected of her.

Of course, she *always* did what was expected of her. When she was a kid, she'd never missed a day of school, no matter how bad she felt or how much she wanted to sleep late. When she'd got her first job nine years ago at the age of sixteen, delivering flowers for Josie's Posies, she'd been the most dependable employee Josie had ever had—but she'd never put her work before her family or friends.

Now a full-fledged floral designer, Carrie had met

Hank when he came in to buy flowers—for another woman.

Hank. How well did she really know him? She gave him another oblique glance. He wasn't like any other man she'd ever met, actually. She'd thought that was because he came from Texas, but maybe that wasn't it at all. Maybe he was just selfish. Maybe she'd be better off without him.

This is a fine time to think about that!

She was starting to panic. Desperately she tried to clear her mind of negative thoughts and concentrate on what the minister was saying. The die was cast. There was nothing, absolutely nothing, she could do about it now.

Besides, she loved him. He was bright and funny and mischievous and ambitious. He loved kids and dogs, and even more to the point, he loved *her.* She knew he did.

So why had he left her at the altar once and come late the second time?

The young minister leaned forward earnestly. "If there is anyone here who knows any reason these two should not be joined in holy matrimony, let him speak now or forever after hold his peace."

In the deafening silence, Carrie glanced around. Everyone was watching her with rapt attention. She saw their thoughts on their faces: *no one ever says anything at this point in the ceremony. Why does the minister even bother?*

Carrie looked back at Reverend Wills, who was

just about to open his mouth to go on. All of a sudden, something inside her snapped.

To her horror, she heard her own voice saying, "I do! I know a reason!"

Chapter Two

CARRIE YANKED HER HAND from Hank's and whirled. Lifting her voluminous skirts above her knees, she ran back down the aisle she'd just traversed with measured steps. A sea of stunned faces registered in her mind but didn't actually sink in. All she could think about was getting out of here—out of this mess, out of this marriage.

Hank caught up with her at the back of the room. "Hold it!" he ordered, catching her by her arms and swinging her around to face him. "What the hell's going on? What's the problem?"

"Let go of me!" She tried to yank her elbows free, without success. "He asked if anyone knew a reason...and I do. So just let me—"

"Not until we get a few things straight." He looked at her with blazing blue eyes. "Did you or did you not agree to marry me—twice, as a matter of fact?"

"Yes, but I didn't know what I was doing the second time!"

Sean and Josie, the best man and matron of honor, joined them at the back of the room, horror plainly written upon their faces. All the guests had swiveled around in their seats to watch with clear fascination.

The minister stared at them, slack jawed. He'd probably never had anyone take him up on that escape clause before.

So what do they think we are? Carrie wondered indignantly. *A television sitcom?*

Hank loosened his hold on her arms. He smiled that smile that charmed birds out of trees, and contacts into spilling their guts even when they knew they'd regret it. "I get it," he said. "You've got bridal remorse."

"I've got what?"

"Cold feet, honey."

"My feet are just fine!"

"I mean nerves—wedding nerves. If you really love me like you said you did—"

"How dare you suggest I don't love you!" She glowered at him, her hands crumpling her skirt into masses of wrinkles. "I've loved you from the moment I met you!"

"And I love you," he said quickly, his face completely free of guile. "This is what we both want, so let's not keep all these nice people in suspense any longer, okay?"

The Reverend Wills approached at that moment. "Are you all right, Carrie?"

"She's fine," Hank said. He took her hand and tried to urge her up the aisle, but she held back.

He wasn't going to get around her this easily! "You don't love me," she accused, ripping her hand from his. "Marriage is forever. I don't think I want to take a chance on a man who—"

"I do *too* love you!" He shoved his outraged face close to hers. "Jeez, what the hell— Beg pardon, Reverend. What the heck do you want from me, Carrie? Blood?"

"I want to be sure we've got a chance of making it work before we stand up there in front of God and everybody and make promises we may not be able to keep."

"Are you after promises or guarantees?" he challenged. "Because I'm not an appliance store. I don't give guarantees."

"Don't I know it!"

Reverend Wills patted the angry bride on the arm. "Calm down, Carrie. Maybe you and Hank and I should find a private spot and talk about—"

"Private?" Carrie glanced at their enthralled audience. "Why do we need a place that's private? Everybody shared my humiliation when he stood me up the first time, so I guess they deserve to be here for the finish."

"That's it!" Hank slapped his temple with a flat palm. "You're giving me back what I gave you, right? You never intended to marry me today. You set me up."

"I did not! I wasn't late for my own wedding, remember? *You* were—twice."

He blinked, then frowned. "But I explained all that. You said you understood."

"*You* said I understood." Grabbing her bouquet of violets from the unresisting hands of her matron of honor, Carrie whacked him across the shoulder. Blue and white petals rained down across his tuxedo and fell upon Josie's pale green carpet. "I understand that if you loved me, you wouldn't have been late—that nothing could have kept you away."

"Nothing except the biggest opportunity of my life." His eyes lit with an inner fire. Grabbing her arms again, he stared into her eyes. "Carrie, it's the opportunity of a lifetime. What my editor came to tell me is—"

"I don't care what he told you! Let me go, you brute." She twisted her head to one side and squeezed her eyes closed for a moment, trying to avoid being swept up in his excitement.

"No, really! The guy they assigned to cover the Fort Knox gold trial won't be able to do it and they're sending me in his place. Do you realize what this means?"

She stopped struggling. "Why won't the other reporter be able to do it? Did you put out a contract on him or something?"

"No! His wife's pregnant and he wants to be with her when the baby's delivered." Hank's expression made his feelings about this decision perfectly clear: the guy must be an idiot.

Carrie melted. "That's wonderful. His wife is a very lucky woman."

Hank grimaced. "But we're talking the crime of

the century—the theft of a zillion bucks worth of gold from Fort Knox, for cryin' out loud—the potential collapse of the gold standard, the poverty of nations. This case has got it all! It's the biggest thing since O.J. and the Oklahoma City bomb trial. He may never get this kind of opportunity again."

"Well, whoopty-do. He'll never get another opportunity to see the birth of his son either." She gave him her most scornful glance.

"And best of all—" he should have looked this excited when she said she'd marry him, Carrie decided "—they've moved the trial to Dallas!"

"That does it." She whacked him again with her bouquet, now mostly stems, and whirled toward her dumbfounded matron of honor. "Do you have that engagement ring?"

"Of course."

Carrie stuck out her hand. "Let me have it." Josie dropped it on her palm and Carrie thrust it at Hank. "I wouldn't marry you if you were the last man on earth. I knew Texas and Boston didn't mix, but me—I *had* to take a chance! Thank heaven I came to my senses in time."

Instead of accepting the ring, he tried to put his arms around her. "Ah, c'mon, honey, you know you don't mean that. You love me—you said so."

"Yes, but *you* love your job first, sports second and me a distant third." She shoved the ring into his pocket, then twisted her head aside to avoid his descending lips. "I'd be a fool to settle for second best, but with you, second best would mean a move up!''

Hank fell back on his old standby: ''But I love you!''

''Not enough. Not nearly enough.'' She turned her back on him. ''Goodbye, Hank, and good luck. I...I wish you all the best with your future endeavors.''

''Jeez,'' he said, his tone suddenly uncertain, as if he might finally be starting to believe her. ''Does this mean the wedding's off—*really?*''

She let out her breath with a deep, ragged sigh. ''As Granny would say, light dawns over Marblehead! Yes, the wedding is off. Go to Dallas and forget you ever knew me.'' She squared her shoulders. ''As for me, I think I'll get a dog. I can count on a dog.''

She waited for Hank to assure her that she could count on him, too, but he didn't. Instead he said in a strained voice, ''If that's how you really want it.''

''Children, children, don't be too hasty.'' The Reverend Wills interjected, briefly putting his hands on two stiff shoulders.

Josie broke in anxiously. ''She's just upset, Hank. Once the two of you have a chance to talk this out, I'm sure everything will be all right.''

''Hey, buddy, maybe if you got down on your knees and promised nothing like this would ever happen again...?'' That was Sean, cajoling.

''What's the point?'' Hank walked around Carrie,

and she, gaze downcast, saw only his long legs in the satin-striped tuxedo trousers. With sudden shock, she realized he was heading for the front door. "I could promise the moon," he was saying, "but promises aren't enough anymore and I'm fresh out of guarantees."

He disappeared into the front hall and Sean, with an exclamation of disgust, hurried after him. Josie put her arm around Carrie's tense shoulders and squeezed.

The front door opened and closed with a bang.

Hank Brady was gone. Carrie would probably never see him again. She knew she should say something to the guests, make some apology, but words wouldn't come except for a whisper to Josie: "Get me out of here, okay? I think I'm going to scream!"

And Josie got her out of there while the Reverend Wills addressed the dumbfounded guests.

EVENTUALLY EVERYONE LEFT except for Carrie and Josie, Granny and Hank's sister, Amanda. The bride-not-to-be had cried, screamed and ripped off her wedding gown. She now sat in her wedding lingerie at Josie's dining room table, a slice of wedding cake before her and a glass of wedding champagne in her hand.

She sucked in a deep, quivering breath and lifted her glass. "Here's to me," she announced. "It was the right thing to do, even if it was the wrong way to do it."

Josie raised her own glass. "Hear! Hear!" She drank. "Whatever you say."

Carrie patted damp eyes with a soggy tissue and glared at her grandmother and at her now-not-to-be sister-in-law. "What's wrong with you two?" she complained. "You're supposed to be cheering me up."

"Why?" Granny demanded tartly. "You brought this on yourself, dear."

"I...?" Carrie thrust out her chin, feeling unfairly maligned. "This is Hank's doing, not mine."

"Your grandma's right!" Amanda's eyes, as blue as her brother's, flashed. "Okay, he acted like a jerk, we're all agreed on that. He was late for his own wedding—not once but twice. So are you trying to tell us you didn't know what he was like when you agreed to marry him? Is it suddenly a crime to be ambitious?"

"Ambitious? The man's a certified workaholic." A tear plopped into Carrie's champagne.

Amanda rolled her eyes. "I had more sympathy for you in December, to be perfectly frank. Now..." She shook her head decisively. "Sorry, but I'm not buyin' it."

Granny nodded agreement. "You could at least have tried to work it out," she said. "You should be more like your mother, Caroline. She knew a woman's place—"

"Don't, Granny. Please don't go there." Carrie clenched her teeth in frustration. Was her grandmother really unaware of all the lonely nights and terrible fights?

"Well," Granny said, "your parents stayed together to the end. I'm just afraid you expect things to come too easily."

"I do not!" She couldn't believe her own grandmother would take *his* side, but then, Granny had never seen her son's failings, either.

"You do, too," Minerva insisted. "Because of what happened in December, you were just looking for something to throw back in his face."

"I was not!" But was she? Could there be a tiny grain of truth in that? Oh, surely not! And yet Carrie hadn't been entirely surprised when he failed to appear at the appointed time. It was almost as if she'd expected it....

"He loves you," Amanda said. "You're the only girl he's ever been serious about."

"And *you* love *him*," Granny added. "You've never let any man get you this close to the altar—and you've let Hank do it twice."

Amanda caught one of Carrie's hands in hers. "Call him. Talk to him. You can work this out."

Josie stood up so suddenly that her chair toppled over with a bang. She didn't even glance at it. "Will you two lighten up?" she demanded. "Give the poor girl a chance to think. She doesn't have to make any more decisions right now."

Carrie appealed to her best friend. "What do *you*

think I should do, Josie? Was I completely unreasonable?''

Josie's full mouth thinned into a tight line. ''I'm the wrong person to ask, Carrie.''

''You're my best friend. If I can't trust you, who can I trust?''

Josie groaned. ''I've been married three times—and divorced three times. I wish I'd had the guts you showed when you stopped your own wedding.''

Carrie shot a triumphant glance at the other two women.

Josie went on. ''In all fairness, I've got to say I loved all three of the bastards, and sometimes I have to wonder if I'd tried a little harder...'' She shrugged. ''Who knows, I might be a happily married woman today instead of what I am—a cynical 'Nooyawka' hiding out in Back Bay Boston and trying like hell not to fall in love again because I don't really do it very well.''

She gave her friend a sudden smile. ''That's not what I want for you, Carrie, so I'm going to let you make up your own mind about this. Whatever you decide, I'm with you all the way.''

They hugged and they cried, and then Granny and Amanda hugged and cried, and then Josie broke out another bottle of champagne. And by the time Carrie realized this was supposed to be her wedding night, she was too far gone to care.

Much.

TWO DAYS LATER, Carrie was back at work and trying to pretend nothing untoward had ever happened. The fact that nearly everyone who walked through the door at Josie's Posies number two in the suburb of Redmond *knew* didn't exactly make that resolution easy to keep.

When Josie herself dropped by at lunchtime carrying cartons of Chinese food, Carrie was more than happy to join her boss for chow mein and sympathy. They'd just settled down with plastic plates and wooden chopsticks when Clancy Gagliardi, one of Carrie's delivery boys, stuck his head through the curtained doorway. He'd started work early but had been so busy that Carrie hadn't had a chance to speak to him yet, beyond handing him his schedule.

"What's doin', ladies?" He gave them his broad, goofy grin. Thin and wiry, he was only nineteen, but completely reliable which was more than could be said for most of their delivery people. Furthermore, he knew Boston and its suburbs and neighborhoods like the back of his hand.

"Not much." Josie grinned. "How's it going out there, Clance? Streets about cleared of all that snow?"

"Most." He sounded dubious. "I just had a close call, though. I went to hang a right and take a Uey and some clown nearly ran over me." He shook his head wonderingly. "Tourist, probably. The guy was wicked nuts." He brightened. "Say, Carrie, thanks for inviting me to your wedding. I had a great time."

Carrie choked on cashew chicken. When she could talk again, she said faintly, "You're welcome—I think. Uhh...what was it about the occasion that you *liked?*"

He gave her a broad wink. Everything Clancy did, he did with a flourish. "The entertainment," he said. "Anybody can get married at a wedding, but it takes real nerve to take a hike." He raised his eyebrows. "When Hank booked out of there, I figured you'd go after him and it'd all end okay anyway."

Nobody said anything to confirm or deny his expectations.

"Uhh...you did, huh?" Now he looked a tad anxious. "You two made up?"

Carrie put down her chopsticks. "I'm afraid not."

"Whoa!" He backed toward the door, eyes wide with disbelief. "I'm wicked sorry to hear that." He looked uncomfortable. "Gotta go. Deliveries to make on Cass Ave. Later." He disappeared behind the curtain.

Carrie picked up her chopsticks again. "People have been asking me about it all day," she said ruefully. "Some have heard and they try to offer condolences without getting maudlin. Those who haven't heard wonder why I'm not on my honeymoon. I find it really uncomfortable."

"I'm sure. But they mean well."

Carrie nodded. "Poor Clance. He meant well, too, but it's awkward." She frowned. "He really seemed surprised to hear we weren't back together again."

"Have you thought about that, Carrie? Amanda and Granny were pushing you a little hard, but a couple of days have passed now and you've had a chance to calm down and think. Are you going to call him?"

"I'm...always thinking about it. But I'm scared, Josie."

"Everybody's scared of something. There's the telephone."

Carrie's heart skipped a beat at the thought of hearing his voice after a desolate two days. She'd missed him; how she'd missed him! She'd never dreamed...

"Not here," Connie decided. "Not now."

"Later?"

"Maybe." She poked at a chunk of chicken. "I'm not sure. I mean, I can hardly expect him to be sitting around waiting for me to call."

"Why not?"

"Well, because... He could have called *me,* after all."

Josie groaned. "Are you kidding? After the way you talked to him? Sorry, honey, but the first move's going to have to come from you this time. That is, if you want him back."

Want him back? More than she wanted to keep breathing! But she wanted him back in a new and improved version, not the same old take-her-for-granted charmer she'd sent packing. She'd had enough of that from her dad, when she'd been growing up.

She thought about Hank the rest of the afternoon—which was hardly news, since she'd thought of little else since that dreadful meltdown on Saturday. By the time she locked up the shop at six and headed for her apartment in Redmond, she still hadn't made up her mind.

The drive home took all her concentration. Although the streets were cleared of snow, banks of the stuff still filled the gutters and there were slick spots on the streets. A white-knuckle driver when weather conditions were bad—which in Boston was much of the time—Carrie concentrated on the business at hand.

She liked snow just fine, as long as she didn't have to go out in it. She liked driving in windy conditions even less, and the occasional thunder-and-lightning rainstorms less still. By the time she got home, she was a nervous wreck.

Home, sweet home for Carrie for the past two years was a "three-decker," as it was called locally: a narrow, three-story brownstone house with each floor a separate apartment. Hers was on the top floor, which she reached by means of an ancient elevator that rose creakily at her command.

Actually, she loved that elevator, with its lacy-metal double doors, marble floor and wooden walls. There was something almost majestic about the way it ascended with a kind of lumbering magnificence.

Once inside her apartment, Carrie draped her raincoat over a rack in the hallway and carried her mail into what Granny called the "pahlah"—or more properly, parlor. Bills, a flyer from a new dry-cleaning establishment, an invitation to a wine tasting... She tossed the stack aside and headed for the kitchen and a cup of tea, deciding she'd worry about dinner later.

Cup in hand, she walked to the telephone located on a small table near the sofa and stood there looking down at it, undecided. Her hand trembled so suddenly that the cup clattered against the saucer. She set it down hastily to keep from splashing the contents all over the dark, flower-patterned carpet.

This was ridiculous.

Grabbing the handset, she dialed Hank's number quickly, before she could lose her nerve. Heart in her throat, she heard one ring, two...

His machine picked up. "Howdy, stranger. This is Hank Brady, ace reporter, telling you I've gone to Texas to cover the Fort Knox gold trial. Leave a message and I'll get back to you when I can—but if you're casing the joint, don't even think about it. I've got security services and alarms and guard dogs and piranha fish and killer bees..."

His voice faded away in a cacophony of dogs barking, cats squalling and sirens screaming.

Numb with shock, Carrie hung up the handset very gently.

He was gone. He hadn't called and hadn't waited

for her to call. He'd left no message for her, hadn't sent her a letter, apparently hadn't given her a single thought. He'd simply packed up and headed for Texas.

She'd been right all along, and as soon as she quit crying she'd be very proud of herself.

Chapter Three

HANK BRADY WASN'T WORRIED.

Sure, Carrie was ticked off at him, but she'd come around. She always did. In the meantime, he had the assignment of a lifetime in his hometown and he was going to abso-damn-lutely make the most of it.

But once he'd rented a place to hang his hat, and established his credentials with the court, and tilted with the bureaucracy, he surprised himself by spending more and more time thinking about that final scene with the woman he loved.

And he *still* couldn't figure out what her problem was. So he'd arrived a few minutes late—big damn deal. Life wasn't built on absolutes. You had to be flexible, go with the flow, be spontaneous, seek adventure!

He concluded that it was only a matter of time before she called him to admit she'd overreacted. But as the days passed, it occurred to him that in his spare time he might want to hurry that reconciliation.

Thus, on Sunday, the first day of February, he called Josie to order posies. He called her at home, not at any of the three flower shops, since they were naturally closed. But would he let a little thing like that stand in his way?

"Yo, Josie!" he said. "It's me, Hank."

"Nope," she disagreed without missing a beat, "your name isn't Hank, it's Mud."

"Very funny, but let's be serious."

"I am serious, but that would be a first for you. I didn't think a guy who screwed up his wedding twice would know the meaning of a word like *serious.*"

Hank sensed hostility. "C'mon, Josie, be nice," he coaxed.

"Why in the world would I want to be nice to *you?*"

"Because I'm trying to make amends here."

"To me? You didn't do anything to *me* except break my best friend's heart."

"Not amends to you, amends to Carrie."

"And you dialed the wrong number? How quickly they forget!"

"I didn't dial...!" He sucked in a deep breath, thrown completely off stride by her hostility. "Look," he announced brusquely, "I want to order flowers, but your store's closed on Sundays, and I wouldn't want to take a chance on running into Carrie by calling there anyway."

"Swell. So you bother me at home. Who's the lucky recipient, if I may inquire?"

"*Who do you think!*" This conversation was getting downright annoying. In case he hadn't made himself clear, he added, "Carrie, of course."

"Silly me—of course. You want to send flowers to the woman you left at the altar in December and insulted at the altar in January. Right. This works for me. What do you want, Mr. Sensitivity?"

"Will you shut up and let me tell you?" When she did, he continued, "I want to send her flowers for Groundhog Day."

"Groundhog Day." Josie sounded stunned at such an innovative occasion for flowers. "When the hell is Groundhog Day?"

"Tomorrow. I'd have thought you'd be loaded with orders."

"It's not one of the biggies," she admitted dryly. "What do you have in mind?"

"I dunno. Something...different. You got any stuffed groundhogs you could stick in it?"

"*Aargh!*" Josie said, then continued in a perfectly normal voice. "Somehow I doubt it, but I'll find something...special. How much do you want to spend?"

"I don't *want* to spend anything. But for Carrie—the sky's the limit. Twenty-five bucks?"

"For twenty-five bucks you can get a plastic fern with a cheap cigar announcing, 'It's a boy!'"

"Okay, a hundred dollars! I don't give a hoot in hell what it costs," he said grandly. "I just want her to know I'm thinking of her."

"Right. And on the card...?"

"How about, 'I'm thinking of you'?" he suggested sarcastically. "And 'I love you, Hank.' That ought to do it."

"I wouldn't be at all surprised. Where do I send the bill?"

"Not so fast! Since I've got you on the line and I'm going to be plenty busy in the foreseeable future, I might as well order the rest."

"The rest of what?"

"The rest of the flowers. I want you to send her the same thing with the same message on Lincoln's Birthday—"

"Which is?"

"February 12. And on Valentine's Day. That's—"

"I know when Valentine's Day is."

"Right. And on Presidents' Day—that's February 16. And Washington's Birthday, February 22—"

"Presidents' Day covers Washington and Lincoln both, if I've got my presidents and holidays straight."

"Yeah, it does, but I don't want her to think I'm cheap. And send flowers on St. Patrick's Day—that's March 17—and on the first day of spring and—"

"It occurs to me that if you don't ever intend to come back to Boston, there's no point in any of this. You're already through March."

By now he was feeling pretty proud of himself for thinking of this flower scam. Carrie was gonna love it. ''I'll be back,'' he said grandly, ''eventually. In the meantime, I don't want to miss a trick.''

''Seems unlikely.''

''Right. And send flowers on April Fool's Day. Uh, do you think that's in good taste?''

''Good taste for polite society or for a man who orders his flowers in bulk to save his precious time?''

''Watch those sour grapes, Josie-girl. Hell, yes, send 'em on April 1, and on April 5 when daylight saving begins and on—''

''That's it.''

''What's the problem?''

''I don't take orders that far ahead.''

''Get outta here!''

''Okay, I don't take more than six orders per customer at a time.''

''Why do I doubt that?''

''I'm losing patience with you, Hank Brady. Just give me your address so I can send you the bills and get you out of my life!''

He was sure she'd normally have insisted on a credit card number, but she wanted to give his address to Carrie. Hank offered the information around a smile and added, ''If Carrie and I haven't made up by the time daylight saving starts, I'll have another order for you.''

''If you and Carrie haven't made up by then, there'll be no point in another order. You didn't ask my opinion, but I think you're wasting—''

"I didn't ask your opinion because I don't want it," he said cheerfully. "Just let her be surprised. Thanks for your help and goodbye."

He hung up smiling, a well-satisfied man. Carrie loved flowers; hell, flowers were her life. This would hold her until he had time to give her his full attention.

Damn, Brady. He patted himself on the back. *You're a genius!*

CLANCY DELIVERED the Groundhog Day arrangement the following afternoon. Working on a funeral wreath in the back, Carrie glanced up and did a double take.

"What in the world is that monstrosity?" she demanded curiously.

Clancy looked at the huge arrangement made up mostly of bird-of-paradise with a little greenery thrown in. A plush pink pig nestled among the stems toward the front. "I thought it was wicked cool," he said.

Carrie groaned and came forward to examine this tribute to bad taste. "What's the significance of the pig?"

"Groundhog Day. Get it? Ground*hog*. This is a hog."

"This is a fluffy pink pig. This is also a joke, right? Who's the lucky recipient?" Plucking the card from the greenery, she read: "To Carrie—I'm thinking of you and I love you. Hank."

Dropping the card in horror, she fell back a step. "Where did you get these flowers?"

"Josie told me to deliver 'em to you."

"*Josie* made this atrocity? And I thought she was my friend!"

"Whoa!" Clancy's eyes went wide. "This is the best-looking arrangement of flowers I ever delivered. Usually you women make all those wimpy little froufrou things—no offense. This one's *manly.*"

"Then be my guest. It's yours." On an irresistible impulse, she plucked the pig from his jungle home, then turned toward the telephone and dialed.

"You mean it? You don't think it'll hurt Josie's feelings if she finds out?"

"Not even a little bit." Carrie waved him away. "Josie, what do you mean sending over that ghastly arrangement with *his* name on it?"

"Calm down, honey. He called me at home last night and placed the order. What could I do? His money's as good as anyone else's, even if it does come from Texas. God, Carrie, he had me so rattled I didn't even ask for a credit card! Now I'll have to send him a bill and wait for him to send a check—"

"He'll pay, all right. He may be a jerk but he pays his bills."

"Are you as angry as you sound?"

"Angrier." Carrie clenched her fingers around the pink pig, trying to compose herself. "Why is he doing this to me? Why can't he just pick up the telephone and admit... Never mind. I don't care what he does or who he does it with. If he thinks one ostentatious basket of flowers is going to change anything..."

"Yeah, one basket," Josie agreed glumly. "Just remember, Carrie, I'm only the messenger."

Carrie remembered those words when Clancy delivered the Lincoln's Birthday basket featuring a rolled and beribboned copy of the Gettysburg Address, and the Valentine's Day basket featuring hearts and cupids ad nauseum, and the Presidents' Day basket with a giant Presidential Seal in chocolate, and the Washington's Birthday basket with cherries wired onto a bonsai tree and a tiny hatchet for decoration.

I'll get you for this, Hank Brady, she vowed, fingering the minihatchet. *I'll get you for this!*

MARCH BLEW IN like a lion in Dallas, Texas, where everything was going just great for Hank Brady, ace reporter. The Fort Knox Knock-Off case was underway and it was he who'd given it the name now adopted countrywide. He'd made strong contacts, was scooping the opposition at every turn, was working night and day and making a huge name for himself very quickly.

Hank was the fair-haired boy, all right. He should be the happiest camper in the mammoth press corps.

He wasn't, and he couldn't seem to get his rotten mood to lift. Even his photographer, Bill Sulewski, was starting to avoid him.

Coming home at the end of one particularly long day, Hank dropped more than a week's worth of mail on the kitchen counter of the closet where he'd been living since he came to Dallas in January. Normally, anywhere he hung his hat was home, but every time he looked around at this place, all he could think about was how horrified Carrie would be if she ever saw it.

Which she wouldn't. Son of a...

Pulling a beer from a tiny refrigerator that also contained a carton of month-old milk, six kinds of chip dip and a week-old pizza, he returned to flip through the mail.

Crap, all of it—except for two envelopes with his sister's scrawl on the front, which reminded him that he owed her a couple of phone calls. But with the hours he'd been keeping, he just hadn't gotten around to it.

Still, his heart beat a little faster. Letters from Carrie would have been better, but maybe Amanda would have news of his beloved.

He ripped into the first envelope, a heavy square of ivory-colored paper. When an invitation fell out, he thought he'd have a heart attack.

Amanda was getting married? To his best buddy, Sean Kelly? On April 4? What the hell was going on?

Holding the stiff paper in equally stiff fingers, he began to swear. He'd kill Kelly, that's what he'd do.

This was happening too fast. Amanda was just a baby. If that bozo hurt her—!

He ripped into the second envelope. The letter inside was dated February 25; it had apparently been longer than he realized since he'd checked his mail. Still angry, he began to read.

Hi, big brother.

Just wanted you to be the first to know that Sean's proposed and I've accepted! We're madly in love and I'm so excited I can hardly stand it! We're going to get married just as soon as we can arrange it, so don't be surprised when you get your invitation. And don't worry—we want a simple ceremony and it won't cost you a penny! (Ha-ha!) Josie's offered us the use of her place, since she says she's had a lot of practice getting ready for weddings, although nobody's actually gotten *married* there. (More ha-ha's!)

Sean's out of town for a police thing in Philadelphia—training of some kind. He asked me to ask you if you'd be his best man. After all, he did the same for you twice! (Ha-ha again!) I told him I knew you would.

That's the news from this end. I'm following your brilliant career in the newspapers and I'm really proud of you, big brother. See you soon I hope.

Mandy

Hank sat there for a long time. Then he dragged the telephone closer and dialed Amanda's number. After four rings, the answering machine picked up: "Hi, this is Amanda Brady. I just hate to miss a call, especially yours, but sometimes it can't be helped. If you'll just leave a message—"

"Hello? Hello?" Amanda's sleepy voice cut off the perky recording.

"Amanda? This is your brother calling. Jeez, you sound like you were asleep."

"Hank? What's wrong?"

"Nothing's wrong. I just got your letter and the invitation to the wedding—"

"You get mail at one a.m. in Texas nowadays?"

"Oops." He glanced at his wristwatch; it was midnight, and Boston was an hour ahead. "Sorry about that. I just got home and I didn't realize it was so late. Want me to call you back tomorrow?"

"I'm awake now." Her voice sounded firmer, if a bit disgruntled. "What did you call about?"

"Uhh...to say I'm happy for you. That is, if you're sure you want to marry that big Irish clown."

Her soft chuckle reassured him. "I love that big Irish clown and I'm looking forward to raising a whole flock of little Irish clowns."

His throat tightened and he had to clear it before going on. "Then I guess it's all right."

"You'll be Sean's best man, won't you? I mean, you can get off to come back for just a few days, can't you?"

He doubted it, but he said, "I'll try. Uhh...you don't see much of Carrie these days, I suppose."

"Sure I do." Amanda's voice sounded suddenly guarded. "We *are* friends."

"How is she?" He held his breath, hoping to hear words like *miserable, lonesome, missing you.*

"She's okay."

That answer did not please him. "Just okay?" he persisted, trying to drag specifics, preferably negative, out of her.

He heard her exasperated sigh. "Okay, if you must know—"

Ah, here it came. He settled back to enjoy the gruesome details.

"—She's doing great. She's happy and...well, I guess you'd say *calm*, and she's never looked better."

"What!" He jerked upright in astonishment.

"And she's going to be my maid of honor. I didn't intend to tell you that until you agreed to stand up for Sean. I was afraid you hadn't gotten over her and you'd try to weasel out."

Weasel out? When hell froze over! Carrie hadn't forgotten him any more than he'd forgotten her, and he'd be damned if he'd let her get away with this—this crock! Amanda might believe Carrie was happy as a lark, but Hank knew better.

Caroline Duncan loved him and he loved her. Period, end of discussion. Mumbling a few more words of congratulation, he hung up the telephone.

And sat there.

And sat there.

He couldn't recall ever feeling so...bereft, as if the bottom had fallen out of his world. He'd learned at his mother's knee that personal fulfillment inevitably followed professional success, and she'd held up his happy-go-lucky father as a horrible example of where lack of ambition landed you. Now, out of left field, rushed the stark realization that his mother had been wrong, wrong, terribly, horribly wrong—and so was he.

He finished the beer and tossed the can in the general direction of an already overflowing trash basket. It bounced off the wall and rolled to rest against a dirty sneaker. Hank barely noticed.

Hell, he hadn't put Carrie third, the way she'd charged.... Okay, maybe second. Now, for the first time, he had to admit to himself that his success was hollow without her.

Dammit, he wanted her back, and apparently a few flowers with love notes attached wouldn't do the trick. He sighed and leaned back until his head rested on the couch cushion. Staring up at the stained ceiling, he thought about his situation.

He *could* get her back. He still didn't doubt that for a minute. He'd just have to give her his full and undivided attention.

And therein lay the rub. Would his editors give him time off for a little thing like attendance at his sister's wedding, with a shot at winning back the woman of his dreams thrown in? And if they wouldn't, what was he prepared to do about it?

THEY WOULDN'T.

They gave him all kinds of reasons, but the bottom line was they had no desire to change horses in midstream—or reporters in midtrial. They'd give him ego strokes and more money, but they wouldn't give him time off.

Hank felt as if he'd been poleaxed.

How the hell was he going to win back the love of his life if he was in Texas and she was in Boston? For a moment he toyed with the idea of trying to get her to come here, even knowing that plan didn't have a snowball's chance in hell of working.

"I *gotta* get some time off or I won't be responsible for the consequences," he bitched to Bill over a quick hamburger lunch.

The photographer rolled his eyes. "You're telling me. Jeez, Hank, you've turned into a regular asshole. Everybody's avoiding you. Hell, I wouldn't be here today myself, but I was afraid if I turned you down, you'd beat me up."

Hank wasn't exactly pleased to hear himself being so described, but had to admit it was close to accurate. "That does it," he said, standing up. "It's D day."

He returned to the table ten minutes later. "I got it," he said with grim satisfaction. "I got five days off."

Bill's eyes went wide with surprise and perhaps a new respect. "How'd you manage that?" he wondered aloud.

"I told 'em I was going nuts and had to get home."

"I can vouch for the nuts part. What did they say to that?"

"They said I was exaggerating. So I raved and ranted to give 'em a sample. Then I told 'em if they'd let me go back for the wedding, I'd return to Texas April 5, the day after, come hell or high water."

"Good. That's good." Bill nodded approval. "And what did they say?"

"They said I'd *better* unless I could be happy writing obituaries and covering grip 'n' grins for the rest of my life."

"And what did you say?"

"I said, 'Trust me. I can do this.'"

And at that moment, he really thought he could.

Chapter Four

CARRIE DIDN'T WANT to be Amanda Brady's maid of honor in the first place, but Hank's sister hadn't left her much choice. "There are only two reasons you'd turn me down," Amanda had said. "The first is that you don't really like me but were willing to put up with me for my brother's sake." Her big blue eyes filled with tears.

"And the other reason?" Carrie asked, desperately hoping for an excuse she could use.

"The other is that you're not really over my big jerk of a brother and you're afraid to face him," Amanda said briskly, tears forgotten. "But then I said to myself, surely you wouldn't let him intimidate you!"

Put that way, Carrie had to say yes.

She consoled herself with the knowledge that there was only an outside chance Hank would return to Boston for the wedding anyway. If his job could come between him and his own wedding, how much chance did his poor sister have of getting him here for hers?

Outside chance being the operative words. With so much big news coming out of the Fort Knox Knock-Off trial, Carrie really didn't think Hank would make much of an effort to return, not for something so mundane as a *wedding*. If she seriously thought he might, she'd...she'd take a vacation to the south seas before agreeing to be a member of this particular wedding party. Even his sister was beginning to have her doubts that he'd show up.

Getting ready for Amanda's bridal shower on the Sunday afternoon before the April 4 wedding, Carrie found herself growing more and more morose. Here she was, almost over Hank, and his sister had to go get married and bring him roaring back into Carrie's imagination, if not her life.

I am *over him,* she assured herself as she bustled through last-minute arrangements. She had to step over her houseguest to do it—a fat old Siberian husky named Killer who lay around with all the animation of a three-toed sloth. She'd known when she agreed to dog-sit for her first-floor neighbor that it would be a pain, but what could she do?

Tossing the dog a biscuit, which he caught on the fly, Carrie looked around with satisfaction. Cake, champagne, streamers, flowers by the armful transformed her apartment into a festive site for Amanda's lingerie party.

So why was she even thinking about Amanda's brother? He'd already be relegated to the dim and distant past if only he'd stop sending those horrible flower baskets. She darted an accusing glance at the strange array of objects on a round table in one corner of the room, fronted by the plush pink pig. All these kooky items plucked from the various floral tributes just reminded her of things better forgotten. If she were smart, she'd get rid of the lot of them.

She checked her wristwatch, determined to change the direction of her thoughts. The guest of honor should arrive in another fifteen minutes and the other guests soon afterward. All was in order, so she might as well—

The doorbell pealed. Carrie frowned. Someone was seriously early. With a final glance around the room, she smoothed her burgundy-colored skirt and went to answer.

Hank Brady stood on the other side of her front door, holding a bouquet of blue and white violets and grinning as if there'd never been a discouraging word uttered between them.

"Hi, honey," he said. "I'm home." And he swept her into his arms and kissed her.

In a state of shock, she let him. Oh, how she'd missed his touch, his kiss, his bold confidence. When he nudged her lips apart with his tongue, she let him. When he touched her tongue with his, she melted into a puddle of pure desire.

When he closed one hand over the curve of her bottom and dragged her hard against him, she let out a little squeak of protest and pushed herself out of his embrace. Outraged, she gave him a strong shove and slammed the door in his face.

Somehow he managed to wedge a foot inside—a

foot encased in one of those damned cowboy boots he used to wear before some of the Texas wore off. "Oww!" he howled piteously. "I think you broke my foot!"

"Good!" She leaned against the door just enough to keep it closed. "Go away! You're trespassing!"

"That wasn't a trespassing kiss, that was a Damn-I'm-glad-to-see you kiss."

"Says who? I don't even know you anymore, you good-for-nothing, two-bit, chiseling—"

"Aha! If you don't know me, where do you get off calling me names? Honey, open the door and let me in so we can talk about this like reasonable adults."

"I have a telephone! If you'd wanted to talk to me, you could have called me anytime."

"I sent you flowers."

"They're ugly! You sent me ugly flowers!"

"Are you kidding?" He sounded astonished. "Your boss personally took care of my order. Those flowers *oughta* be good-lookin', they cost me an arm and a—ow! I think you're about to cripple me, here."

"Of all the crybabies." She flung open the door and glared at him. "There, you're free. Now go away."

He stood before her with one foot cocked at an unnatural angle and the bouquet of violets looking as if they'd been run over by a truck. All their little stems were broken and their blossoms drooped around the hand that thrust them toward her.

"For you!" He smiled triumphantly. "Flowers and an abject apology. What more could it take to make a woman happy?"

"I refuse to accept your flowers *or* your apologies, neither of which are sincere."

Turning her back on him, she stalked to the middle of the long narrow living room, her heels clicking on the hardwood floors. She whirled to face him warily, already on the defensive.

He limped after her. "C'mon, Carrie, let bygones be bygones. Can't you see it from the other person's point of view?"

She blinked, frowned, realized he was about to do a number on her and stiffened her spine. "Oh, no, you're not pulling that on me again. What's to see? You walked on me like a rug and now you come strolling in here as if you'd never been away, saying—"

"Sweetheart, honey, dear, that's not how it is at all." He hobbled closer. "We're not talking about some little ol' assignment here, we're talkin' about the chance of a lifetime—"

"We're talking career versus wife," she interrupted. "Let's be honest."

"I wanted it for both of us," he countered, skipping over the honesty issue. "Sure, I'm ambitious, but I need to make enough money to support a wife and—" his voice softened "—children. And can you blame me if I want you to be proud of me?"

"Nobody's proud of reporters. They rate one notch above used-car salesmen in public confidence, for Pete's sake."

"I'll bet that really hurts the wives and children of used-car salesmen," he said, as if incensed on their behalf. "Honey, baby—"

"Get away from me and take your mangy flowers with you!" She felt on the verge of breaking down; if he didn't go away soon she was going to lose it.

He frowned at the splayed collection of posies. "I thought you liked violets."

"I do! So why have you been sending me bird-of-paradise and ranunculus and—"

"What the hell is a ranunculus?" He looked genuinely alarmed.

The fact that he also looked handsome and sexy as hell registered somewhat belatedly. With a leather jacket to ward off a chilly March wind, he wore jeans as if born to them, a cream-colored sweater and the boots. All he lacked was a Stetson hat.

His long-lashed, blue eyes narrowed knowingly. "I almost made you smile," he accused. "C'mon, Carrie, admit you're glad to see me."

"I am *not* glad to see you." She sniffed. "I never wanted to see you again."

"But now that you have, you're falling for me all over again, right? It's all you can do not to fling yourself in my arms and—"

Killer let out a sound that, according to his owner, was indigenous to Siberians. It sounded part groan, part gasp and part growl. Hank jumped in surprise and swung around to stare down at the supine animal.

Carrie did not fail to note that he'd forgotten to favor his "injured" foot.

"What in the *hell,*" he demanded, pointing, "is *that?* A furry rock?"

Laughter sputtered in her throat, but she'd choke before she'd let it out. "That's a dog," she said when she could speak again. "His name is Killer and if I gave him the order, he would."

"Jeez," Hank said, "when you threatened to replace me with a dog I didn't believe you."

"I don't *care* if you believe me as long as you go—right now."

"Carrie—"

"I'll sic my dog on you, I swear I will!"

"Sweetheart—"

"Killer, attack!" She pointed a stiff arm and stiffer finger at Hank, praying the dog would deign to at least lumber to his feet.

He didn't. Instead he once again let loose with that all-purpose combination grunt 'n' groan 'n' growl.

Hank ignored the dog to appeal to Carrie. "Doesn't it mean anything to you that I'm going crazy without you? That I can't eat, can't sleep, can't work—"

"Ha! The day you can't work is the day they plant you six feet under." She turned her wrath on man's best friend. "Killer, attack or you're going to the pound. And don't think I don't mean it!"

"Okay." Hank sighed and his tone turned philosophical. "I made up that part about not being able to work, but the rest of it's true. When I'm *not* working I just wander around like a man in a daze, trying to think of ways to get you back."

"You'll *never* get me back. Two strikes and you're out."

"Where'd you learn to play baseball, sweetheart, darlin'?" His indulgent smile sparkled. "Everybody gets three strikes before they're out, even criminals." He advanced upon her. He had to step over Killer to do so. The dog, a ninety-pound lump of fur, whined and ducked. "I've got one more strike coming to me and, so help me God, I won't blow it."

She backed away. "Don't you dare touch me. I'll call the police! I'll—"

The doorbell rang and her eyes grew wide with relief. "Why are you still here? I'm having a shower for your sister this afternoon and you'll ruin everything."

"Amanda? That's great."

He appropriated her door as if it belonged to him. Flinging it open, he swept his wide-eyed sister into an enthusiastic embrace.

"Hank!" Amanda shrieked, clinging to him while

he whirled her in a circle. "I didn't know you'd gotten into town already!"

"I came straight from the airport to the arms of the woman I love," he said, eyeing Carrie over his sister's shoulder. "I didn't think you'd mind."

"Mind? I'm thrilled! Then you two are back together again?"

"No!" Carrie cried, just as Hank insisted it was true. They were still arguing about it when the rest of the guests started arriving.

HANK WAS THE ONLY MALE among eleven females at the shower, and he loved it, managing to dominate the proceedings with wit and charm. No one seemed to mind except Carrie, the hostess, and possibly Josie.

Only Josie managed to avoid the clichéd response of every other guest upon spotting Hank: "You're back together again!" Then Carrie would have to explain, and then Hank would object to her explanation, and then the guest would stifle a knowing grin and insist that she understood perfectly. But none of them understood at all, Carrie thought, growing ever more desperate to convince them—and maybe herself.

Once everyone was assembled, champagne and toasts were the order of the day, with Hank leading the charge. "To my sister, who's getting a helluva guy. If he loves her half as much as I love Carrie..."

Significant glance, knowing smiles, groans from Carrie and Killer.

Hank repeated it in case anyone had missed it the first time around. "As I was saying, if Sean loves Amanda half as much as I love Carrie, she's a very lucky woman." He gave Carrie a *so there* glance.

Everyone sipped champagne and looked at Carrie, who refused to partake until she'd set the record straight. Filled with determination, she raised her glass, surprised to find that her hand trembled.

"To Amanda," she announced. "Your brother wouldn't recognize love if it spit in his eye, but I know that you and Sean do. Here's to a lifetime of happiness." She looked straight at Hank. "Which is much more likely if both the bride and the bridegroom show up at the wedding within shouting distance of the stated time."

A challenging light sparked in his eyes; she should have remembered how competitive he was. He lifted his glass and drank, then held it high again.

"To Sean, who'll be getting a woman who loves him enough to consider his needs as well as her own."

Everyone drank and heads snapped back toward Carrie.

"To Sean, who'd never dream of putting his job before the happiness of the woman he loves."

"To Amanda and Sean, who realize that the actual wedding ceremony itself is the least important ingredient in a successful marriage."

"To Amanda and Sean, who know that—"

Amanda broke in a bit breathlessly; she'd been listening to the escalating and argumentative toasts with as much fascination as everyone else. "Oh, my goodness!" she exclaimed. "I think that's probably enough toasting. I can hardly wait to get to the gifts, so if nobody has any objection—"

"Speak now or forever hold your peace," Hank muttered, and all of a sudden he wasn't grinning or joking or being charming.

Carrie's stomach clenched painfully at the possibility that perhaps he'd actually been hurt when she called off their wedding in the most public manner imaginable. She'd expected him to be annoyed, confused, even angry, but it had never, in all honestly, occurred to her that he'd been *hurt*.

Yet she did believe that he'd loved her...at least a little. But hurt? Not Hank Brady. He was too self-contained and self-absorbed to feel such a vulnerable emotion.

Wasn't he?

She watched him surreptitiously while Amanda opened her gifts: seven pink satin camisole gowns with matching satin-padded hangers, two lavender satin camisole gowns with matching satin padded hangers, and two fire-engine red bustier-and-thong combinations that made her blush.

Hank sidled up to Carrie during the oohing and aahing and whispered in her ear, making her jump nervously. "Did you get stuff like that at your shower?"

"Yes." She hissed the word.

"Sure would like to see you in that red getup."

"In your dreams, buster."

"Nah," he murmured, his warm breath tickling her ear. "I see you there every night, honey lamb, and it ain't nearly enough."

She wanted to groan. This man did not play fair. Instead she sprang to her feet. "Time for cake, everyone!"

Josie beat her into the kitchen.

"What in the hell is going on?" the tall blonde demanded. "Are you taking up with that man again?"

"No, I am not taking up with that man again, as you so quaintly phrase it." Carrie reached for the silver-and-crystal cake knife that had been a gift from Granny, who'd refused to take it back when the wedding went kaput. "I'm *trying* to keep from killing the brother of the bride, which would very likely cast a pall over the festivities."

Josie nodded. "Very likely. I'd still enjoy seeing it, though."

"Life's full of little disappointments. Will you carry the cake or are you just here to harass me?"

Josie laughed and reached for the decorated sheet cake. "Hey," she protested, "I'm on your side. I think the guy should be drawn and quartered for what he did to you. I also think he's drop-dead gorgeous and, given fifteen minutes, could charm the pants off ninety-nine women out of a hundred."

"Then I'm that hundredth," Carrie said, ignoring the indisputable fact that he'd charmed the pants off her any number of times. But that was in the past. She was a much sadder but wiser woman now. Not even a sweet-talking Texan was going to get her in the sack once she'd seen his true colors.

Cake held high, Josie led the way back into the living room. There a decorated card table waited with silverware and wedding-design paper plates. While everyone admired the cake, Carrie comforted herself with the knowledge that this shower was nearly over. Once everyone went home, she could brush Hank off the way he deserved.

The bride-to-be cut the cake and then Carrie and Josie served it. Hank hung back until everyone had been taken care of, then sidled up to his sister.

"Can I have the piece with all the frosting roses?" he inquired.

Amanda gave him a startled glance. "You don't like frosting. You don't even like cake. You like pie." But she set to work cutting off a large slice just the same. Sliding it onto a plate, she handed it to him.

He grinned. "I don't like frosting, but Carrie does. I'm gonna share."

Carrie, who was standing nearby and had heard the entire exchange, sniffed haughtily. "No, thanks. I'll get my own cake."

"It's more fun to share," he wheedled.

"No, thank you." She glared at him.

"Oh, dear," Amanda said anxiously. "Are you two going to have trouble getting along? Because if you are..."

Carrie took pity on the bride. "Don't worry," she said. "We'll avoid each other. It'll only be for a few days."

"We can't avoid each other." Hank took a bite of cake, grimaced, smiled belatedly. "Delicious."

"Liar," Carrie said, well aware of his preference for pie. "What do you mean, we can't avoid each other?"

"You're the maid of honor and I'm the best man. I'd say that means we'll have to not only see each other but be civil." He winked. "I can do it if you can. Hell, I can do it even if you can't. I *am* a sensitive, giving, nineties kind of guy."

Carrie stared at him in a state of shock. Of all the low-down, contemptible tricks! She spared a quick glance at Amanda, who looked both scared and hopeful.

So what was Carrie going to do about this turn of events without ruining, or at least raining on, the bride's big day?

Distressed, she reached out with her fork and scooped a yellow frosting rose off Hank's chunk of cake, popping it into her mouth. By the time she realized what she'd done, that rose was history and he was looking at her with laughing, knowing eyes.

Chapter Five

CARRIE WHISPERED URGENTLY in Amanda's ear, "I've got to talk to you!"

"Huh?" Amanda glanced around, her expression almost dazed. The shower was winding down and the poor girl apparently had so much on her mind that she was having trouble concentrating on the here and now.

Carrie was sympathetic, but pressed ahead. "I've got to talk to you about—you know."

Amanda blinked. "I don't think I *do* know. Want to clue me in?"

"Him!" Exasperated, Carrie jerked her head toward Hank, holding court at one end of her green velvet couch. Four or five women clustered around him, staring with worshipful expressions while he regaled them with insider tales of the Fort Knox Knock-Off trial.

Amanda's distracted expression softened. "Wasn't it sweet of him to come back for my wedding? And to serve as Sean's best man, too. You've got to admit, it was asking a lot but he came through. That's my brother!"

Carrie would not be distracted from her purpose. "Why didn't you tell me he was going to be best man when you asked me to be maid of honor?'' she demanded. ''I have no desire to stand next to him in Josie's house in front of a minister again, even if it *is* someone else who's getting married. *I do not want to do this*—trust me on that.''

''Oh, I do trust you.'' Amanda clasped her hands together earnestly. ''Believe me, if I'd known he was going to accept, I'd have told you when I asked you to be in the wedding party. But he hadn't said he would at that point and I saw no reason to change my plans on the off chance he'd finally get around to accepting.''

''Still...''

''Carrie, you know how close I am to my brother. After Dad left and Mom died, Hank was all I had. He practically raised me.''

And it hadn't been easy. Amanda had still been a minor and Hank a college student. He'd fought the entire state of Texas on his sister's behalf—and won. Of *course* Amanda adored him. Carrie sighed. ''That's not really the point,'' she stated.

''Of course not. The point is, you're my best friend. Well,'' Amanda amended, ''my best friend who doesn't live in Texas. Or maybe I should say my best friend who lives in Massachusetts—oh, you know what I mean.''

Carrie did, and it brought a resigned smile to her lips. ''I'm very fond of you, too, Amanda, over and above the fact that I detest your brother. Under the circumstances, couldn't you do me a tremendous favor and find someone else?''

Amanda's eyes teared up; they were doing that a lot these days. ''I couldn't possibly,'' she wailed. ''Don't even suggest it. Besides, you've already got your beautiful dress and everything.''

Carrie's ''beautiful dress'' was a typical wedding monstrosity with princess seaming so tight she could barely breathe and a big bow draped over her bottom. It was candy pink; the two bridesmaids' dresses were identical, only in apple green.

''That's true,'' she admitted, ''but maybe you could find someone who's the same size. I wouldn't mind at all—I mean, I'd hate not getting to wear it and I'd hate not being part of your wedding, but it should be perfectly clear that I'm very uncomfortable being around your brother again.''

''Don't be silly.'' Amanda smiled and flapped a hand dismissively. ''Today was difficult because you were caught by surprise, but now you're ready for him.'' She frowned. ''Aren't you?''

''Well, yes, sure, but—''

''Then, like I said, there's no problem.'' The doorbell pealed, followed by a heavy knocking. ''There's Sean!'' Amanda flew to let him in.

All Carrie wanted was to get everybody out of her apartment so she could think about all this. Everything Amanda had said made sense, but Carrie knew sense had nothing to do with it.

She still reacted to Hank Brady like a match

scraped across sandpaper: he might rub her the wrong way but he still sent her up in flames every time he touched her. She missed him in other ways, too—missed his good humor and optimistic outlook.

"Hi, Carrie, Josie." Sean Kelly, big and bluff and Irish, grinned. He had one arm around his bride-to-be, who was pressed possessively against his side and was loving it.

Sean spotted his brother-in-law-to-be. "Hank! Why, you old—" a quick glance around changed what he'd intended to say "—son of a gun! When did you get into town? Why didn't you call?"

The two men shook hands and pounded each other on the shoulder.

"Got in a few hours ago," Hank said. "I came straight here to see my girl."

"Your *what?*" Sean stared at Carrie with pure astonishment.

"What am I going to have to do," Carrie demanded rhetorically, "carry around a sign that says I Am Not Hank Brady's Girl?"

"Who you gonna believe," Hank asked Sean, "your best friend or some crazy woman who walked out on her own wedding?"

"I didn't walk out, you *drove* me out." She appealed to the group at large. "Promise me that none of you will go around spreading false rumors that this man and I are anything more than—"

"Good friends?" Sean interjected helpfully.

"Lovers?" Hank suggested hopefully.

"Bitter enemies?" Josie put in her two cents worth sarcastically.

"I was going to settle for *casual acquaintances,*" Carrie said, rolling her eyes in exasperation.

Sean grinned. "Whatever." He kissed Amanda on the cheek. "Are you ready to go to the Martins', sweetheart?"

"Sean, honey..."

"Uh-oh," he said. "I sense a change of plans."

"It's just that I talked to Emily earlier and told her I'm exhausted from all the work for this wedding and she suggested I just go on home after the shower and try to get a little rest."

"I'll come with you," he offered eagerly.

She laughed and shook her head. "I said *rest!*"

He looked crestfallen. "Oh. In that case...Hank, some of the guys are going over to shoot hoops at Andy's. Wanna come along?"

Two things registered instantly with Carrie. First, Sean had turned down a chance to shoot baskets in favor of spending time with Amanda and her friends; and second, Carrie wouldn't have to worry about Hank anymore, today at least, because he *never* passed up any activity that featured a ball.

She picked up the remains of the cake and started for the kitchen, determined to ignore the painful flood of memories about what Hank had so cavalierly called "the traditional wedding-day basketball game."

Therefore she was caught completely off guard

when she heard Hank say, "Sorry, Sean, but I think I'll hang around and help *my girl* clean up."

The subtle stress on "my girl" kept his greater meaning from sinking in for a moment. When it did, Carrie gasped and nearly dropped the cake. Holding it in a white-knuckled grip, she turned to face him.

"Don't be ridiculous. I don't need any help."

"Yes, you do," he said, his expression placid.

"I don't! I want you to go."

"Oh, my," Amanda said, "they're at it again. I think we'd *all* better go."

The remaining guests murmured assent and headed toward the entry hall, where they'd hung their coats.

Carrie left the cake in the kitchen and hurried to follow them to the door. "There's no hurry," she said, feeling suddenly anxious at the thought of being left alone with *him*. "Have another glass of champagne. Have another cup of coffee."

They ignored her entreaties. One by one they hugged her, thanked her, left her. Even Josie rolled her eyes, sighed and departed. Finally only Amanda and Sean remained.

"Thank you so much." Amanda accentuated her thanks with a hug. "You don't know how much your friendship means to me, Carrie."

"Me, too." Sean grinned over the pile of lingerie boxes in his arms.

"And I just know you can get along with Hank," Amanda added. "For my sake..."

They left. Slowly Carrie turned to face her nemesis, her incorrigible, unconquerable nemesis—the man who'd just put her ahead of a game of hoops with his friends. And if he thought that was going to impress her...he was right.

HE COULDN'T BELIEVE she was still mad at him, but she was. Facing him with snapping brown eyes, her soft mouth forced into a grim line, she still managed to look more appealing than ever.

He'd always thought she was gorgeous, but never more so than at this moment...when he wanted her more intensely than he'd ever wanted anything in his life. Stepping toward her, he said her name.

She jumped back as if he'd waved a club at her. "You've got to go!"

"What's the rush? I said I'd help you clean up and I will."

"I don't need your help." She marched past him and began to collect champagne flutes and cake plates. "You never helped before, so why start now?"

"Because I'm trying to make brownie points," he said cheerfully. He picked up a handful of silverware. "Is my subtle ploy working?"

"No!" She almost smiled, but he saw her catch herself in the nick of time. She'd always been a sucker for ingenuousness. "Once all this stuff is picked up, will you go?"

"Maybe."

"Then let's hurry."

She did, he didn't, but it still took only a few minutes. Even the floor was clean without benefit of vacuum cleaner, what with Killer's keen appetite for cake crumbs. When there was nothing left to do, Carrie faced Hank with her hands on her hips.

"Okay, thanks and goodbye."

"That's a bit abrupt, don't you think? How about a cup of coffee for the road?"

"Sorry." She stuck out her cute little jaw. "It's time for Killer's walk."

"I'll go with you."

"You don't want to do that." She bent to snap a lead on the husky's collar. "The ground's still muddy from the rains we had last week."

"Been a bad winter, has it?" He pulled her coat from the hook in the front hall and held it for her.

"The usual. We had a serious snow-and-sleet storm in February, and March has been wet."

He shrugged into his leather jacket. "Any thunderstorms? I know how much you hate that."

He saw the annoyance on her face—annoyance that he knew her well enough to say that. Hell, that was only the beginning of what he knew about her.

"Look," she said, "I'm really not interested in standing around discussing the weather with you." Opening her apartment door, she led Killer to the elevator.

Hank tagged along. "March is almost over," he said, ignoring her dictum. "As you used to say—"

"I don't *care* what I used to say."

The metal elevator doors clanked open and she dragged a less-than-enthusiastic Killer inside. Hank crowded in with them, making the available space seem even smaller than it was.

"April showers bring May flowers," he quoted, without regard for her stated lack of interest.

She turned her back on him. The elevator started its descent with its customary groans. Killer braced himself, heavy claws grating on the marble floor and silver eyes wide with anxiety.

Hank bent to stroke the dog's head but kept his attention on the woman, standing there so stiffly. "And when it rained, you used to say it was raining violets."

For a moment he thought she wouldn't answer, and then she said in a low voice, "Granny's the one who always said that. Actually, what she says is 'No matter how dreary it looks now, it'll soon be raining violets.'"

"I can only hope." Hank straightened, swaying imperceptibly toward her. "Carrie—"

"We're here."

And indeed, the cracker box in which they stood shuddered to a halt that nearly threw Killer onto his face. When the door rumbled open, the dog led the charge out of the elevator and out of the building.

Hank followed, wondering when a few of those violets were going to rain down on him. So far he didn't seem to be making much progress on his own.

Not that a little thing like that ever stopped him.

IT TOOK BOTH OF THEM to drag Killer back inside the elevator for the trip up to the third floor. "Jeez," Hank puffed, "how do you manage that animal on your own? Maybe I better hang around. You need me."

"I do *not* need you. Under normal circumstances, I tempt him with doggy treats. I just forgot today."

She saw Hank's thoughts in his eyes: *Because you were thinking about me.* "And it *wasn't* because I was thinking about you. I—I'm out of doggy treats. But Killer's owner is coming back tomorrow, so it won't be a problem."

"This monster isn't yours? But you said—"

"I was angry when I said I was going to get a dog."

"You're obviously still angry. What do I have to do to—"

"I'm not angry. I just don't want to go through this again."

"Again?" His blue eyes narrowed. "Are you talking about December or about your father?"

Her jaw tightened. "I should never have told you about my father."

"Why not? You were a little girl and he broke your heart, but I never will. I'm not like him, honey. I—"

"Stop!" She couldn't listen to any more of this. "Actions speak louder than words."

"Carrie—"

The elevator clunked to a stop, and he followed her out into the hall and then inside the apartment. She released the dog and let Hank take her coat, thinking that she'd made herself quite clear and surely now he would go. Surely now he would admit that everything was over between them. Surely now he would...take her in his arms.

He took her in his arms, this man who had chosen her over basketball, at least this time.

"Stop that," she commanded breathlessly. "If I won't marry you, I certainly won't sleep with you."

He nibbled at her throat. "I don't want to sleep with you, but I do want to take you to bed."

"Not a chance." She slipped her hands around his waist beneath his sweater. His skin felt warm and smooth and firm. "Hank Brady, you were the biggest mistake of my life. I'm over you now and no way am I going to—"

"You're not over me." He unfastened her top button and guided her back a step. Holding her by the shoulders, he kissed the cleft between her breasts. "Did you get this at *your* lingerie shower?" He eyed her lace-and-satin bra.

"Certainly not." Her mouth was so dry she could hardly speak and she fought the instinct to close her eyes and let her head roll back. "I returned all that stuff...well, I tried to. Most people wouldn't take it back. But I did manage to get the majority of the wedding presents returned to the proper p-people."

He swooped her up in his arms before she could do anything about it. "That's good." He dropped kisses on her eyelids, then carried her into the bedroom and laid her on the bed.

She groaned. "I told you I wasn't going to do this," she said, tugging at his sweater. "Why don't you just go quietly away and stop screwing up my life?"

"Because—" he tossed the sweater aside and made quick work of her dress, as well "—I love you, remember?"

"I'm not the one who forgot, you did." She fumbled at his tooled leather belt; he fumbled with the hooks on her bra. "Hank, this is ridiculous!"

"Is it?" He dropped over her, pressing her body deep into the mattress, one knee between her legs. "Sure doesn't feel ridiculous. In fact, it feels..."

Heavenly. She knew exactly how it felt. Like coming home, only to a better place; like making love beneath a shower of violets; like surrendering to the power of love.

The chill that had surrounded her heart since that horrible day in January slowly thawed beneath the heat of his hands and mouth and body. At some point she stopped fighting, even in her heart, and simply accepted the mutual need that lifted them until, in her entire universe, there was only the two of them locked together in love.

HANK KNEW HE'D WON. Lying there in the gathering darkness, he held Carrie in his arms, determined not to gloat. Silently he vowed that he'd never let her get away from him again, not if he lived to be a hundred. And it wasn't just the sex, either.

At which thought, he had to smile. Whatever troubles they'd ever had were mostly ones of communication. In bed, they'd been in total sync. That obviously had not changed.

He stroked a hand down her back and over one rounded hip, eliciting a luxurious groan. "Hank Brady," she murmured in a sexy, satisfied voice, "you're no good. I told you we couldn't do this. I told you to go away and leave me alone."

"Did you? I guess I didn't hear." He kissed a closed eyelid. "Once I saw that you'd kept my groundhog, I knew that no matter what you said, you still—"

"Groundhog! What are you talking about?"

"That pink groundhog in the living room. You kept other stuff from my flower baskets, too. I'm flattered." But not surprised.

She stifled laughter. "That's a pink pig. I don't think there's any such thing as a pink stuffed groundhog."

"Whatever you call it, it worked." He nipped at her earlobe. "I've missed you, darlin'. Did I mention that?"

"How can I be sure? You've been talking ever since you got here. I think I'm suffering from dialogue overload.'' Laughter lay just beneath the surface and she snuggled closer to him.

This was the way it was supposed to be, and he was going to take charge and make sure it stayed this way.

''Okay,'' he said, ''here's the plan.''

''You've got a plan?'' She sounded surprised and not particularly pleased.

''I've always got a plan,'' he said, an understatement. ''The way I see it, there's no need to make a big deal out of it.''

She went still in his arms. ''Out of what?''

She might be slow catching on at times, but she was adorable enough to make up for it. ''You and me and us getting married. We've tried the formal route a couple of times without much success, so my feeling is, it's time for a new approach.''

She withdrew a tiny fraction, really only a slight shifting of position. Her voice changed, lost its soft edges. ''Would you care to explain what you're getting at?''

''Simple. I've got to return to Dallas the day after the wedding, but as soon as the trial ends, we'll fly to Las Vegas and get married there.''

He waited for her to say something.

She didn't.

He grew impatient for her approval. ''So? What do you think?''

''I think...'' Suddenly she shoved herself away from him and sat up on the far side of the bed. One arm came up and she pointed toward the door with a trembling finger. *"I think you'd better get out of here before I kill you!"*

"No, no," he protested, astounded that she still didn't seem to get it. "My plan is perfect. We don't even need to tell anyone in advance. That way we won't have a lot of pressure to get everyone we know all involved in our business. We'll just *do* it—get married and then come back and announce a done deed."

She rose in all her naked glory. "If you don't get out of here I'm calling the police!"

"But *Carrie...!*" His confidence evaporated. What the hell was going on here? They'd just made mad, passionate love and now she was telling him to buzz off? "Hey, what's going on? You can't just use me and toss me aside. I've got feelings, too." *Good approach, Brady. You've still got it!* "If you'd rather risk another wedding extravaganza here in Boston, I'm game. I was thinking of you, after all."

"No, you weren't." Grabbing a robe draped over a chair, she threw it on and whirled to face him.

"I was, too!" Hank picked up his jeans and slid into them, although he'd rather thought they might have another round of lovemaking. Hoped, anyway.

"You were thinking of your job, as usual. Did you listen to yourself? You said *after the trial is over.* Well, to hell with the trial! I'm not going to run *my* life by your *work* schedule and that's final. I told you, I'm sick of being your third priority."

Tight jawed and stunned, Hank yanked on his clothes. "You're wrong about that," he stated over his shoulder. "Didn't you notice? You've moved up to second and sports have dropped to third. Damn it, Carrie—"

A lamp crashed against the wall alongside his head. He whirled toward her in time to catch the slam of the bathroom door.

For a few minutes he stood there in a cold sweat, holding a boot in one hand. For the first time, he realized that he was plenty worried.

When he'd left town in January, he'd been convinced Carrie would see the error of her ways and be waiting to take him back.

She wasn't, despite the fact that she'd let him coax her into bed. Somehow he doubted he'd be able to do that again.

Winning her back was going to be tougher than he'd ever imagined. Maybe even impossible...

Chapter Six

CARRIE SLUMPED on the edge of the bathtub long after she heard the front door slam behind him. Finally she succumbed to Killer's whining and came out, dry-eyed but desolate.

She'd cried her way through January; her tears had finally tapered off in February. Now in March, she supposed she had no tears left to shed.

If she had, she'd shed them now, for she must be the biggest fool in the universe. She stared at the messy sheets and remembered, and her cheeks flushed with humiliation and despair. How could she have let him cajole her into bed only hours after his return? Had she no pride?

Feet dragging, she forced herself to open a can of dog food for Killer—the traitor. As an attack dog he was a total washout. Then she packed the pink pig and other holiday-flower memorabilia away in a cardboard carton, dressed and took Killer outside again. Standing hunched in a steady drizzle, she forced herself to face a few facts as cold and hard as the weather.

Fact number one, she still loved Hank Brady even if he was a jerk, and supposed she always would. Number two, although he *had* chosen her over basketball, she was still one peg below his work and he obviously didn't even know what was wrong with that picture.

Bottom line: there was absolutely no chance they could make it as a couple. Carrie would not wind up like her mother, endlessly waiting....

Now it was up to her to avoid, evade and ignore Hank until Sean and Amanda were married—a matter of days. Then Hank would go back to Dallas and she'd go...crazy, probably, but that was a chance she had to take.

WEDNESDAY, April Fool's Day, Clancy's delivery to Carrie was a bit different from the usual overblown floral offerings. This time Hank had sent a simple but lush basket of clover decorated with a plastic pick featuring a good luck four-leaf clover. Slowly she opened the note in his familiar handwriting and read: "I may be an April fool but I love you anyway. Here's hoping this four-leaf clover brings me luck—and you. Hank."

SEAN CHUGALUGGED his beer, burped and glared at his best man. The bachelor party had been a roaring success; only one guest and the guest of honor were still on their feet, so to speak. Everyone else had gone home or was stretched out in an attitude of slumber. The stripper had come and gone, the beer had come and nearly gone, and it was two o'clock on Friday morning.

"So what's your problem?" Sean demanded of Hank, slurring his words slightly. "I was having a real good time until I looked at you, ol' pal. You're about as much fun as a root canal, you know that?"

"Don't mess with hyperbole, good buddy," Hank suggested dryly. "In a battle of wits, you're only half-armed at the moment."

"Oh, yeah?" Sean stuck out a belligerent chin. "If you weren't my gal's brother, I'd—I'd..." He seemed to forget where he was going with that thought and sighed. "You got troubles, huh?"

"You could say that."

"Woman troubles," Sean suggested wisely.

"Yep."

"Carrie, huh?"

"Yep, one more time."

"I saw how she's been treating you." Sean nodded his red head.

"You mean, like a leper?" And Sean didn't know the half of it. She'd actually returned his April Fool's tribute with a tacky note saying she didn't need luck, she just needed him to stop hounding her. That's exactly what she'd said: *hounding her.*

Sean was too far gone to pick up on Hank's state of mind. "Yeah, just like a leper," he agreed, blinking and squinting as if trying to clear his vision. "Hell, you'll figure somethin' out. A woman ish only a woman, but a good woman ish a pain in the heart forever."

"Sean, old pal o' mine, you're drunk."

"Nope, I'm *plash*tered. Mind if I grab a little shut-eye..." He keeled over sideways on the sofa, starting to snore almost instantly.

Hank stared at him, shook his head in pity and stood up. Looked like this party was over.

Looked like the other one was over, too. Fighting vague feelings of desperation, he tossed his nearly full beer can into the trash, checked to make sure all the bodies were breathing and let himself out of the apartment.

He still had a little more than two days before he had to be back in Dallas. Hell, all kinds of things could happen in a little more than two days.

THE REHEARSAL at Josie's place was torture. Carrie fought memories and tears through the entire thing. If the practice was this difficult, how would she ever get through the real wedding?

It defied logic.

Hank leaned over to speak in her ear in that way that always sent shivers down her spine. "Nice-lookin' couple."

She darted him an exasperated glance and sidled a step away. Half of that nice-looking couple had obviously overindulged at the bachelor party the night before. Sean's bloodshot eyes peered woozily at the proceedings and he followed directions like an automaton.

Amanda seemed oblivious to his discomfort. Perfectly at ease, completely without nerves, she smiled and chatted brightly.

Carrie envied her.

Amanda, with Josie at her side, waved to get the attention of those in attendance: Sean's parents, maid of honor and best man, two bridesmaids and two groomsmen, the minister and the pianist. Amanda's own parents had died several years ago, so she had only her brother to lean upon.

He stepped to her other side now and gave her a kiss on the cheek. "You doin' okay?"

"Of course. Why wouldn't I?"

He shrugged. "So what's next on the agenda?"

She smiled. "The rehearsal dinner. Sean picked Luigi's." She gave her intended an adoring glance.

Sean turned green at mention of his favorite Italian restaurant, gulped hard and nodded gamely.

Amanda raised her voice. "Luigi's, everyone. You all know where it is. Josie, do you want to come with us?"

"No, thanks. I'll drive the bridesmaids."

"Great. Then Hank and Carrie, you'll come with me and Sean. Does anyone else need a ride?"

It quickly became apparent that no one did. Thus Carrie found herself in the back seat of Sean's Blazer sitting next to Hank and wishing she was anywhere else, anywhere at all. Determined to avoid any personal exchange between them, she looked out the window. Depressed, she gave desultory attention to Sean's favorite rock and roll radio station, to keep her mind off the man beside her.

"Carrie..." Hank picked up the hand resting in her lap.

"Shh!" She snatched her hand away. "The weather report's coming on. Pray for sunshine."

"...Nor'easter bearing down on Boston, and the weather gurus say it'll hit late tonight."

"Carrie," he said impatiently, "there's nothing we can do about the damned—"

She shook her head to silence him while the radio announcer continued with his depressing message. "...Three days of rain and thunder and lightning and just general crud...."

Hank fidgeted until the guy on the radio finally put on an Elvis Presley record. Then he spoke in a voice so low it was almost lost beneath the music's throb. "I know you're pissed off at me, but if you're waiting for an apology because we ended up in bed, hell will freeze over first. I don't regret a thing."

"I don't want an apology. I don't want anything from you."

"I don't believe that."

"I don't care whether you believe it or not."

"You want guarantees and all I can give you are promises."

She darted him an incensed glance, then turned back to the window. A cabby made a U-turn in front of them: a Uey, Clancy the delivery boy called that popular Boston maneuver. Sean swore loudly and swerved to avoid a collision.

The sudden movement threw Carrie hard against Hank's shoulder. For an instant, she reveled in the contact; then she pulled sharply away.

And reacted to what he'd just said. "Guarantee, promise—you're playing word games. What's the difference?"

"Plenty. Guarantees come with tires and refrigerators, not with marriage. Promises come from people, and people are fallible. You have to work at a promise."

"My mother used to say that promises are like piecrusts—easily broken."

His mouth tilted down at one corner. "Everybody's mother used to say that and I guess it's probably true. But because a thing is fragile doesn't mean it's not worth working for and nurturing and protecting. Carrie, sweetheart, I can't think of anything that requires more work and comes with more built-in pitfalls than a marriage."

This didn't sound like the Hank she knew talking. She looked at him through narrow, suspicious eyes. "Did you think all that up yourself?"

He looked stricken, but that was one of his best responses, as she well knew.

"You cut me to the quick," he said. "With my sister getting married, I guess I've been thinking about...you know, *life.*"

She laughed. "You're joking, right?"

"No, really, I—"

"We're here," Amanda sang out from the front seat. "We have a private room reserved, so let's go see if everything's properly set up before the rest of them get here."

Carrie was grateful for the interruption. Hank's promises *were* like piecrust. He could dress them up with all the pretty words he could think of but she would never, ever trust him again.

End of story.

"I'M A REFORMED MAN," Hank said, his expression solemn.

Seated once more in Sean's back seat, they were on the way to Carrie's apartment following an interminable rehearsal dinner, during which Carrie had exerted all her energies in avoiding and ignoring him.

"You certainly are *not* reformed," she retorted. "You're the same old workaholic you always were. You even left in the middle of dinner to call your editor."

"It wasn't in the middle, it was at the end. All the good stuff was over. Everybody was just milling around."

"That's *your* interpretation. I say it was in the middle."

Sean steered the Blazer onto Carrie's street. Hank glanced out the window, his manner distracted.

"Look," he said, a desperate tinge to his tone, "I'm doing my best to be thoughtful and attentive and—"

"Charming?" Carrie interjected.

"Sure, why not?" He looked surprised she'd even bring it up. He fumbled in the pocket of his leather jacket. "I'm trying to win you back, Caroline Duncan."

"I told you that's out of the question." But her heart constricted at hearing that possibility voiced.

He extracted a small jeweler's box. "I kept your engagement ring."

"Good idea. You can have it resized for some other woman, when you find one willing to accept you on your own terms." Ah, but even as she said it the third finger on her left hand itched for the familiar presence of that ring. It had nearly killed her to return it.

"Dammit, I don't want some other woman!"

"You will," she said. "Sooner or later..." Her heart constricted at the truth of her words.

"We're here," Amanda announced, turning down the blaring radio. "You'll be at Josie's tomorrow at one, right, Carrie?"

"You can count on it. Don't worry about a thing. You're almost home free."

Amanda laughed. "What? Me, worry?"

But walking through the rain to her front door with an unusually quiet Hank escorting her, Carrie sighed. Knowing what had happened in January, how could Amanda *not* worry?

Before the antiquated elevator, Carrie turned to Hank with a deliberately blank expression. "Thanks for seeing me in," she said. "I'll be fine now."

"I could come up and walk Killer for you."

"Killer's back with his owner."

"Then I could come up and—"

"Good night, Hank." Stepping inside the elevator, she pressed a switch.

"Don't do this, Carrie." He said it as if he meant it. "I'm getting a little tired of banging my head against your stubborn refusal to—"

The metal doors closed with slow deliberation, blocking out the voice as well as the brooding expression on the face of the man she loved.

All she could think about was *sooner or later.* Sooner or later he'd find someone else, and when he did, he'd leave her alone.

From the sound of his final words, the operative word was *sooner.*

"I CAN'T DO THIS!"

Amanda stood in the middle of Josie's bedroom, above the living room where she and Sean were shortly scheduled to exchange wedding vows. Dressed in her beautiful formal wedding gown and clutching a lacy white handkerchief, she stared at her maid of honor with horror in her blue eyes.

Carrie blinked in astonishment. "Of course you can! What in the world...?"

Amanda shook her head so hard that the crown

of orange blossoms tilted crazily. Carrie made a grab for it before it could topple from her hair.

"I can't. I didn't know what I was agreeing to," Amanda whimpered.

Carrie repositioned the pins to secure garland and veil. "Did anything happen after you dropped me off last night?"

"No. Yes."

Carrie gave the trembling woman a hug, trying to offer comfort. "Which is it?"

Amanda chewed on her lower lip. "We kind of...got into a fight, I guess you could say."

"About...?"

"He got drunk at that bachelor party."

"Practically everybody got drunk at that bachelor party. I agree it's disgusting, but that's what guys do. Guys I know, anyway."

Amanda looked stubborn. "Hank didn't."

"That surprised me, to be honest. He got blotto at his own bachelor party—both of them, actually."

"He's a changed man," Amanda said with fervent belief. "But Sean...if he could get wasted after promising me he wouldn't, maybe I don't really know him at all."

Mystified, Carrie stared at the bride. "You've known him ever since you moved to Boston two years ago. Good grief, you two have dated for more than a year. What's *really* going on here? You seemed so calm last night."

"I w-w-wasn't." Amanda's teeth chattered, probably with nerves. "I've been trying so hard to keep my cool, but after we dropped you and Hank off, I asked Sean, in a very civil way, why he broke his promise and h-he said, 'Don't start with me, Amanda!'"

"That's just a figure of speech!"

"Oh, no, he meant it." Amanda grabbed the ruffles on Carrie's pink dress and hung on. "Maybe we should just live together for a while and see how it works out. Maybe that's what we should do. Marriage is so—so permanent. If you're just living together—"

"Amanda, get hold of yourself!" Carrie caught the distraught bride's hands and pried them from the crushed ruffles. Perhaps the time had come to be firm. "You know you don't mean that."

"I do!" Amanda glanced around as if seeking an escape route.

"All right, then." A bit of reverse psychology might be in order. "Let's get out of here, then."

Amanda blinked. "Do you mean it? You think I shouldn't marry him?"

"Absolutely," Carrie said firmly. "Since you don't love him, you'd be insane to—"

"Who says I don't love him?" The bride stared with wide and horrified eyes. "Just because you didn't love Hank enough..."

That would hurt later, when Carrie had time to think about her own feelings. At the moment, there was a disaster to be averted. "Amanda, honey, you and Sean are not Hank and me,'' she stated. ''You've just got cold feet—lots of brides do.'' She patted Amanda's pale cheek. ''But don't you think you're being the tiniest little bit unreasonable? Sean made one mistake and your brother made a hundred, so you really can't compare them.'' She shrugged. ''On the other hand, if you no longer love him—''

''But I do! I love him so much I ache with it. Oh, I'm so confused.'' Amanda groaned. ''I just want to be sure, and I'm not.''

''If you want a guarantee,'' Carrie said gently, ''buy a washing machine. If you want a husband, you'll have to go on faith and promises.''

For a moment, Amanda stared with mouth agape. Then she threw herself into the arms of her maid of honor. ''Oh, Carrie,'' she cried, ''that's so wise. Thank you!''

Carrie just stood there, hardly believing she'd just quoted the man who'd broken her heart.

''JEEZ,'' SEAN WHEEZED, ''I think I'm gonna toss my cookies.''

Hank glared at the tall man with the black tuxedo and the green face. ''You do and I'll knock the crap out of you, so help me God. Get hold of yourself, man! The ceremony's set to begin in ten minutes.''

Sean shook his head slowly, as if any quick moves would make good his warning. ''She won't be there. It'll be just like you and Carrie all over again.''

Hank didn't know if the poor slob meant the first time, when Hank arrived late, or the second time, when Carrie left early. Either way would spell disaster.

"She'll be here," he snarled. "What the hell is your problem?"

"We got into a real row last night after we dropped you and Carrie off," Sean admitted unhappily.

"About what?"

"Damned if I know." He added as if it were an afterthought, "The bachelor party, maybe."

Hank frowned. "But she seemed fine about that at the rehearsal."

"Yeah." Sean sighed. "Women. Go figure."

Go figure, Hank echoed, but only in his thoughts. "You love her, right?"

Sean blinked and licked dry lips.

"Look, you SOB," Hank barked, "this is my little sister we're talkin' about here. Do you love her or don't you?"

"I love her," Sean said in a barely audible whisper.

Hank breathed a sigh of relief. "In that case, we're gonna walk out there and smile and act like everything's just hunky-dory. You got that?"

"I...got that."

"And if you even *think* about yackin' or otherwise screwing up this glorious occasion, just look at me and remember that if you do anything—*any-*

thing—to mess up this wedding, I am gonna kick your ass from here to Texas. Got that?"

Sean grinned, the first time since Hank had walked in. "Thanks, pal. I needed that."

Hank wished someone had given him equally good advice, but what the hell? It was too late now.

WALKING DOWN THAT AISLE in Josie's tastefully decorated living room and seeing Hank waiting for her was probably the hardest thing Carrie had ever had to do—and she had to do it *smiling*. Taking her place, she ignored him, turning to watch the bride's measured progress.

Amanda looked pale but self-possessed. Carrie glanced at Sean—pale but *not* self-possessed. In fact, he looked as if he might keel over at any moment. She turned toward Hank in alarm—and wished she hadn't.

Hank looked great—fabulous, in fact—in a classic tuxedo and white shirt. In his lapel he wore a boutonniere from Josie's Posies, made of a red rose and baby's breath. Her glance crossed his and he gave her a slight smile so impersonal that it sent chills down her spine.

And in that moment she knew he'd given up. He wasn't going to bother her anymore. She should be...if not happy, at least relieved.

So why did she feel like crying?

The bride reached her bridegroom's side. Stepping forward, Carrie lifted the fingertip-length veil and arranged it gracefully in a cascade down Amanda's back. Only then did she take the time to look—really *look*—at the bride.

Amanda glowed, and as Sean stared into her face, the haunted expression on his slowly lifted. Pure, unadulterated joy replaced it. Taking her hand in his, he mouthed the words *I love you.*

Quick tears blurred Carrie's vision and she stood there in a daze, barely hearing the words of the ceremony. Thoughts of Hank flooded her mind: all the good times they'd had together, all the joy of falling in love and deciding to commit the rest of their lives to each other.

And then she was hit by disappointment so bitter that she could barely stand here with him only a few steps away. She spared a quick glance in his direction. He was listening to the minister with that utter concentration he brought to everything he did.

Suddenly the minister's quiet voice cut through Carrie's wandering thoughts like a diamond through glass: "—Knows any reason these two should not be joined in holy matrimony, let him speak now or forever after hold his peace."

The words jarred her and she flung back her head, her gaze locking with Hank's. From out of the blue, light dawned over Marblehead, as her grandmother was so fond of saying, and Carrie realized that the room had become deathly quiet.

Tearing her gaze from Hank's, she saw that the

bride and the bridegroom and everyone else in the entire room was staring at her and holding their breath, as if they fully expected her to yell "Stop the wedding!" and go rushing down the aisle.

Chapter Seven

WITH EVERYONE IN THE ROOM staring straight at her, Carrie swallowed hard and forced herself to smile as if she didn't have a care in the world. She heard—or imagined she heard—a collective sigh of relief from those assembled. After what seemed like an eternity, the minister proceeded with the ceremony.

But later, while toasting the newlyweds with champagne in Josie's enormous family room, Carrie reminded herself that she must remain strong for a few more hours. Then she could go home and fall apart, secure in the knowledge that she wouldn't be seeing Hank Brady again for a very long time—perhaps ever.

On the outside chance that his plans had changed, she forced herself to approach him where he stood watching the bridal couple accepting congratulations and best wishes. "So when will you be flying back to Texas?" she asked casually, as if she didn't care much one way or the other.

"Tomorrow afternoon," he replied, matching her lack of inflection.

"That's good." She couldn't quite manage a smile, but did keep her voice impersonal. "Now that we've got them married, I suppose we can all get back to our own lives.''

''Looks like.'' He straightened. ''If you'll excuse me, I see someone I need to talk to.''

And he walked away.

HELL, YES, Hank told himself, he was as eager to get back to his own life as she was to return to hers. Texas was looking better by the minute.

He was still brooding about it when the disc jockey hired for the occasion put on the first record. A slow and dreamy melody filled the room. Alone on the small portable dance floor, the bride and bridegroom shared the first dance, to enthusiastic applause.

When the second dance began, Hank recognized his duty and went in search of Carrie. He offered her his hand, without a smile, because by this point a smile was more than he could handle.

She took a step away. ''Oh, I don't think—''

He unclamped his tense jaws only long enough to speak. ''This is the best man asking the maid of honor to dance, not Hank asking Carrie. Sorry to inconvenience you, but I think they all expect it.''

''Oh, God.'' Her head drooped for an instant, then snapped up to reveal a bright smile. ''Of course. Thank you for reminding me of my duty.''

She took his hand and he led her onto the tiny dance floor, where she went into his arms as naturally as if she belonged there—which, of course, she did. Only when he drew her close did he realize how very tense she remained, her back and shoulders rigid.

Deliberately he whirled her around the floor, then settled into a sedate rhythm. Over his shoulder, she seemed to be concentrating on the newlyweds, not on the way it felt to be held in his arms.

Hell, he could tell her that feigned indifference wasn't going to work. If she was half as aware of him as he was of her—

"Please," she said, interrupting his thoughts in a breathless little voice, "not quite so tight."

"Sorry." He loosened his hold until they were dancing a foot apart.

She bit her lip. "You're really angry with me, aren't you."

"What makes you think that? Just because I returned to Boston thinking I could win you back, only to have you laugh in my face—"

"I didn't laugh."

"I interpreted it that way. So okay, the handwriting's on the wall. We're finished. Maybe I can accept that, but I don't have to like it."

"Hank—"

"Oh, hell!" His fingers bit into her waist. "Meet me for coffee tomorrow at eleven at the Silver Skillet."

"Why on earth should I?"

"Because you loved me once, or said you did. Because you owe me at least that much. Because if you don't, I'm going to cause a scene right here and now and I know how much you'd love that."

"You wouldn't!" She stared at him, brown eyes wide and defenseless.

"Yep," he said, "I will. I deserve one more chance to make you see things my way."

"You're insane!"

"I'm determined. There *is* a difference. Yes or no?"

"Please—"

"Yes or no!"

"All right, yes!" She glared at him. "But I don't like being coerced. Don't expect me to be in a receptive frame of mind."

"Just be there or—"

"Hank! Dance with your sister."

Without missing a beat, he whirled Carrie into Sean's arms and took Amanda in his own, thinking that he couldn't wait to get on that airplane headed for Texas. Still, there was at least one tiny ray of hope....

IT WAS RAINING when Hank got home and it was raining when he got up Sunday morning. "April showers," he muttered, looking out the apartment window. "More like April torrent. Bah! Humbug!" Up to five inches, the guy on the radio had said—just general crud.

Thunder cracked, lightning flashed—and *Hank* flashed onto a mental image of Carrie quaking in her shoes. She hated thunder and lightning, or maybe the more accurate word was *feared*. He reached automatically for the telephone, then yanked his hand back. He'd be seeing her in an hour. Over coffee in a public place, perhaps he could finally make her see...

Dammit, he *had* to make her see. He glanced at his wristwatch and saw that it was already after ten. His plane didn't leave until one o'clock. If she was there promptly at eleven—and Carrie was always prompt—there'd be time for him to say his piece and still make it to the airport, assuming he talked fast.

But first he'd check and see how things were going in Texas. Picking up the telephone handset, he dialed Bill Sulewski. His photographer answered on the second ring.

"Hank! Damn, I'm glad to hear from you. You're coming back on that one o'clock flight, right?"

There was something in his voice that brought Hank's antennae to full alert. "That's the plan. You sound a little rattled. What's going on?"

"Nothing. Nothing at all." But this time the voice concealed a smile.

"Okay, buddy, out with it. What do you know that I don't?"

"Nothing! Not a thing. I'm just relieved."

"Relieved? That's a strange choice of words."

"Okay, glad. Whatever."

"Spit it out, Bill. I've got this sixth sense that tells me you're holdin' out on me."

Bill groaned. "I'm not even supposed to know."

"Know what?"

Bill hesitated. "What the hell...since you're coming back, what will it hurt if I tell you?"

"Tell me what?" Hank had a hard time not yelling at this point.

"I guess I should. I mean, they are ganging up on you."

"Who's ganging up on me?"

"You know, the bigwigs. They didn't like it when you insisted on taking the week off when they were all set to give you that political column you're always whining about."

Hank wasn't whining at the moment, he was groaning. That column was the dream of his life. "Go on," he said through gritted teeth.

"Well," Bill said warily, obviously picking up on Hank's mood, "they got pissed off."

"I lost the column." Hank's gut clenched. His ultimate professional goal had gone down the tubes while he chased after a woman who refused to listen to reason.

"Yeah, but then I guess they had second thoughts. The way it stands now, if you're on that one o'clock plane like you're supposed to be, you'll get your column as soon as this trial ends."

Hank's heart soared. "Are you serious?"

"*They're* serious. But if you're not on that

plane...now how did they phrase it? 'Your future as a hotshot reporter with this newspaper will be in serious jeopardy.'"

"And you got all this from...?"

"Hey," Bill said with a laugh, "gotta protect my sources."

"Didn't you say your girl works in the publisher's office?"

"Jeez, Hank, don't even suggest it! I wasn't supposed to know anything about this. And if anybody asks, I'll say I don't. See you Monday at the courthouse." The telephone line went dead.

Hank hung up numbly, almost wishing *he* didn't know anything about it, either. All it did was make an impossible choice even more difficult. The lady or the job...

Or maybe he'd get lucky. Maybe Carrie would be both punctual and willing to listen. Maybe Hank would get *real* lucky.

Hell, he thought with more than a touch of disgust, whoever said that hope sprang eternal sure had it right.

CARRIE TURNED OFF the answering machine the minute she dragged herself out of bed Sunday morning to face a dark and stormy day. Although she'd agreed to meet Hank for coffee at eleven, she'd never intended to show up. She'd only agreed in order to avoid a scene.

The telephone began ringing at 11:05 and never

stopped. Red-eyed from lack of sleep and trembling in reaction to storms raging inside and outside, she turned her back on the annoying instrument and went to pour herself another cup of coffee.

At least she'd survived the wedding. The worst was over. Hank would get on an airplane in a few hours and fly away. Then her life could return to normal. Well, as soon as she managed to forget that she'd let him into her bed again, life could return to normal.

The telephone kept ringing. This was driving her crazy! She had to get out of here, she decided. With the shrill ringing in her ears, she stamped into the bedroom and threw off her gown and robe, dragged on jeans and a sweatshirt. She'd go to Josie's, she decided.

Grabbing her anorak, she flung open the front door and stopped dead. Hank stood there, his hand raised as if to knock. At sight of her, his eyes went wide with surprise, then narrowed. He sucked in a quick angry breath. "You were supposed to meet me at eleven," he growled. "What the hell happened?"

He advanced; she retreated back into her apartment. Rain rolled off his trench coat and puddled on the floor. He shook his head and raindrops flew in all directions.

She gave him a shove. "You've got no right to be here. Don't you have a plane to catch?"

"Let me worry about that." He took another step.

"Why didn't you show up at the Silver Skillet at eleven like you said you would? Why haven't you been answering your telephone?"

"I never intended to meet you," she said angrily. "And I didn't answer the phone because I knew it was you, although apparently..." Apparently someone else was calling, her, too, because she'd opened the door and found him standing there with the clamor of the telephone in her ears.

First things first. She glowered at him. "Don't you have a heart? Honestly, Hank—" She stopped short. "How did you get in here, anyway? I didn't buzz you in."

"I ran into your second-floor neighbor going out as I was coming in and she remembered me."

"I'll have to speak to her about that—" A burst of thunder made Carrie jump almost into his arms, which attempted to close around her. "Don't do that!" she cried, fighting free from his embrace. "Please go away! I don't want you here."

"Carrie," he said, "I love you. I never stopped loving you. I want you to marry me."

She closed her eyes for an instant to regroup. "I can't marry you. You don't love me enough."

"Maybe it's the other way around—you don't love me enough. Enough to trust me, I mean."

"In spite of everything that's happened, I *do* love you." She said it like a shameful confession. "But I'll get over it, because I don't intend to spend the rest of my life with a man whose number-one priority is his job, not me. My mother tried that, and believe me, it doesn't work. I'm sorry but that's how I feel.''

''You *are* number one with me,'' he said. ''Maybe the only way to prove that is to—hell, to quit my job and start over someplace else.''

''That's right,'' she said indignantly, ''make a grandstand play. Can't you just accept the fact that we're finished?''

''I'll sign a prenuptial agreement,'' he argued. ''I, Hank Brady, love you, Caroline Duncan, more than this or any other job I ever had, have or will have. I love you more than basketball and football combined.'' He stuck out an arm and shoved up the sleeve to reveal a strong brown wrist. ''Hell, get a knife! I'll sign it in blood!''

''Don't you dare make fun of me.'' She pushed past him. ''I'm going to Josie's and you can go to the devil, for all I care.''

He followed her into the hall. ''I wasn't making fun of you, I swear to God. I love you madly and I want to spend the rest of my life—''

''Give it up, Hank.'' She punched the button for the elevator.

The metal doors clanged open and she stepped inside. He followed. She sidled to the back of the small cage, not wanting to stand any closer to him than was necessary.

''Okay,'' he said grimly. ''You don't have to draw me a picture. You don't have to hit me over the head with a baseball bat.'' The door closed with the scrape of metal and the elevator lurched into motion. He glared at her and added, ''I just don't know why you'd say you'd meet me and then—''

The floor dropped from beneath her feet and the lights went out.

Carrie screamed and grabbed for anything she could hold onto. There *was* nothing, and she found herself tumbling to the marble floor when the elevator suddenly stopped with a horrible creaking and groaning of gears.

Gasping, she crouched there in the dark, trying to decide if she was dead or alive, injured or merely scared to death. What had happened? Had the elevator cable broken?

''Carrie?''

Hank's voice came out of the utter blackness, bringing hope with it. ''Hank! I'm here.'' She stretched out a hand and touched him—his knee, she thought. ''What happened?''

''Something's wrong with the elevator, obviously. The storm must have caused a power failure. It's darker than the pits of hell in here.'' His hand touched her arm, moved down to her hand and lifted it to his mouth for a kiss. ''Are you all right?''

''I...I think so.'' Even in the darkness, she closed her eyes to more fully savor the feel of his lips on her fingers. ''God, I hate thunder and lightning!'' She shuddered. ''I don't know why storms frighten me so, but they have ever since I was a little girl.''

But then, suddenly, she remembered: herself at five or six, clinging to her mother during an electrical storm and begging for Daddy to come and save them both. Only Daddy was still at the office....

Hank tugged at her arm. "Come on over here, then, and let me protect you."

Her shaky laugh surprised her; she was so scared she didn't know how she managed it. "Do you know how politically incorrect that is? I don't need a man to protect me. I can d-do it myself."

"Then come over here and protect *me.*"

His tone was charged with feeling. Drawn to him by an irresistible force, she scooted toward the sound. Her chin bumped into some part of him—his thigh?—and he pulled her up onto his lap, held her against his heart.

"Thank God you're all right." He sighed with a satisfaction that seemed to come straight from his soul.

She let herself relax against him. After a moment, her heart rate slowed. "Are we going to die?" she asked in a low voice.

He chuckled. "Not a chance. We've still got a lot of livin' to do."

For some reason, she took comfort in that. "How l-long do you think we'll be stuck in here?"

"I don't know. Maybe I should start punching buttons and see if—"

"No, don't!" She clung more tightly to him. "Don't leave me here in the dark."

His arms tightened around her. "I won't, Carrie. I'll *never* leave you, unless you make me."

"This isn't the time for that."

His laughter bounced off the walls of the small enclosure. "There's never been a better time. Carrie, when we got into this elevator, I had just about conceded defeat where you were concerned. Then the elevator dropped and I thought it was all over—we were dead."

She groaned. "Could it fall again? I mean, how safe are we now?"

"I don't know. All I know is that when the end seemed near, I didn't think about my job. I thought about you."

"Oh, Hank..." She felt herself melting.

"I'm sorry I hurt you, Carrie. I'll try to make up for it if you'll let me, but I will *never* give up on us."

She felt the cold return of reality. "How can you make up for it when you've never even realized what it is that upset me so?"

"I didn't before, but I do now." He began to stroke her back. "There I was, sitting in that coffee shop waiting. You *said* you'd be there but you didn't come. The more time passed the more upset I got. And then I thought maybe something had happened—you'd been hit by a car crossing the street or something."

Laughter just one notch shy of hysteria bubbled in her throat. "The old dead-in-a-ditch scenario."

"Yeah, I guess." His blank tone said he didn't have a clue what she was talking about. "But then I thought, if I feel this lousy over a cup of coffee, how did you feel standing around in your wedding gown waiting for me?"

She felt a shudder run through him.

He nuzzled her temple. "I'd blown the best thing that ever happened to me, but I'd be damned if I'd slink out of town without facing up to it. That's why I came—to say I understood too late, and that I'd go away and never bother you again."

"And then the sky fell." She slid her arms around him and rested her head on his chest.

"Yes. When this elevator dropped, I don't know about you but my life really did flash before my eyes." He stroked tendrils of hair away from her face. "I've learned my lesson. More than anything in the world, I want another chance with you. Can we try again?"

She thought about that, really thought hard, trying not to drag all those old feelings into the equation. "*Maybe* we can start over," she said at last. "I want to...but I'm afraid to take another chance."

"Don't be."

He tilted her chin and kissed her, and the final barrier safeguarding her heart crumbled. Clinging to him, she kissed him back without reservation, reveling in the taste and texture of his mouth. For a long time they sat there in the dark on the floor of the incapacitated elevator, kissing and touching and discovering each other all over again.

On the verge of complete surrender, Carrie felt a slight tremble in the floor beneath her and struggled to sit up. "Did you feel that? I think we moved a little!"

"The earth moves every time I touch you." Hank tried to kiss her again. "Here, I'll show you."

She stifled skittish laughter. "I'm being serious. Shh!" She listened for a moment but heard nothing more. "How long do you think we've been stuck here?" she asked.

"An hour, maybe? Who cares? I'm not bored, are you?"

"No, but I'd still like to know what time is it."

"It's April. That's close enough." He reached for her.

"You've got one of those watches that lights up and I want to know what time it is," she said stubbornly.

"All right, if you insist." A green glow appeared briefly. "It's one-fifteen. Satisfied?"

"*I* am, but what about you? What time is your plane?"

"Who cares? Come here."

This time he succeeded in dragging her back onto his lap. His hand brushed across the tip of her breast, sparking an electric charge.

"But Hank," she argued halfheartedly, "Your flight leaves sometime this afternoon, doesn't it? If we're stuck here much longer you may miss your plane."

He slid one hand up beneath her shirt and curved it over her breast. "At the moment, I'm not thinking about airplanes," he murmured.

She ran her hands over his throat and up across his cheeks, reveling in the feel of him. "Then what *are* you thinking about?" she asked breathlessly.

"Important stuff." He kissed her temple. "Like what a terrible mistake I made when I let you down. Honey, my dad was a lovable bum who never figured out a way to support his wife and kids that didn't involve hard work—and he was allergic to that. I thought ambition was a good thing and too much ambition was even better. I guess I needed to learn the hard way that there are things in life even more important than a big paycheck or a major byline."

She melted. "Oh, Hank..."

He held her close. "You were right, though. I did put you last although I never intended to. I never will again, Carrie, I swear it. I love you. Will you say you'll marry me—again?"

Throwing caution to the wind, she showered him with kisses. "Yes!" she cried, "Yes, yes and yes! I'll marry you, Hank."

He let out a long, emotional groan. "I may be the happiest man stuck in midair in all of Boston," he said. "Why don't we seal the deal, right here in our lucky elevator...."

The lights flickered—flickered and flashed on again. With a lurch, the elevator began to move. Carrie shrieked and clung to him. After what seemed like an eternity, they jolted to a stop.

For a moment they sat there, holding their collective breaths. Then she cried, "We're saved!"

"I was saved when you said you'd marry me," he corrected her.

Untangling themselves, they stumbled awkwardly to their feet on shaky legs. Through iron lace, they could see wind and rain lashing the trees beyond the front door. Hank punched the button and the door slid open obligingly.

Arm in arm, they stepped off the elevator. Already the sense of unreality was fading and Carrie found herself wondering how much of what had passed between them in the elevator was just the adrenaline talking.

Dared she believe all he'd said? Actions did speak louder than words, after all. He *said* she came first with him, but did she? When the chips were down, would he choose his work over his wife? By agreeing to marry him, had she just made the same mistake as her mother?

Someone was running toward the front door, head down against the battering rain. It was Josie, Carrie saw with surprise.

Hank held the door for the newcomer, the wind nearly snatching it from his hands. Josie almost fell inside. Struggling to catch her breath, she finally managed to speak.

"Damn, Carrie, when did you stop answering your telephone?" she gasped, shoving wet hair out of her eyes.

"That was you calling? I didn't want to talk to Hank so I turned off the machine."

"Well, I *do* want to speak to Hank. I figured he might be here."

"You found me," Hank said. "What's the problem?"

"Your editor is trying to locate you and he's in a real snit. He said he'd tried calling Carrie—"

"Oh, dear," Carrie groaned.

"Yeah," Josie agreed darkly. "You really messed things up by turning off your machine today of all days. How the guy got my number, I have no idea."

Hank shrugged. "You're on my emergency call list, right after Carrie and Amanda. So what did he want?"

"To say he knows you weren't on that one o'clock plane, because he went to the airport to give you some stuff—I don't know what, something to take to Texas with you—and you never showed up."

Carrie was struck speechless. Hank had already missed his plane? She couldn't believe he'd be so calm about it.

Hank did indeed seem unperturbed. "Thanks for letting me know, Josie. You're a pal."

"Hank!" Carrie grabbed him by the lapels and shook him. "You knew you'd missed your plane but you didn't care? You really do love me more than you love your job!"

"Yes, and I'll still love you when I'm an unemployed journalist."

"But you're not unemployed," Josie interrupted. "That's the rest of the message. He said if I found you first, I was to tell you that if you're on the four o'clock plane to Dallas, you've still got a job. He said the earlier plane couldn't take off because of this rotten weather, so he's giving you a break."

"He calls this weather rotten?" Hank threw back his head and laughed. "Josie, it's raining violets!"

Carrie, happy in his arms, couldn't have agreed with him more.

Epilogue

HANK AND CARRIE MADE IT to McCurran Airport with only minutes to spare. Standing at his gate and waving goodbye, she realized that she'd never been happier in her life.

He made her happier still when he wheeled around at the entrance to the passenger loading bridge and loped back to her, ignoring the airline employee calling after him to hurry.

He kissed her hard and quick. "I love you," he said. "I'll call you as soon as I get to Dallas."

He sprinted away, gave her a final wave and disappeared through the gate, the last passenger to board the plane. She walked to one of the glass walls overlooking the airfield, hardly able to see for the tears in her eyes.

This time they were tears of happiness.

She wasn't a child, after all; she knew a person's work was important. She could handle that just as long as she knew she was *the* most important thing in his life—that he would always be there for her, as she would be for him.

She watched until the plane began to back away from the jet bridge. Although she knew Hank couldn't see her, she blew him a kiss before heading for the exit.

Walking to her car, she looked up into leaden skies and smiled. A few wayward drops of water struck her cheeks, but she didn't brush them away.

Because it really *was* raining violets—at least in her heart. She could hardly wait to call Granny in Florida and tell her she'd been right all along.

SHE'S THE ONE!

Kate Hoffmann

Chapter One

STEEL GRAY CLOUDS SCUDDED across the sky, whipped by a damp wind off the Atlantic. Chase Donnelly leaned against the railing of the porch and stared out at the choppy water, following a whitecap until it dissolved on the sandy beach far below him.

How many times as a boy had he stood in this same spot, on the sprawling veranda of his grandmother's huge Victorian summer house, and stared out at the sea, dreaming of adventures in faraway places? Summerhill had been his second home for as long as he could remember.

He had first come here as a child. On the night before the last day of school, he and his two brothers would pack their bags, stuffing a summer's worth of toys into their duffels, along with a few T-shirts and pairs of shorts. They'd leave for Nana Tonya's the minute school let out, Nana's chauffeur picking them up in the Bentley to make the drive from Boston to Woods Hole.

The summer officially began the moment Winston drove the Bentley onto the car ferry for Martha's Vineyard. Chase would hop out of the back seat and run to the bow, hanging his arms over the gunwales and turning his face into the spray. The tangy sea breeze would seep into his skin and ruffle his hair, and the waves beneath the bow of the ferry would set his body swaying in an instinctive response.

His life in Boston, so staid and proper, would slowly disappear behind him and the summer would rise up ahead—sparkling blue water, white sand dunes and rustling sea grass. Endless sunny days full of adventure in his little sloop, with its sun-bleached sails and wooden mast. Life had never been so good or so right. And he'd wanted it to last forever.

Chase chuckled softly and shook his head. To hear his family tell it, he still lived the summers of his boyhood. According to his father, he'd never grown up. But Charles Donnelly III knew nothing about his eldest son, Charles IV. All his father knew was profits and losses, strategies and maneuvers. He knew the family business more intimately than he knew his own family.

"Daydreaming again?"

Chase turned to find Nana Tonya standing in the doorway, her white hair slipping from the tidy knot at the back of her head and whipping around her gently lined face.

"It won't be long until I can sail over for a visit, Nana. I put the boat in the first of April."

She slowly approached, leaning heavily on her cane. "And what then? Will you keep on sailing like you did last summer? And the summer before?" Chase could still detect traces of her Romanian accent in the pleasant lilt of her voice.

Chase smiled. 'There's a good idea,'' he said.

''Your father wouldn't think so.''

He touched his grandmother on her shoulder. ''I'm sorry. This is your birthday party. We're supposed to be one big happy family. The last thing I wanted to do was get into it with Father.''

Nana reached out and ran her palm along his cheek. ''I expected nothing less,'' she said.

Chase arched an eyebrow. ''That famous second sight of yours hard at work again?'' Nana Tonya took great pride in her Gypsy ancestry and her ability to see the future. The rest of the family found it an embarrassment, especially when she talked about her visions so openly. But Chase found it charming.

''Your fights have become a family tradition,'' Nana said.

''Holidays, birthdays, anniversaries. I provide the entertainment.''

Nana shook her head wearily. ''You will never be able to make him happy until you settle down and take your rightful place in the family business.'' She paused and sighed. ''And he will never make you happy until he understands the man that you are. With you two, there is never room for compromise.''

''So what do you see for me, Nana?'' Chase teased. ''Tell me my future.''

''I don't have answers to your questions, Chase.''

''All right, how about stock tips? You've steered me right on more than one occasion. Made me lots of money. I'd even settle for a baseball score. Are the Sox going to win their season opener?"

Nana patted his cheek again, then turned to look out at the ocean. "You know that my visions are not like television. I cannot turn them on and off at will."

Chase draped his arm around her shoulders and stared out at the horizon with her. "How did you ever find a place in this family, Nana? You and your Gypsy blood marrying into all this stuffy Boston tradition."

"I fell in love with your grandfather and he fell in love with me. I remember when Charles told his family that he wanted to marry me. He was always the rebel, and they thought he'd chosen me because I was so unsuitable. You are a lot like my Charles," she said, a wistful smile touching her lips.

"But you made it work, Nana. You fit in."

"I did it because family was the most important thing in the world to me." She stared at the horizon for a long time, her expression still and serene. Then she suddenly shivered and turned to him, her brow furrowed. "Tonight you will dream of the woman you will marry."

Chase blinked in surprise. His sharp laugh died on the breeze. "Come on, Nana," he chided. "Don't tease."

Nana shrugged. "I have seen it. Just now."

"You're serious?"

"Believe what you will."

"I always take your visions seriously," Chase replied, "because you're always right. But I wanted a stock tip. I'm not looking for a wife."

She slipped her arm through Chase's. "A wife might do you some good, Chase Donnelly." She gave his arm a squeeze. "We must go inside now. Your mother has probably set fire to my birthday cake and I must make a wish and smile about growing another year older."

They walked back into the house, arm in arm. The cozy dining room grew silent when Chase appeared. The family was still gathered around the table, right where he'd left them fifteen minutes before. Chase's father, two younger brothers and their wives were all in their Sunday best—tailored suits and designer dresses. Always the rebel, Chase had arrived in wrinkled chinos and a faded polo shirt.

"There's the lady of the hour," Chase's father cried, jumping up from his spot at the far end of the table. He took his mother's hand and led her to her place at the head of the table, shooting Chase an annoyed glare as he pulled out her chair. "Maybe now we can act like grown-ups?"

Chase grabbed his napkin from his spot and sat down. "Oh, let's not. Nana deserves to observe our family in its natural state, don't you think?"

Chase's mother glided into the room with the birthday cake and sent him a warning look. "Nana, you shouldn't have gone outside without your wrap. You'll catch your death."

Nana Tonya leaned back in her chair. "After ninety years, I think I'm capable of taking care of myself, Olivia. Chase and I were having a nice talk."

"Was he pumping you for stock tips?" John asked. The middle boy in the trio of brothers was the most like their father—conservative, self-important and cynical. Patrick, the youngest, hadn't yet revealed his true colors. Though he showed a proclivity toward John's character traits, he still occasionally looked to Chase as a role model.

Nana bent closer to the cake and blew out half the candles, leaving the remainder of the task to Olivia. "I told Chase that tonight he would dream of the woman he'd marry."

All eyes at the table turned toward Chase, and he saw a tiny smile quirk the corners of Nana's mouth.

Patrick's jaw dropped. "Chase? Marry? I'd sooner put money on Donnelly Enterprises going bankrupt than on my big brother tying the knot."

Chase shrugged. "What's so hard to believe? You don't think I'd be able to settle down? I'd like to find a woman and get married. I'm no different from any other man." He cursed the defensive tone in his voice, loath to be baited into another argument.

"Sure," John replied. "You'd make a helluva husband, if you could only stay in one place for more than a week and confine yourself to one woman."

"When I meet the right woman, I'll know," Chase muttered. "I just haven't yet."

"I'll be surprised if you can find her in the crowd," John countered.

Olivia pointed at John with the cake knife, clearly aggravated with having to referee another battle within the Donnelly clan. "Boys, this is Nana's night. Can we please just change the subject?" Usually Chase's father stepped in, but he was quietly observing the interchange between his sons.

"You have absolutely no career aspirations," John continued, ignoring his mother. "You jump from one thing to another."

"I don't choose to work in the family business," Chase replied. "But that doesn't mean I don't work."

"You can't call that import business a career," Patrick commented, getting into the spirit of baiting the black sheep. "How much do you make in a year?"

"He's a cheese salesman," John said. "When he's not sailing around the world and chasing women. How much do you *think* he makes?"

"I have interests in a company that imports wine and gourmet foods, not just cheese," Chase said, trying to keep his voice even. "And do I have to remind you that Great-grandfather Donnelly delivered milk and cheese door-to-door on a handcart when he was a kid? Our family has a long-standing business relationship with cheese."

"Owning a small import business doesn't come close to running a division of Donnelly Enterprises. When was the last time you set foot in our offices?" John asked.

"I can't remember the last time I was invited," Chase countered.

Chase's father tossed his napkin on the table and stood, cursing softly. "Well, I'm inviting you now, dammit. You're a stockholder and board member. It's time you took some interest in the business. You'll report to John's office tomorrow morning."

"Is that an order?" Chase asked, his jaw tense with suppressed irritation.

Chase's father's expression turned cold. "Do what you want. But if you expect to maintain your seat on the board, then I'd suggest you spend a few days a week learning a little more about the family business." With that, he walked out of the room.

An uneasy silence grew at the table, Nana Tonya watching Chase with a curious gaze. As always, John and Patrick's wives pasted polite smiles on their faces, maintaining a safe distance from family squabbles. And Olivia, ever the peacemaker, cleared her throat before she began to slice the birthday cake.

"Why don't we have our cake and coffee in the solarium?" she suggested brightly.

As the family gradually rose from their places, Chase remained in his spot, as did Nana Tonya. A few moments later they were alone in the dining room. He braced his elbows on the table and studied his grandmother shrewdly over his steepled fingers. "Somehow I get the idea that you orchestrated this whole thing."

"Believe what you wish," she said, an enigmatic smile on her lips.

LATER THAT NIGHT, asleep in his old bedroom at Summerhill, surrounded by memories of his childhood, Chase Donnelly dreamed of a woman with hair the color of spun flax and eyes as blue as a Pacific lagoon. She stood on the bow of his sailboat, her flowing white dress fluttering in the breeze, her skin kissed golden by the sun.

She smiled and walked toward him, his name like a siren's song on her lips. And when she stood near enough to touch him, she reached up and slowly unbuttoned her dress. The sheer fabric fell off her shoulders and puddled around her feet before the salt breeze caught it and blew the dress overboard. She laughed, the sound sweet and musical, lifted by the wind.

And then she fell into his arms, all warm skin and soft curves, and he kissed her. He knew he could never let her go, this woman, this wanton. His wife.

"THIS IS A WEDDING we're talking about, not a corporate takeover!"

Natalie Hillyard didn't respond at first, but continued down the sidewalk, dodging and weaving through the lunch hour pedestrians in downtown Boston. Her sister, Lydia, tried to keep up with her pace, but by the time they'd reached the lobby of the Donnelly Building, she was hopelessly out of breath, her face pink with the cold.

Natalie finally stopped and gave her sister a chance to recover. "I don't see what you find so surprising. I have my entire wedding on a flow chart. I've timed every decision, every purchase and every event to the precise minute and dollar amount. And my flow chart says that you and I have to visit the florist after work at 5:37 p.m." She paused. "Is that purple streak in your hair going to be gone by next month?"

Lydia reached up and touched her bangs. By the way they dressed, no one would ever guess they were sisters. Natalie was dressed in a tailored suit and cashmere overcoat. Save for the purple streak, Lydia was adorned in black befitting her image as an art student.

"Well, maybe your flow chart should have told you to call me a few days ahead of time and let me know. I can't go, Natalie. I've got class."

Natalie set her briefcase on a marble bench in the atrium lobby. "I have all your classes on my scheduling software and you don't have a class tonight. You're my maid of honor, Lydie. The books say that you're supposed to help me with these things!"

"Nat, this is a wedding. The most important day

of your life. You shouldn't have to do everything by the book."

Frustrated, Natalie sat down on the bench, the tension of planning the wedding finally catching up with her. "I'm sorry. It's just that this day has to be perfect. You don't know Edward's family. His mother would have been happy to plan and pay for the entire wedding herself, but it's important for me to prove my competency. Once I'm married to Edward, I'm going to have to organize our social events. I don't want her thinking I'm a complete nitwit."

"And you want to marry into this family?" Lydia ran her hands through her shaggy blond hair—hair the exact color of Natalie's, except for the purple streak. "It's easy to be a blueblood if you've got a heart made of ice. That future mother-in-law of yours hasn't thawed in years."

"Lydie, don't say that. They're going to be my family now. For the first time in my life, I'm going to have the security of a real family."

A hurt expression crossed Lydia's face. "*I'm* your family. Since Mom and Dad died, we've had each other, and that's always been enough. Nat, we've been through a lot in the last twenty years and we've survived. What do you need that stick Edward for? He doesn't deserve you."

"He's waited for me, through grad school, and then until I had my career established. He's a good man, Lydie, and I owe it to Edward to plan the most perfect wedding there ever was."

Lydia gasped. "Do you hear yourself? You *owe* it to Edward to marry him? You're supposed to marry Edward because you're madly in love with him and can't live without him. So far, I haven't once heard you say you love him. And you two spend more time apart than together."

Natalie bristled, Lydia's insight ringing truer than she wanted to admit. "You're twisting my words, because you don't like Edward. I happen to care for him...very deeply."

"See that? You can't even say the word!"

"Love? There, I said it! I love Edward."

Lydia crossed her arms over her chest and studied Natalie shrewdly. "I don't believe you."

"Well, I don't care. Besides, love is highly overrated. Edward and I respect each other. We share the same goals, the same outlook on life. Our marriage will be built on trust and companionship, not on lust."

Lydia groaned. "Oh, God, Nat. This is worse than I imagined. Tell me that you at least have a good sex life."

"My sex life is none of your business," Natalie said stubbornly. "And what's wrong with how I feel? Our parents supposedly loved each other, but they fought like cats and dogs right up until the very end."

Lydia reached out and took Natalie's hand. "I

know that marrying Edward seems like a good idea, but I think you're marrying him for all the wrong reasons. Financial security and a houseful of interfering in-laws aren't good reasons."

Natalie glanced at her watch, then slipped out of her coat and draped it over her arm. She picked up her briefcase and smoothed her skirt. "I'm late. We're late. You were supposed to bring me back from lunch fifteen minutes early so that my staff could throw a bridal shower for me."

"That was supposed to be a surprise," Lydia said, frowning.

"I *hate* surprises. Besides, I've had it on my flow chart for a week. I'm going to be late for the festivities. I'll see you tonight? Five thirty-seven at City Florists?"

Lydia nodded and Natalie kissed her sister on the cheek, then headed for the elevator, her thoughts occupied with Lydia's questions and doubts. Maybe she wasn't madly in love with Edward, but they would base their marriage on something much less fickle than emotion. She had always been a practical person, someone who preferred fact to fantasy, good sense to sentiment. And she'd been lucky enough to find a man who shared her pragmatic outlook on life.

Most people might call Edward stuffy and maybe even a little boring. But in him, Natalie found all the stability and security she'd lost the day her parents had died. From that instant on, her life had been filled with endless upheaval as she and her little sister were shuffled from relative to foster home and back again. Edward would always provide a good home for her and that's all she really needed to be happy.

Glancing at her watch again, she pushed the button on the elevator, then tapped her foot impatiently. She really was behind schedule. Hopefully, the ladies in the office would present her with one large gift rather than lots of little gifts to be unwrapped, a waste of precious time. Why they'd insisted on throwing a wedding shower, she wasn't sure. They were her staff, not her friends. The work setting was no place to make friends.

The elevator finally arrived and Natalie swept inside. The doors were just about to close behind her when she heard a male voice call out, "Hold the elevator!" When an arm snaked between the doors setting off the sensor, she reached out and pushed the button to close them. She didn't have time to wait for stragglers. He could catch the next elevator.

The door began to shut, but the man stuck his hand in again. Back and forth they went, the doors closing and opening and closing and opening until the stranger finally cursed out loud and shoved his shoulder between them. Natalie snatched her hand from the control panel and moved back, pasting a polite smile on her face.

He stepped into the doorway, annoyance flooding his handsome features. But then he stopped short and stared at her, unblinking and unabashed. He opened his mouth to speak, but then snapped it shut, frowning. Still he watched her, and she couldn't help but look back. After all, he was incredibly handsome, with chiseled features like she'd only seen in fashion ads.

A bizarre current of attraction crackled between them and a shiver skittered up her spine, but still she couldn't look away. He had the most beautiful green eyes that she'd ever seen—clear and direct, without a trace of artifice. Throughout her childhood, to protect herself and her sister, she had been forced to evaluate strangers in such a way, to read the motives behind their eyes. There was nothing to fear from this man, of that she was certain.

Then why did she suddenly feel so breathless? Sure, he was handsome. Any woman would find him attractive. But it was the way that he looked at her, as if he were slowly undressing her with his eyes. Never in her life had a man looked at her like that—not even Edward. Nor did she expect him to, for Natalie knew she wasn't particularly pretty.

She forced herself to glance away, to fix her eyes on the control panel to her right. But she was drawn inexplicably back to him, sneaking another peek when the doors began to close. For an instant, she wondered if she should get out. But she was already seven minutes late, and Natalie hated to be late. She also hated people who ignored the unspoken rules of elevator etiquette. This handsome stranger didn't face the door and turn his attention to the lights above it. Instead, he continued to stare at her, almost as if he recognized her.

Natalie took a small step sideways, wondering if maybe they did know each other. But she would have remembered this man—those perfect features, the deep tan that hinted of a winter spent in southern climes. His dark hair, blown by the wind, was longer than proper business style dictated, brushing the collar of his leather jacket.

Her gaze slid over his long, lean body before she turned her eyes up to the lights above the door. Instead of a suit, he wore jeans and a khaki-colored shirt and—her gaze ground to a halt—a tie with a hand-painted hula dancer. She stifled a smile and looked down at her shoes.

''Do we know each other?'' His voice, rich and warm, echoed through the elevator car.

For a moment, she wondered if he was talking to her. But then she realized that he had to be—they were the only two people in the elevator. Her heart skipped, not out of fear, but out of some strange excitement. She turned to speak, then looked away.

All her common sense told her to ignore this man, but she couldn't. Except for the tie, he didn't seem like the type to test his favorite pickup lines on strange women in elevators. But why would he turn his attention on her? ''No,'' she finally murmured. ''I don't believe we do.''

''Funny. I could have sworn...''

She glanced over at him and found herself smiling. "I have a very good memory for names and faces. And I'm sure we've never met."

They continued the elevator ride in silence and had nearly reached her floor when the stranger leaned in front of her and flipped a switch on the control panel. The elevator bumped to a halt.

"This is going to sound strange," he said, "but I think I know where we've met."

She should have been frightened now, caught in an elevator that was going nowhere, a strange man her only companion. But she wasn't. For all the common sense that Natalie possessed, she knew this man didn't mean her any harm. In fact, she felt flattered by his attention. "I'm sure we haven't..."

He raked his fingers through his hair, then held out his hand. "All right. It was in my dream last night." He paused. "You. You were in my dream. We were on a sailboat and I was...well, that doesn't really matter."

Natalie smiled again. This was certainly the most original line she'd ever heard, though she would have expected something smoother, more sophisticated. But she did take some small pleasure in the fact that, for the very first time, a man was trying a line on her. "This is all very amusing, but I'm engaged."

Her statement seemed to take him by complete surprise and he frowned. "But you can't be," he said. "You're supposed to marry me."

Natalie's eyes went wide and suddenly her common sense returned in full force. This man was not just handsome. He was crazy, whacko, a certified lunatic. She quickly reached over and flipped the switch he'd touched. The elevator began to move again, but only until the stranger flipped the switch again.

Natalie's anger rose. Who was this guy? And what right did he have to hold her hostage in an elevator? "Listen, mister, I don't know what you want, but if you don't—"

"Wait! Just hear me out. I swear, I'm not crazy."

"I don't want to listen to you," she cried. "I'm late and I'm engaged. And nothing you say to me is going to make a difference."

He closed his eyes and shook his head. "You're right." He reached across her and started the elevator once again. "It's just that my grandmother had this vision. And she's never wrong. And then you were there, in my dream. And now you're here. And somewhere between the birthday cake and this elevator, I've completely lost my mind." He cursed softly, then gave her a sideways glance. "You wouldn't want to have dinner with me tonight, would you?"

Natalie couldn't help but laugh. The sound bubbling from her throat surprised her, for she rarely found much that genuinely amused her. But this handsome stranger had an uncanny way of undermining her customary self-restraint. "I told you, I'm engaged."

"And I'm Chase," he said, holding out his hand. "Short for Charles. It's nice to meet you. Maybe we could meet for coffee after work?"

Hesitantly, she clutched her hands together in front of her, certain that the moment she touched him her resolve would disappear and she'd fall victim to his considerable charms. "I—I don't care what your name is. And I don't drink coffee. I'm engaged."

"Tea, then? I know—you're engaged. But if you don't drink something, you're going to get dehydrated."

She shook her head, tempted to say yes, but determined that she would not allow herself to consider his offer. She looked up at the numbers above the door. Why was this elevator moving so slowly? And why was this man, this Chase, this *stranger* having such a disconcerting effect on her?

Natalie Hillyard did not speak to strangers! Not on the street, not in the subway and not on an elevator. Not even if the stranger was the most handsome man she'd ever met. She didn't accept impromptu invitations and she certainly didn't fall for tired old pickup lines.

"Water," he said. "We could go out and have a nice glass of water."

"No!" she replied. To her relief, the elevator doors finally opened on her floor. She hurried out, glancing over her shoulder to make sure he wasn't following her. But he just stood, his shoulder braced against the open door, and gave her a wave. "You'd like me," he said. "People say I'm a really nice guy."

"And I'm engaged!"

Chase laughed, the warm sound filling the hallway. She reached for the door to the reception area and pulled it open, determined to put as much distance between her and this sexy stranger as she could.

"We will meet again, sweetheart," he called as the door slowly swung closed behind her. "It's destiny."

Chapter Two

"IT'S ABOUT TIME you got here! You were supposed to come this morning."

Chase shoved his hands in his jacket pockets. He hadn't expected a warm welcome. "Nice to see you too, baby brother. Sorry I'm late. The elevator was...temporarily stuck."

"Our elevators are always in perfect working order," John said, his bluster an exact imitation of Chase's father. "I'm going to have to speak with maintenance about this."

Chase waved him off. "Leave it for later. It's not important."

"Never leave for tomorrow what can be done today," John replied.

"Wait, let me write that down," Chase said. "I want to embroider it on a pillow."

John sighed in exasperation. "I can see that this is going to be a waste of time. I don't know why you bothered to show up."

Chase clapped his brother on the shoulder. "Don't despair, Johnny. Now that I'm here, I'd love to take a tour of the office. You can introduce me to all the little people."

Actually, there was only one person Chase was

interested in meeting. Somewhere in the office he'd find his dream girl, the pretty blonde who had left him standing at the elevator door just moments ago.

When he had first stepped inside the elevator and caught sight of her face, he'd felt as if someone had punched him hard in the gut. His breath froze and his vision blurred, and for a moment, he had tried to convince himself that she didn't look familiar at all, that she was merely an attractive stranger.

But his dream the night before had been so vivid, leaving every detail of her face and her body imprinted on his mind. She was the one—the one his grandmother had told him about. She was no longer a dream, but a real flesh-and-blood woman. And if Nana's prediction was to be believed, she would someday be Chase's wife.

Though he'd learned to believe in Nana Tonya's visions, he still couldn't help but search for a logical explanation for the woman's appearance. Had he met her before? Did she merely resemble the woman in his dreams? Or was she, as his grandmother claimed, part of his destiny?

He didn't have answers for the jumble of questions that followed, but he knew he had to see her again. She'd been bound for the corporate offices of Donnelly Enterprises. If he was lucky, she was an employee with a desk and a nameplate. And if she wasn't, the receptionist would certainly remember her arrival—and her name.

"I suppose we could start with a tour of the offices,'' John grumbled. ''I could introduce you to our management team, although many of them will still be at lunch. If you've been reading our corporate newsletter, you know that we've consolidated several divisions under—''

''Can the commentary, brother. Just give me the tour. I'll ask any questions as they come up.''

The tour seemed to drag on for hours, although Chase knew it wasn't taking nearly as much time. He found corporate life exceedingly dull. Marketing, operations, data processing, personnel; endless offices and endless introductions...

As they entered the finance department, Chase was ready to give up and trust that the receptionist could provide him with more illuminating information. He turned to John, but then a group of women crowded into a small, glass-walled conference room caught his eye. He stopped short as one of the women held up a lacy black negligee.

''She's the one,'' Chase murmured, stopping to stare through the window.

''What?''

''Who is that?'' he asked. ''There. With the lacy underwear.''

John shook his head in disgust and clucked his tongue. ''I wouldn't have expected such unprofessional behavior from Natalie Hillyard. But I guess all women lose a little of their common sense before their wedding. She's getting married next month, but thank God, she's not taking a honeymoon. Ms. Hillyard is our director of finance. Runs the whole department. In a few more years she'll be in line for a vice presidency—that is, unless she decides to dump her career for kids and a house in the suburbs."

"She's beautiful."

John frowned as he stared through the window. "Beautiful? Natalie Hillyard?"

Chase nodded. Though most men would probably miss it, Natalie Hillyard had a simple perfection about her, an inner radiance that seemed to illuminate features that many men might find unremarkable—pale hair and high cheekbones, wide green eyes and delicate mouth. But Chase saw much more. A vulnerability that she managed to hide behind a dispassionate expression.

"Don't even think about it, Chase. She's engaged and she's a very competent, valued employee. M.B.A. from Boston College. Comes to work at seven every morning and doesn't leave until seven at night. Definitely not your type."

"Her name is Natalie Hillyard?"

"Donnellys do not pursue employees of the company. If you even approach her, I'm going to tell Father."

"You always were a tattletale, Johnny." Chase sighed. "Come on, you can introduce me."

Chase stepped through the door of the conference room, taking in the balloons and crepe paper decorations, the cake displayed on a long credenza. The festive chatter stopped the moment the ladies noticed his presence, but Chase's attention was firmly focused on Natalie Hillyard. He grinned, then nodded at the lacy confection she held in her hand. "Very nice," he said. "The latest in business attire, I presume."

The flush of color that had accompanied her perusal of the gift drained from her face and Natalie Hillyard blinked in surprise. "It's you," she murmured, white-knuckled fingers clutching the lacy lingerie.

John cleared his throat and stepped in front of Chase. "Ladies, I'd like to introduce my older brother, Charles Donnelly IV. Chase, these women work in our financial department."

Chase slowly circled the room, shaking hands with each one and enjoying a personal introduction. Low whispers followed him and he knew they were speculating about his sudden appearance. According to his father, Chase was the subject of endless gossip, though he rarely set foot in the office.

When he reached Natalie Hillyard, he again held out his hand. "Miss Hillyard. Best wishes on your upcoming wedding." He glanced down at the open boxes of lingerie, then fingered a pale green teddy. "The green suits you," he said, leaning closer so that only she could hear his words.

Color came back to her cheeks and her hand grew limp in his. "It—it's a pleasure to meet you, Mr. Donnelly."

"Chase," he said. "After all, we're old friends, aren't we?"

She murmured his name once before fumbling with the open boxes of lingerie. Chase watched her for a long moment, then turned back to John. "Nana tells me that I have an office here. Why don't you show me where it is? I can count my paper clips while you get back to work."

John sighed in exasperation, then turned and headed out the door. Chase took one last look at Natalie Hillyard, then smiled to himself. To hell with corporate policy. A guy didn't dream of the girl he was supposed to marry, then just walk away from her without another word.

"Ladies, it was my pleasure."

The group burst into a clamor of conversation the moment he stepped out of the room. He didn't even bother to speculate as to the subject. If Natalie Hillyard hadn't heard of his reputation by now, she certainly would by the end of the day. Chase winced inwardly. For once he wished that his reputation hadn't preceded him.

They reached an office three doors past John's and entered. The interior looked much like his brother's office without the requisite family photos and college rowing trophies. Chase circled his desk, then flopped down into his chair and propped his feet up on the smooth mahogany surface. He wove his fingers together behind his head. "Nice," he murmured. "Do I have a secretary?"

John, being devoid of a sense of humor, found nothing funny about Chase's question. He crossed his arms over his chest and sent his brother a warning glare. "Don't bother the employees and don't make any long distance calls on business phones. If you have any questions, I'm 8674 on the intercom."

Chase swiveled around in his chair. "Does the computer work?"

"You can access anything that's not confidential—even executive-level information. There's a list of commands in your top desk drawer. Use the last six digits of your social security number as your password."

Chase waited until his brother closed the door before he spun around in his chair and flipped on his computer. He grabbed the command list from the desk drawer and set to work. "Natalie Hillyard," he murmured. "Let's get to know each other a little better."

A few minutes later, he had a personnel profile, a résumé of sorts that gave her educational background and history with the company. Her address and home phone was easy enough to get from the company directory. He scribbled it on a piece of scrap paper and shoved it in his pocket.

But then he bumbled into something completely unexpected, better than her home phone number. The computer system at Donnelly Enterprises included a scheduling program for employees to keep track of their business appointments. Sweet Natalie also kept her personal schedule on the computer.

"City Florists," Chase read. "Five thirty-seven. Tonight." With a satisfied smile, he hit the print command and waited for the rest of Natalie's schedule to appear.

As he watched the paper slip from the printer, he wondered at his sudden obsession with this woman. It wasn't as if he was certain they were meant for each other. But he was curious. Would she turn out to be the same extraordinary woman he'd made love to in his dreams? Or would fantasy prove to be much more alluring than reality?

Chase had had his share of fantasy females—beautiful, sexy women who drifted in and out of his life as regularly as the tide. Not one of them had captured his attention as Natalie had. She was a mystery, a cool facade impenetrable at first contact. Yet there was so much more hidden beneath the surface. Why did the thought of exploring her depths fascinate him so?

Whenever he'd imagined himself married and raising a family, he'd always pictured a woman like Natalie by his side—tall and slender, fresh faced, confident and intelligent. A woman he could spend a lifetime getting to know, someone more complex than just a pretty face and a sexy body.

Chase leaned back in his chair and stared at the ceiling. What the hell was he doing? He'd shared no more than a few minutes with Natalie Hillyard and already he was picturing her as a permanent fixture in his life. Had he completely lost his mind?

She was engaged, a point she'd made patently clear more than once. Pursuing her would probably turn out to be a total waste of time. Still, there had to be something to Nana's vision. He'd dreamed of a woman and that woman had appeared before him the very next day, in the flesh. A man couldn't ignore such a singular event. Chase had always been one to test his own destiny and now was no exception. He needed to prove that Natalie Hillyard was not the woman of his dreams—or he'd have to marry her.

Chase flipped off his computer and grabbed the copy of Natalie's schedule. He methodically folded it in thirds, then shoved it in the back pocket of his jeans as he reviewed his options.

Natalie was an employee of Donnelly Enterprises and, according to John, took her job very seriously. No doubt she'd be reluctant to date a Donnelly, but since Chase didn't work for the company, that problem could probably be overcome. Beyond that, he'd simply need to deal with her insistence that she was happily engaged and about to be married.

What had John said? She'd be married next month? Chase snatched the schedule from his pocket and flipped through the pages. "April 4." He cursed softly to himself. That was only two weeks away. Two weeks to determine if Natalie Hillyard really was his destiny. And if she was, what then? Somehow he sensed that life would be a lot easier if he just forgot about his dream girl and walked away.

But Chase Donnelly had spent his life making every dream he had ever had come true. He wasn't about to toss this one aside.

A COLD SPRING RAIN dampened rush hour as Natalie approached City Florists at precisely 5:36 p.m., one minute before she'd told Lydia to arrive. Their appointment wasn't until quarter to six, but on average, Lydia arrived for most events approximately eight minutes late. It was always best to take her sister's tardy habits into account.

Natalie's first visit to the florist had been exactly three months prior to her wedding date, but she had insisted on approving a sample of the centerpieces to be certain the lilies fit in exactly with her color scheme. Mother Jennings would not tolerate tiny imperfections.

Given the choice, Natalie would have been happy with a small civil service. Without family of her own, the wedding was no more than a party for Edward, his parents and their numerous friends, relatives and business associates. But one did not become a Jennings without a very proper and very formal ceremony and reception.

Natalie pulled open the door, then wrestled her umbrella inside. As she turned, she caught sight of the only other customer in the shop. He stood with his back to her, speaking to the clerk behind the counter. There was something so familiar about him—the dark hair brushing his collar, the leather jacket, the blue jeans that hugged his—

She froze. What was *he* doing here? Cursing softly, she scurried behind a huge palm, peering through the fronds at the man who had bedeviled her thoughts for the entire afternoon. Chase Donnelly turned to look at a bucket of daffodils, and Natalie stared, transfixed by his handsome profile.

Time after time she'd caught herself thinking about their encounter in the elevator, about the odd attraction she'd felt toward him, the jolt of electricity that had tingled through her body when he'd taken her hand. She couldn't recall ever experiencing such an immediate and disturbing sensation. Even when she'd first met Edward there had been only a mild interest. But this man—Chase Donnelly—was different than any man she'd ever met.

"He's dangerous," she murmured to herself.

"Who's dangerous?"

Startled, Natalie turned to find Lydia standing at her shoulder and staring toward Chase. She grabbed Lydia by the arm and yanked her behind the potted palm. Lydia gave a little yelp and Natalie clapped her hand over his sister's mouth. "What are you doing here?" she whispered.

"You asked me to come," Lydia said, tugging at Natalie's fingers.

"You're early."

Lydia slapped at Natalie's hand. "What are you doing? And why are we whispering?"

"He's here," Natalie said in a miserable voice. She sneaked another peek through the fronds. "Over there. Looking at the daffodils."

"Who?"

"Chase Donnelly. I—I met him in the elevator. I mean, I didn't really meet him. We—"

"Donnelly as in Donnelly Enterprises?" A frown marred Lydia's forehead. "Why are you hiding from him?"

"I'm not hiding."

"Is he your boss?"

"Technically, he doesn't work for the company. But he's on the board of directors, so he could have me fired if he wanted to. And after the elevator, and then the wedding shower, well, I—"

"What elevator? Nat, you're babbling and you never babble."

"Do you think he followed me?" Natalie shook her head "No. He couldn't have. He was here when I got here. He didn't follow me. It's just...a coincidence." She paused and sighed. "Fate," she murmured. "Destiny," she added, recalling his words to her.

"Then why are you hiding in the bushes? He probably won't even recognize you."

"Oh, he'll remember me," Natalie said, glancing at Lydia. "He says I'm supposed to marry him. He dreamed it in a dream. Something about his grandmother and birthday cake. I didn't quite understand. It was all a little...overwhelming."

Lydia's eyes grew wide and she turned to stare at Natalie. "You're kidding. Your boss told you that you were going to marry him? Is he crazy?"

"Probably. And he's not my boss. He's just related to my boss," Natalie repeated. "Maybe that's why he never comes into the office. Maybe the family keeps him hidden away because he has...mental problems." She drew a long breath. "Could a guy that handsome really be a lunatic? He has the kindest eyes. And a little dimple in his chin and..." Lydia stepped out from behind the plants, but Natalie pulled her back. "Where are you going?"

"I'm going to check him out."

"If you talk to him, tell him to leave me alone. Tell him I'm engaged."

Natalie watched as her sister casually strolled over to the counter. Lydia had always been much more assertive than Natalie, more willing to take chances. And she'd always been more comfortable around strangers—especially men.

At first, Lydia stood at a safe distance, studying Chase surreptitiously while she spun a rack of greeting cards. But then, to Natalie's consternation, her sister struck up a conversation with him. Before long, they were chatting amiably. A thread of what felt like jealousy snaked through her and she turned away, scolding herself silently.

What was wrong with her? All these strange feelings welling up inside of her did nothing but frighten and confuse her. She was never one to act on impulse, to behave irrationally. But this man brought out the worst in her character, flaws she'd never known about.

"Natalie?"

She spun back around. To her mortification, Lydia was crossing the shop with Chase in tow. Frantically, Natalie glanced toward the door, calculating the odds on making a clean getaway. But she couldn't run. She needed to put an end to this ridiculous situation as soon as possible.

"Natalie, look who I just met!" Lydia cried. "It's Chase Donnelly. Chase, you know my sister, Natalie Hillyard."

With a smile quirking the corners of his mouth, he held out his hand, daring her once again to place her fingers in his. She found herself transfixed by his handsome face, her gaze skimming over the strong planes and angles, lingering on his vivid green eyes and the cleft in his chin. Her mind swam, a whirlpool of confusion and attraction and frustration. Their gazes locked.

"It's nice to see you again, Natalie," he said, a teasing tone in his voice.

His fingers were warm and strong, and a familiar tingle seeped up her arm, numbing her nerves like a potent drug. She felt a slow blush creep up her cheeks as she struggled to find her voice. When she tried to draw her hand away, he held tight to her fingers. "What—what are you doing here...Mr. Donnelly?"

"I just stopped in to order some flowers," he replied. "For my grandmother."

"Did you hear that, Natalie?" Lydia said, her voice sounding a million miles away. "He's buying flowers for his grandmother. Isn't that nice?" She lowered her voice and bent near. "Not the actions of a crazy man, I think."

"Yes," Natalie breathed. "Very nice."

Chase slowly rubbed his thumb along the back of her hand and Natalie lost herself in the enjoyment of the simple caress. "I'm really glad we had another chance to meet. It gives me an opportunity to apologize for my behavior this morning in the elevator. I'm sure I must have sounded like a real kook."

"Yes," Natalie replied, staring down at her hand. "I—I mean, no. Not at all."

"Would it be too forward to ask if you'd care to join me for coffee after you're finished here?" he asked. "I'd like to make it up to you."

"Yes," she murmured, willing to say anything to stop the barrage of sensations that raced through her body. "I mean, it wouldn't be too forward to ask."

"Good. I'll meet you then. At Jitterbug's. It's right down the block. In a half hour?"

"Jitterbug's," Natalie replied absently. "Yes, it's right down the block."

With that, he let go of her hand and started toward

the door. He turned back once and smiled at her, then walked out of the shop. She wasn't sure how long she stood there, staring at the door and rubbing the back of her hand. Had it not been for Lydia, she probably would have stood there all night.

"Oh my," Lydia said with a sigh. "Did you just accept a date with him?"

Natalie blinked. "No, of course not," she replied, her mind frantically racing through their conversation. "I didn't, did I? I told him it wasn't forward of him to ask. But I didn't accept."

"I think you did."

Natalie grabbed her sister's elbow and clutched it tightly. "I can't meet him for coffee. I'm engaged."

"Don't yell at me! You're the one who accepted the invitation."

"Why didn't you stop me?" Natalie demanded. She pulled Lydia toward the counter at the back of the store. "Have you forgotten why we're here? We're here to discuss the flowers for my wedding."

"What wedding? I think you should forget Edward. I like this guy much better."

"Forget Edward? How can I forget my fiancé?"

"Where is he, anyway?" Lydia asked. "Shouldn't he be here, helping you with the wedding? He's never around when he's supposed to be."

"Edward is in London on business, where he will be for the next week."

"Good. Then you can meet Chase for coffee after we're finished here and no one will be the wiser."

"Lydia, why are you doing this? If rumor is to be believed, Chase Donnelly is a certified Casanova."

"Because I think you deserve better than Edward Jennings and that pack of vultures he calls a family." She sighed longingly. "And this guy is *definitely* better, don't you think?"

Natalie glanced back at the door, then cursed this sudden impulsiveness that had come over her. What was she doing? Her whole life had been planned out, beginning with a fairy-tale wedding to a man she'd known for years. And now, out of the blue, she had accepted a date with a complete stranger—and a reputed playboy to boot.

"Prewedding nerves," she murmured. "All brides go through their moments of doubt, don't they?"

"Sure," Lydia said, "although most of them just have a good cry and then feel better. But a date for coffee with a handsome man—that's another approach."

The truth was, Natalie wanted to go. She wanted to find out why Chase Donnelly had such a hold on her, why her attraction to him seemed to overwhelm every bit of her common sense and decency. And she wanted, once and for all, to put an end to all the silly feelings he stirred up inside of her.

She moaned and pressed her fingers into her temples. "I won't go. I can't go. After all, I'm engaged."

HE WAS SITTING at a table by the window when she arrived. His hair was damp from the rain and he had slicked it back from his face with his fingers. His profile was even more handsome, his tan skin gleaming in the bright lights of the café.

Drawing on her resolve, Natalie strode over to his table. She held her breath as he looked up at her, but she deliberately avoided his eyes. "This is a mistake," she said, her voice firm and even. "I didn't mean to accept your invitation. I misunderstood."

He leaned back in his chair and crossed his arms over his chest, sending her a dubious look. "But you're here now," he noted. "If you didn't want to come, why didn't you just stand me up?"

Natalie shifted, asking herself the same question and unable to come up with an answer. "I—I..." She swallowed hard. "That wouldn't be polite. After all, I do technically work for you. It's best to cultivate a proper professional relationship, don't you think?"

He considered her reply for a long moment, the silence growing between them until she was forced to look into his eyes. "Come on, Natalie," he said with a charming grin. "Admit it. You're as curious as I am."

She tipped her chin up. "About what?"

"About this thing that's going on between us."

Natalie stiffened and tried to maintain her composure. "There's nothing between us. You're a complete stranger to me. I don't even know you. How can there be anything between us?"

"We're attracted to each other," Chase said, so bluntly that he made it sound like fact. "I felt it the minute I walked into the elevator. You're just too stubborn to admit it."

Natalie closed her eyes and shook her head. "No...no, I'm not."

He picked up his coffee cup and took a sip. "You're not stubborn or you're not attracted to me?"

"Attracted," she said.

"Then I'll ask you again. Why are you here?"

Natalie had had enough of this cat and mouse game he insisted on playing. "All right!" she said, her jaw tight with annoyance. "Maybe I am attracted to you. But that doesn't mean I'm going to act on my feelings. I want you to forget about our encounter in the elevator. And I'm going to forget about accepting your invitation for coffee. We'll just pretend like none of this ever happened."

Chase shook his head. "I can't do that, Natalie. I won't. Not until I know for sure."

"I have to leave," Natalie said, confused by his cryptic words.

As she turned, Chase shoved his chair back and grabbed her hand. She tried to pull away, but he held tight. Gently, he twisted her around until she faced him. He hooked his finger under her chin and forced her to meet his eyes.

For a moment, she was certain he was going to kiss her. Her gaze slipped down to his mouth, to sculpted lips that were parted slightly. If this simple touch had such a profound effect on her, how would she ever be able to resist his mouth and his tongue, the feel of his hands on her body?

"I don't want you to kiss me," she murmured.

A smile touched the corners of his mouth. "I wasn't planning to. Not yet."

Natalie glanced up to see humor sparkling in his eyes, and she felt a warm flush of embarrassment heat her cheeks.

"Just stay, for a little while," he said. He pulled out her chair. "Sit. We can talk."

Worn down by the power of his charming smile, she reluctantly did as he asked. He motioned a waitress over to their table and Natalie placed an order for a café *latte.* She wrapped her arms around herself and waited for him to speak.

"Why don't you take off your coat?"

"I'm not planning to stay long."

The waitress reappeared with Natalie's coffee, thankfully providing a distraction from the silence that had settled at their table. The hot brew burned her throat as she hurried to drink it. The sooner she finished, the sooner she could leave.

"When I stepped inside that elevator, you took me by surprise."

Natalie looked over at him, only to find Chase studying her intently.

"It was like we'd already met. Do you believe in fate, Natalie?"

She would have liked to believe in fate. It would have explained her parents' death and all the things in her childhood that had followed. But Natalie could only believe in cold, hard facts. The skid marks from her parents' car. The truck driver who had fallen asleep behind the wheel. The police knocking at the front door late at night. And the awful feeling of desertion she and Lydia had had. She'd been thirteen when it had happened, all alone in the world except for her six-year-old sister.

Natalie shook her head, brushing aside the bitter memories. "No, I don't. Everything happens for a reason and you just have to look closely to find a logical explanation."

"And our meeting?"

"I was returning from lunch—I was late. And you were...what were you doing in the office?"

"An attempt at family harmony," he said.

"So it wasn't fate. We were both supposed to be right where we were."

"And now we're here. Having coffee together. So, Natalie, why don't you tell me about yourself?"

"I'm engaged," she repeated, for what seemed like the millionth time.

"And what would your fiancé have to say if he knew you were having coffee with me?"

Natalie opened her mouth to reply, then snapped it shut. To be honest, Edward probably wouldn't say a word. He wasn't prone to jealousy, not that she'd ever given him a reason to be jealous. Edward never displayed an excessive level of emotion. He was a very...controlled man. "We trust each other completely," she finally answered.

Chase chuckled. "If you were my fiancée, I wouldn't be so magnanimous."

Natalie had always wondered what it would be like to have a man feel so passionately about her, to care for her so much that he'd be jealous. But then, Chase's remark shouldn't surprise her. He seemed to be driven purely by impulse, by emotions that she couldn't even begin to fathom.

"But you aren't my fiancé," Natalie said. "You aren't even my friend. I've heard all about you, Chase Donnelly, and don't think I can't see right through your charm."

"Then tell me the truth, Natalie. Are you really happy with this fiancé of yours?"

Her head snapped up and she met his gaze. "Edward is everything I've ever wanted in a husband," she said, trying to keep her voice sure and even. "And nothing anyone says is going to stop me from marrying him."

Chase stared at her for a long moment, then pushed back from the table and stood. "All right.

Fine." He reached into his pocket and withdrew his wallet, then tossed a few bills on the table. "Hell, I thought I'd give it a shot. A guy can't ignore destiny, can he?"

Natalie shook her head. "No, I guess not."

Chase smiled ruefully, then bent down and brushed a kiss on her cheek. "It's been wonderful not falling in love with you, Natalie Hillyard. Take care of yourself."

With that, he turned and walked out the door into the drizzling night. She watched him through the window, craning her neck as the other pedestrians gradually hid him from view.

She took a deep breath and slowly arranged the items on the table—first her coffee cup and saucer, then her napkin and spoon—putting everything in perfect order. When she'd finished, she placed her palms on the table and gathered her thoughts.

"I've just had a very bad day," she murmured to herself. "Tomorrow, everything will be back to normal. My life will be right on track."

She sat in the coffee shop for a long time, staring out the window and trying to convince herself of the truth of her words. But somehow, she knew that nothing would ever be the same again. She knew that she would always wonder where this day might have led, had she been willing to throw caution to the wind and take a chance.

Chapter Three

THE DELIVERIES BEGAN arriving the next morning, just as Natalie was finally getting to sleep. She had passed a restless night, tossing and turning, plagued by fitful dreams—of a dark-haired man with a roguish smile juxtaposed with her wedding, a day filled with mistakes and mishaps and a driving rainstorm.

Exhausted, she had rolled out of bed in the middle of the night and sat down with all her wedding files, alphabetizing her response cards, adjusting her budget and pouring over the seating charts that her future mother-in-law had provided. But the more she thought about her impending nuptials, the more restless Natalie grew.

She had tried in vain to call Edward in London, hoping that a quick conversation with him would put all to rights. But after numerous attempts to reach him, she had finally dozed off on the sofa, the shopping channel blaring away on cable. Not long after the sun had risen, she was awakened by the doorbell.

Dragging herself to the door, Natalie pulled her robe around her and brushed her hair out of her eyes. She expected the paperboy or someone collecting for charity, but instead she found a huge bouquet of yellow daffodils awaiting her.

Natalie didn't need to look at the card to guess who they were from. Edward had never in his life sent her flowers, and she was certain he had no reason to start now. The daffodils could be from only one person—Chase Donnelly.

Perturbed, she gathered the bouquet in her arms and wandered back to the kitchen to find a vase. Fifteen minutes later, the next delivery arrived, followed by another every quarter hour. But there were no more flowers. Just a strange assortment of items—fresh baked baguettes and cheese, a tin of oysters, three different bottles of wine, a box of expensive Belgian chocolates, a basket of fresh fruit.

With every delivery, Natalie scanned the street, checking to make sure her nosy neighbors in Redmond were tucked safely inside their houses. Living in the same small town as Edward's parents caused Natalie no end of stress. But Edward had insisted on buying the huge house on Birch Street, determined to fashion a life in the exact image of his very proper parents.

Of course, it would have been highly *im*proper for Edward to share a residence with Natalie before they married, so he had left her alone there in the huge, cavernous house, empty of furniture and badly in need of refurbishing. Once they were married, they would work on the house together, he promised. And though Natalie would have been quite happy with a tiny little cottage in the country, life with Edward meant living in a hundred-year-old mansion that seemed perpetually empty.

By eleven, Natalie's foyer looked like an explosion in a delicatessen. For some strange reason, Chase was under the impression that the way to a woman's heart was through her stomach, and he intended to see her very well fed. Had she known his phone number, she would have called to demand that he cease and desist.

When the doorbell rang again, Natalie had just stepped out of the shower. Cursing Chase Donnelly and his gifts, she hurried to the door and flung it open, ready to give the delivery man an earful. But it was Chase, leaning against the doorjamb, a devilish grin on his lips. "Good morning," he said. "You look pretty with your hair all wet." He bent closer and stole a quick kiss, the same way he'd done the night before. So casually, as if he'd kissed her a hundred times in the past.

Clutching her robe at her throat, Natalie scanned the street, then dragged him inside, slamming the door behind him. "What are you doing here? How did you find me?"

He glanced around the huge foyer, his gaze taking in all the gifts scattered about the floor. "Is that any way to greet a friend?"

"You're not my friend," Natalie said, stamping her bare foot on the cold marble floor.

"Then is that any way to greet an acquaintance you barely tolerate?"

"How did you find me?"

Chase shrugged. "I could say I hired a private detective. Or that I followed you home last night. But to tell the truth, I hacked into the employee files at the office." She watched as he wandered toward the wide central staircase, peering into each room along the way. "You actually live here? This place is huge."

"Edward and I bought it a month after we set our wedding date. You have to leave. If anyone saw you come in I'll—"

"So, does he live here, too? I'd really like to meet him. Is he home?"

Natalie shook her head. "He's out of town on business. He'll move in after the wedding. Right now, he lives with his parents."

"Too bad," Chase murmured. "It always pays to know the competition." He slowly turned and raised his eyebrow. "You know, it would take an army to keep me out of my bride's bed before the wedding. He must be a very disciplined man."

Natalie sighed in frustration, certain that Chase's comment was meant more as an insult than a compliment. "Why are you here? I thought I made it clear last night that I didn't want anything to do with you."

"You did. But I didn't believe you. Let's just say you were less than convincing. Especially when we were holding hands in the flower shop. Remember that?"

"Vaguely."

"You wanted me to kiss you. I could see it in your eyes."

"I—I wanted nothing of the sort."

He stepped closer until they were nearly touching. She could feel the heat of his body, the soft caress of his warm breath at her temple. Natalie wanted to step away, but she couldn't bring herself to move. All her resolve slowly melted beneath his intense gaze.

She wasn't prepared for what happened next, yet it seemed the most natural thing in the world. He kissed her, long and deep, his mouth consuming hers in a flood of pure desire. Natalie's knees went weak and he grabbed her around the waist and pulled her up against his lean, hard body. Her mind spun in confusion, but no matter how hard she tried, she couldn't summon the power to push him away.

Passion like she'd never experienced before raced through her blood, setting her nerves on fire, testing all her notions of self-control. Her every thought now centered on his mouth, on the taste of his tongue, the play of his lips across hers. She felt instantly alive and aware. She felt wanted and needed, beyond all common sense and propriety.

Natalie had kissed only one man in her entire life with any degree of passion, and that had been Edward. But nothing she had ever experienced with

Edward came close to the power of Chase's mouth on hers. Like an addictive drug, his kiss numbed her brain until she could do nothing more than succumb to the wonderful surge of pure sensation.

But then a brief instant of clarity returned as she realized the magnitude of her actions. With a tiny cry, she pulled out of his arms and brought her fingers to her swollen lips. "I—I've cheated," she said, misery flooding her voice. "I'm engaged and I've just cheated on my fiancé."

Chase stared down at her for a long moment, the passion that glazed his eyes slowly clearing. Then he bit back a curse. "I—I'm sorry, Natalie. I shouldn't have done that. It wasn't fair."

"No, no. It's my fault," Natalie said, turning to pace the length of the foyer. "I wanted you to kiss me." She stopped and pressed her fingers against her temples. "I don't know what's happening to me. I'm supposed to be engaged and I'm kissing a perfect stranger."

Chase grabbed her by the arms and forced her gaze up to his. "If you really felt something, Natalie, and you ignore it, the only person you're cheating is yourself."

"I have no choice. What just happened was a mistake. An error in judgment. We'll just...put it behind us. Like it never happened."

"But it did happen. And I'm glad it did."

Natalie pulled away from him and shook her

head. "Thank you for all the lovely gifts, but I think you'd better leave now."

Chase reached out and cupped her cheek in his palm. "Do you really want to marry this guy?"

She stiffened beneath his touch. "I made a promise to Edward and I intend to keep it."

Chase turned to the door, angry. "He doesn't deserve you," he muttered beneath his breath.

"And you do?" she demanded, her voice trembling. "Tell me, are you prepared to marry me? To give me a home and a future?"

"We barely know each other," he replied, his back still to her.

She stepped up beside him and grabbed his arm, forcing him to face her. "That's precisely right. We've known each other for less than twenty-four hours. And you want to destroy a relationship that's been part of my life for years. I'm not going to let you do that."

"Prove to me that you love him," Chase challenged. "Spend the day with me. I promise I won't try to kiss you again. I won't even touch you. But I can't let this go, Natalie."

"What right do you have to intrude on my life? Why are you doing this to me?"

"I don't know," Chase murmured, raking his fingers through his hair. "I wish I did. Maybe if we spend some time together, I'll be able to figure it out."

"No," she said, her chin set stubbornly.

"One day," Chase countered. "And then I'll walk away. I promise."

She closed her eyes and drew in a long breath. She wanted to refuse him, to push him out the door and make him go away. But a tiny voice inside her urged her to ignore common sense and appease her own curiosity. If she didn't, she'd be left to wonder about this man for the rest of her life. She couldn't allow this impetuous kiss to poison her happy future with Edward. "One day," Natalie finally agreed. "I'll spend one day with you and then you'll leave me in peace."

Reluctantly, Chase nodded.

"And no more kissing?"

Chase grinned. "I promise. For now, we're just friends."

SPRING HAD COME EARLY to the Northeast, the last weeks of March more lamb than lion. The snow and ice had given way to warm sun and cool rain, days that held all the promise of the summer to come. Traces of green sprang up in the most unlikely places, and Chase once again felt the lure of the sea, the same instinct that had tugged at his soul since childhood.

They had gathered up all the food in Natalie's foyer before they left and dropped it in the trunk of Chase's battered Porsche Speedster. Then, on a whim, he'd put the top down. Natalie had reluctantly climbed in, fearful of the cold but even more fearful of her prying neighbors. She'd spent the first part of their ride slouched down in the front seat, her hood pulled up to hide her face.

But now, as they raced along the old roads that connected tiny villages southeast of Boston, she pushed her hood back and turned her face up to the sun. Chase couldn't help but appreciate the sheer beauty of her blond hair whipping around her face, her eyes bright and her cheeks pink with cold. This day was more perfect than any in his memory and he wanted it to last forever.

Never mind the fact that he didn't know what the hell he was doing, speeding toward the sea with a woman who had promised herself to another man. All he knew was that it felt so right to be with her and he'd do anything in his power to make sure they'd be together again.

"You're beautiful," he called, taking his eyes off the road to get a long look at her. He wanted to reach over and touch her, to weave his fingers through the hair at her nape. But after the kiss they'd shared, he knew better than to push her. She was engaged and trying desperately to hold on to what she believed was her happiness. If he was patient, she would soon see that Edward was not the man for her.

"You shouldn't say things like that!" Natalie scolded.

"Why? It's the truth."

A blush crept up her cheeks and she gave him a

hesitant smile, then shook her head. She seemed so uneasy with the compliment that he wondered if Edward had ever taken the time to flatter her.

"Where are we going?" she called above the wind.

"Someplace special."

She accepted his explanation without question, then continued to watch as the landscape turned from wide fields and forests to the flat sandy land that edged the Atlantic. Sand Harbor lay nestled on the western shore of Cape Cod Bay, a tiny seaside village off the same highway that wound its way to the very end of the peninsula.

Chase had chosen to live in Sand Harbor more for the snug marina than for its proximity to Boston. He'd purchased a small cottage near the water, and when he wasn't off on one of his sailing adventures, he settled into a quiet life, doing most of his business from home.

But he wasn't anxious to show Natalie the little house on Cape Street. Instead, he turned the car toward the waterfront and the tangle of ramshackle piers and crumbling quays. He stopped the Speedster in front of a chain-link fence, then hopped out and circled the car to open Natalie's door. He held out his hand to help her out, but she deliberately avoided his touch.

"This is someplace special?" she asked.

"Be patient." Chase popped open the trunk and grabbed the bags of food, then slammed it shut with his elbow. He walked to the gate, Natalie at his heels, then fumbled with a rusty old padlock. The gate creaked open and she followed him inside.

"What is this place?"

"It's a boatyard," Chase said. "And right there is my boat. The *Summer Day.*"

Natalie stared straight ahead at the thirty-five-foot sloop, its hull held aloft in a wooden cradle.

"I thought we'd have our picnic here. If the weather were warmer, I'd sail you to some secluded beach, but for now, this will have to do. I've still got to paint the hull before I put her in for the season."

"I—I've never been on a boat before. I've always been afraid I'd get sick."

Chase laughed. "Well, there's no chance of that here." He placed the sacks of food on the ground, then grabbed a ladder, tipped it up and rested it on the gunwale. "You go on up and I'll hand you the food."

When he'd settled Natalie and their picnic supplies in the cockpit, Chase climbed down into the cabin and retrieved a pair of wineglasses and a corkscrew. When he returned, Natalie had crawled up to the bow and was standing there, the wind in her hair, staring out toward the harbor.

He watched her for a long time, recalling the dream that had sent her to him. Except for the jacket and the jeans, she looked exactly like he remembered. She looked like she belonged here with him.... The truth of Nana Tonya's prediction became more real with every second he spent with Natalie.

"You're the first woman I've ever had on my boat," he called. "Except for my grandmother."

Natalie turned and smiled at him, brushing hair out of her eyes. "I find that hard to believe," she teased. "According to office gossip, you're the type who always has a woman on your arm."

"But never on my boat," he said. "When I sail, I want to be alone."

She started back toward the cockpit, grabbing the shrouds for balance. "Then why did you bring me here?"

"Because you belong here. You've been here before."

She gave him a skeptical look but let it pass. "It sounds like your boat means a lot to you."

Natalie sat down and he poured her a glass of wine. "Most guys save up for a car," Chase said, "but not me. When I was a kid, I put my pennies away for a boat. I bought this one when I was sixteen. It was a mess, barely able to float. I worked on her for six years, every day of my summer vacation. The summer I graduated from college, I sailed her down the East Coast to the Carolinas. I promised to come back and take a job with the company, but I just kept sailing. For three years."

"How did you live?"

"Odd jobs, here and there."

"So you just ran away from life, from your responsibilities?"

"I embraced life and all its possibilities," Chase said.

Natalie looked out over the boatyard and sighed. "When I was younger, after my parents died, I used to dream about running away, about leaving all my problems behind and starting a brand-new life as a different person."

"What's stopping you now?"

"I've grown up," she said. "I have commitments—a career, a relationship, a new family. Stability and security. That's what I want. And that's what I'll have."

"And these things will make you happy?"

"I think so. I'm not sure. I've never had them before."

Chase leaned back and swirled the wine around in his glass, watching the sunlight glint through it. "I think you're selling life short, Natalie. You strike me as a woman who would enjoy a little adventure. A little danger."

"You're seeing only what you want to see," she murmured. "You don't know me at all."

Chase looked at her long and hard, trying to find the truth in her words. But even if she'd managed to fool herself, she couldn't fool him. Natalie Hillyard was not as she appeared. Chase sensed that there was a very different woman hiding behind her composed facade. An endlessly fascinating woman he was determined to discover.

THE DAY PASSED SO QUICKLY that Natalie was surprised to see the sun slipping below the horizon. A light lunch and a half bottle of wine had given her a warm, contented feeling she was reluctant to abandon. But she had given Chase his one day and that day was fast fading.

She had expected to feel relief, satisfaction that he'd finally be out of her life for good. But all she could muster was a sense of regret, a twinge of doubt and the fear that she might never feel so at ease again. Chase was fun; he laughed and teased and made her feel special. He told her silly stories and took pleasure in her reactions. So many times during the afternoon she'd looked up to find him watching her, his eyes slowly taking in every detail of her face, as if he were trying to commit it to memory.

But she didn't want the time they spent together to be just a memory. She wanted to hang on to it, like a lifeline; to have something to savor, if happiness somehow eluded her.

How could she have doubts? She'd made her choice and her choice was Edward. Yet a man she'd known for barely two days had thrown her life into chaos. Did she love Edward? Or was she merely settling for what she believed she wanted, as Chase predicted.

Chase Donnelly wasn't at all what she had expected. Office gossip had painted a rather overblown picture of a degenerate playboy bent on seduction. He seemed to take great amusement in that perception, constantly baiting her until she wasn't sure whether he was testing her or teasing her. But in the end, he'd let down his guard and shown himself to be a sweet and considerate man.

But what was it that *he* wanted? Was his passion for her so strong that he was willing to ignore her engagement? She'd never thought herself capable of eliciting such feelings from a man. But then, she'd never met a man like Chase before.

"Are you ready to go?"

She glanced up and smiled. His hair, blown by the wind, fell around his face and he brushed it back, then held out his hand. "For your first time on a sailboat, I'd say you did very well. Next time, we'll have to try it with the boat in the water."

There won't be a next time, she wanted to say. But she couldn't put her thought into words. She wanted to believe that she'd be happy; she wanted to know that there would be more beautiful spring days just like this. But she feared that Edward might never be able to give them to her.

"I should get back," she murmured, shoving her hands in her jacket pockets. "It's getting late."

Chase helped her down the ladder, taking care to touch her only when necessary. But she couldn't ignore the feel of his hand splayed across the small of her back as she made her way down, his warm fingers burning through her clothing to imprint on her skin.

They drove back the way they'd come, but this time Chase put the top up. Without the sound of the wind to distract her, the ride was filled with an uneasy silence. Natalie crossed her arms over her chest and sank down in the seat, a cold shiver pulsing through her body. With every mile that passed, a slow dread sank more deeply into her consciousness.

She was making the right decision. How could she possibly walk out on a marriage to a stable, reliable man for some sailor whose grandmother had had a vision? She would have to be crazy. Besides, what did she really know about Chase, beyond the stories that he'd told her about his childhood and the rumors that circulated at the office?

The two of them were polar opposites. He preferred to live his life without a plan, taking off for parts unknown at the slightest whim. She preferred a comfortable routine. He believed in destiny, in a silly dream that his grandmother had foretold. And she believed in practicality. No two people could be further apart in temperament and ideology than Natalie Hillyard and Chase Donnelly.

"I had a nice time today," she said, glancing over at him.

He smiled, but kept his eyes on the road, the passing cars bathing his features in white light and shadow. "So did I. I'm glad we got a chance to know each other a little better."

"And lunch. The food was wonderful."

"Only The Best. That's the name of my business. We import gourmet foods, a lot of French wines, cheeses. The perfect business for someone who enjoys eating."

"Edward is a banker," Natalie said, regretting her statement the moment it came out of her mouth.

She could see Chase's jaw tighten in the dim light from the dashboard. "Sounds boring."

She smiled, then shrugged her shoulders. "Yeah, I guess it is. He likes money, so it's a perfect job for him. And his father is a banker. Family tradition. The whole family loves money."

"And do you love him?" Chase asked. "Or the money?"

She heard the challenge in his voice, but decided to ignore it. "I've never really had much money until recently." Natalie bit her lower lip. "As for Edward, we're right for each other."

"You're sure of that?"

"I don't want this day to end with an argument," she said softly.

They passed the rest of the ride in silence, Natalie's mind whirling with confusion and doubt. She was almost relieved when Chase pulled up in front of the house on Birch Street. She would have preferred to get out of the car alone, but he hopped out and opened her door for her. He walked her to the front steps, stopping to stand in the shadows of the porch as she fumbled in her pocket for her keys.

When she finally found them, she looked up at Chase and forced a smile. "So, I guess this is goodbye." Natalie tried to make out his expression, but his features were hidden by the darkness. "Thank you—for today. And I—I hope you find the woman you're looking for."

His voice was soft, drifting out of the darkness. "I already have."

She wanted to turn and run inside, but she couldn't just leave him like that. "I—I can't be that woman, Chase. I'm sorry. I hope you understand."

He reached up to touch her and she stepped back. But slowly he brought his hand closer to her cheek, so close she could feel the warmth radiating from his skin. Still he didn't touch her.

"I would kiss you if I could," Chase murmured.

"But you can't."

He brought his other hand up, but again he didn't touch her. "I would hold your beautiful face in my hands, like this. And I'd bring my mouth down on yours. And you would taste so sweet and warm."

Natalie shivered and instinctively turned her face into his hand, but he drew it away before their skin made contact.

Then, he bent slowly, until his mouth hovered over hers, until she could feel his breath on her lips. "And as I kissed you, I'd pull your body against mine. You'd fit perfectly, every soft curve made just for me."

"Chase, please." Her words came out in a strangled plea, but she didn't want him to stop.

"And after I had learned every inch of your body by heart, I'd make love to you. We would be so good together, Natalie. So perfect for each other."

She reached up to place her fingers over his lips, to stop him from driving her mad with such talk. But he turned his head away. She could see his profile in the dim light from the streetlamps. His expression was cool and distant, filled with icy control.

She let her hand drop to her side, then closed her eyes. "I wish I could be more like you. More impulsive, more impetuous. If I was, I would kiss you right now. And we would walk up to my bedroom and we would make love to each other. But that's not who I am, Chase."

"How do you know? How will you ever know if you allow yourself to settle for this life you've constructed?"

"You don't understand. There are plans and invitations and gifts. It's too late."

"It's never too late," Chase said. "You've got the rest of your life ahead of you, Natalie. Are you willing to spend it with a man you don't love?"

Tears of frustration pushed at the corners of Natalie's eyes and she fought them with all her might. She wanted to shout at Chase, to slap his face and to scream that she *did* love Edward. But she'd known the truth for far too long and had simply chosen to ignore it, to believe that she would grow to love her husband over time.

Chase reached into his pocket and withdrew a business card, then pressed it into her hand. "If you ever need anything, night or day, I want you to call me. I promise to come, Natalie. Anytime, anywhere. All you have to do is call."

Natalie drew a shaky breath and slipped the card into her jacket pocket. "Goodbye, Chase." With that, she turned and hurried up the steps. Her hand shook as she shoved the key into the lock. By the time she'd gained the safety of the foyer, her whole body had begun to tremble.

"Put him out of your mind," she murmured to herself. "You've made your decision and there's no going back now."

Chapter Four

THE HOUSE ON BIRCH STREET was dark except for a single light illuminating a corner window on the second story. A crisp wind rustled the budding trees, and Chase tugged at the collar of his leather jacket to block the cold. He had stood in this same spot for the past three nights, staring at Natalie's bedroom window until the light went out and she went to bed.

He had tried to stay away, but he'd been drawn here against all his resolve. Why couldn't he forget Natalie as easily as she'd forgotten him? She was going to marry her fiancé and nothing he could do or say would change her mind. Yet some deep-seated instinct told him that he had to stop her. Why?

Was he so certain that they were destined to be together? Or did she simply represent a challenge, a prize he desired, yet couldn't hope to attain? He had always expected that he'd fall in love someday, but he hadn't anticipated that it would knock him down like a runaway train. He wasn't even sure if he loved her, only that, in the farthest corners of his heart, he believed they deserved a chance to be together.

Had they met in a different place and a different

time, he might have courted her slowly, letting love unfold at its own pace. But the clock was ticking and every hour that passed brought them both closer to an irreversible event—her marriage to Edward.

Chase ran his fingers through his hair, then leaned back against the hood of his car. What could he hope to offer her that Edward hadn't? Chase had lived his life avoiding responsibility. Perhaps if he held down a regular job, if he put some money in the bank and bought himself a few business suits, he might at least look the part. But the thought of spending every day behind a desk at Donnelly Enterprises brought a bad taste to his mouth.

Besides, office gossip was a difficult thing to overcome. He'd always been known as the black sheep in the family, the ne'er-do-well. Would they even give him a chance, or would he be doomed from the start? He'd fought so long and hard against the pull of his family's expectations that to give in now seemed like the ultimate hypocrisy.

With a curse, Chase turned to pull open the door of his Porsche. But he couldn't leave. He had to see her, to try once more. He started for the front door, but then took a detour around the corner of the house. The oak tree stood like a sentinel, the boughs nearly touching her bedroom window. Chase scrounged for a handful of acorns, then shinnied up the trunk.

When he was level with her bedroom, he pitched an acorn at the glass. It bounced off with a resounding ping and he waited. Three more acorns hit the window before he saw her silhouette against the lacy drapes. The curtains parted and Natalie peered out into the darkness.

He threw one more acorn to catch her attention, then waved. The window sash flew up and she bent over the sill and squinted into the darkness. "Chase?" Her voice was soft on the chill wind and sent a current of desire shooting through him. "What are you doing out there?"

"We have to talk," he said, sliding out on a branch until he sat in a patch of light from the bedroom window.

"Why didn't you just ring the doorbell?"

"Because I knew that when you answered I'd have to pull you into my arms and kiss you. I've been thinking about you, Natalie. I can't stop thinking about you."

She sighed. "You *have* to stop."

Chase straddled the bough and slid closer to her. "And I've been thinking about making a few changes. About settling down and taking life a little more seriously."

Natalie smiled ruefully. "That's funny. Because I've been thinking that I take life far *too* seriously. Maybe you're the one who has it right and I've got it wrong."

"I could change. If I had a good enough reason."

She shook her head, her hair tumbling around her

face. His fingers clenched as he imagined the silken feel of it, the sweet smell.

"I don't want you to change, Chase. Especially not for me. I spent my life becoming the person I am. Edward understands me and I understand him. There won't be any surprises between us. It will be all right, I promise."

Chase swore softly. "And when you kiss Edward, what do you feel, Natalie? When he touches you, does he set your blood on fire?"

"Passion isn't all there is to a marriage."

"Then tell me how you felt when I touched you. Be honest with yourself."

"I—I felt regret," she said. "Regret that I'd broken Edward's trust." She paused. "Regret that I hadn't met you years ago. With you, I might have become a different person."

Chase inched a little farther out on the branch, close enough that he could look into her eyes. "I think I love you, Natalie."

Her eyes went wide and she shook her head. "You don't even know me."

"I know that you can't marry Edward."

"We've had this discussion before," she warned.

Frustrated, Chase pushed out to the end of the bough. He was about to speak when a sharp crack sounded. Slowly, the branch gave way beneath him and he dropped like deadweight to the grass below.

Natalie screamed his name, but all he could hear was the sound of his breath being forced from his body. He tried to draw another, but the wind had been knocked out of him. Flat on his back, Chase closed his eyes and forced air into his lungs.

By the time Natalie reached his side, he'd managed to draw a few deep drafts of cold night air, restoring his health but severely damaging his pride.

"Are you all right?" she cried, taking his face between her palms and staring deeply into his eyes. "Lie still. Let me look at you."

Chase did as he was told, savoring the feel of her warm fingers on his face. He groaned as she bent over him and slowly ran her hands down his body, limb by limb. Her touch sent his senses reeling.

"Is anything broken? Where does it hurt? Did you hit your head?"

"I'm fine," he growled, trying to ignore the flood of desire that had pooled in the vicinity of his lap. She had no idea what she was doing to him. And no idea what he wanted to do to her.

Grabbing her around the waist, he tumbled her beneath him, stretching his body over hers and pinning her hands above her head. She twisted and wriggled, but her efforts to get away were feeble at best, her rhythmic movements becoming less unconscious and more deliberate with every second that passed.

"Let me go," she murmured, arching up against him, driving him mad with need.

He bent closer, his mouth nearly touching hers. "Do you really want me to?"

Her lips parted and her breath came in short gasps. He could hear the pounding of his own pulse and he fought for control. Had she just given him a sign, one word, he would have taken her right there on the lawn. But a flash of light against the house caught his attention.

Chase turned to see a police car slowly patroling the street. A spotlight glowed from near the driver's window and he cursed, then rolled off Natalie into the shadow of a large bush.

Natalie struggled to her feet, then brushed the dead grass and leaves from her damp nightgown. From Chase's vantage point behind her, the patrolman's light shone through the thin fabric, outlining her long legs and the soft curve of her hips, the spot where her thighs met. Chase smiled to himself as she waved to the police car, the sweet flesh of her breasts pressing against the nearly transparent fabric.

A voice boomed out of the darkness. "Miss Hillyard? Are you all right?"

Natalie crossed her arms over her chest, giving Chase a deeper appreciation of her backside. "I'm fine. I thought I heard a prowler, but it was just a stray dog. Nothing to worry about."

Chase reached out and grabbed at her ankle, growling softly. With a quiet oath, she pulled away, then stomped on his fingers for good measure.

"Would you like me to take a look around?" the patrolman called.

"No, everything is just fine. I'm fine, we're all fine here. Good night."

They both watched as the policeman slowly continued his patrol of Birch Street and greater Redmond. When the car was finally out of sight, Natalie bent down and grabbed the collar of Chase's jacket. "I want you out of my bushes and out of my life. Go home, Chase Donnelly. Now!"

He grinned and grabbed her hand, then kissed her palm. "I'm in love with you, Natalie."

"I said, go home. Get a good night's sleep. I'm sure you'll feel differently in the morning." With that, she lifted the damp hem of her nightgown and made for the front door.

Chase rolled on his back and stared up at the sky. "You're starting to like me, Natalie Hillyard," he called. "I can tell. It won't be long now."

"Go home!" she shouted.

Chase chuckled, the pushed himself to his feet. He brushed the damp earth from his jacket and jeans, then whistled a cheery tune as he walked toward his car. All and all, he'd had a fairly decent night. He'd told Natalie that he loved her and she'd once again told him to leave her alone.

But there was something in her tone that gave him hope. A little chink had appeared in the armor that she wore with such brazen determination. If he were a betting man, he'd have to lay money on the notion that Natalie Hillyard was starting to fall in love with him as well.

"A SILVER CHAFING DISH!" Natalie cried. "Mother Jennings, this is exactly what I wanted."

"A proper wife can never have too many chafing dishes," Mrs. Jennings intoned. Edward's elderly aunts and his cousins agreed, examining the fine silver as it was passed around the room. For Natalie's part, she wasn't sure what on earth she'd do with six silver chafing dishes, but she suspected she'd find out soon enough.

"I've never seen so much silver in my life," Lydia muttered from her place next to Natalie on the sofa. "But where's the silver toilet brush? And the silver monkey wrench? Surely you put that on your list of must-haves."

"Stop it," Natalie whispered. "They'll hear you."

Lydia snorted in disgust. "Let 'em. If you ask me, they're all a bunch of uptight biddies with nothing better to do than nose around in your life."

Natalie pushed up from the sofa and smoothed her skirt. "If you bid—" She cleared her throat. "If you *ladies* will excuse me, I'll be back in a moment." Lydia stood up to follow, but Natalie waved her off. "Mother Jennings, why don't you tell Lydia all about that crystal vase we received from Edward's second cousin? Lydia adores fine crystal."

Lydia shot her a murderous look before Natalie slipped out of the room. She slowly wandered through the foyer to the rear of the house. To her relief, the powder room was empty and she closed the door firmly behind her.

Running her hands through her hair, Natalie stepped over to the mirror and glanced at her reflection. But the image that stared back at her took her by surprise. Her face was pale and drawn, lined with tension. She touched the corners of her mouth and attempted to smile, but all she could muster was a grimace.

To be honest, she hadn't felt any measure of happiness since the last time she'd seen Chase, four days ago. Her mind flashed back to that night beneath her bedroom window. Natalie slowly ran her hands along her body, trying to recall what it felt like to be beneath him, to feel his hard desire cradled against her hips.

The longer she stared into the mirror, the harder it was to recognize the woman staring back at her. "What am I doing?" Natalie whispered, reaching out to touch her reflection. "I don't belong here."

Suddenly, she couldn't remember how to breathe. Bracing her arms on the sink, Natalie bent over and tried to calm her racing heart. "I don't love him. And I don't want to marry him. And I certainly don't want to call that old battle-ax 'Mother.'"

Her gaze fell on the telephone above the toilet. She'd grown up in a house that had one phone. Edward lived in a house with a phone in every bathroom and two in the garage. Natalie snatched up the handset, then rummaged through her purse until she found her day planner. She flipped it open and slowly dialed Edward's number in London. It would be nearly eleven there. Edward always went to bed promptly at ten.

She just needed to hear his voice. That would calm her nerves and wash away the doubt that plagued her mind. He should never have left her so close to their wedding day. How was she expected to handle all the stress and the prewedding jitters on her own?

After three rings, he picked up.

"Edward?" Her voice cracked.

"Yes? This is Edward Jennings."

She nervously picked at a thread on her skirt. "Edward, it's Natalie."

He cleared his throat and she could imagine him sitting up in bed. "Natalie! Why are you calling?"

Natalie frowned. He sounded so cool and distant, the same way he sounded when she interrupted him at work. "I—I'm fine, Edward," She pressed her hand to her forehead and cursed. "Actually, I'm not fine."

"Natalie, can we talk some other time? I'm very busy right—"

"Edward, you were sleeping."

"Yes, well, I've had a long day and—"

Natalie took a long, deep breath. "Edward, I...I—"

"What?" he snapped. "What is it?"

She wasn't sure what possessed her at that very

moment—whether it was his curt tone of voice or his reluctance to put her worries above his sleep. "I want to call off the wedding. I'm breaking our engagement. I can't marry you." A long silence hissed over their transatlantic connection as she waited for him to reply. "Edward? Are you there?"

"We'll talk about this when I get home," he said. "For now, I want you to calm down and consider your behavior. You're being irrational and impetuous. For God's sake, Natalie, grow up."

"I have considered my behavior," Natalie said stubbornly. "Believe me." She swallowed hard. "It's over, Edward. I'm sorry to tell you this by phone, but I can't go through with it. The wedding is off."

She waited, trying to still her trembling hand and her pounding heart. But he didn't say a word, didn't offer a protest or even a hint of surprise. Instead, she heard a click on the other end of the line and then, a few seconds later, a dial tone.

Natalie expected to feel some regret, some sadness. But as she stood with the phone in her hand, the only thing she could muster was a surge of anger. She'd called him for comfort, for reassurance. And all he could give her was a few indifferent words and irritation at having his sleep interrupted.

She dropped the phone in its cradle and began to pace the perimeter of the bathroom, growing angrier by the second. "It's over," she murmured. "I've done it and it's over."

Beyond that fact, all she knew was that she had to get out of the Jenningses' house. Had she brought her own car, she would have ducked out the back and made an easy escape. But Mrs. Jennings had insisted on sending a car for her so that Natalie might have help when it came time to return home with her gifts.

"Lydia," Natalie murmured. "I'll take Lydia's car."

But Lydia was trapped in the parlor, listening to an endless diatribe about silver patterns and fine crystal and the proper way to clean a chandelier. There was no way to get a message to her without facing the rest of the guests and making up some lame excuse to leave. Natalie had never been a proficient liar.

She snatched up her day planner from the edge of the sink and rifled through it until she found the card she'd tucked inside. Anytime, he had told her. She punched out Chase's cell phone number, then said a silent prayer that he would answer. He picked up on the second ring.

Natalie swallowed hard and tried to calm her racing heart. "Chase? It's Natalie."

She closed her eyes and let the sound of his voice wash over her. "I didn't think you'd call. God, Natalie, I've missed hearing your voice."

"You said to call," she replied, "if I needed you. And I do. I need you to come and get me. Right away. I'm in Redmond at 721 Kensington, right across from the square. Can you come?''

''I'm in the car now. I'll be there in fifteen minutes,'' he said.

Natalie let out a long breath, then smiled. ''Thank you.'' She hung the phone up, then sat down on the toilet to wait, nervously tapping her foot. The time ticked by on her watch and she tried to keep calm. Ten minutes had passed when she heard a knock on the door.

''Natalie? Are you in there?''

She opened the door a crack. The hallway was empty except for her sister, and Natalie quickly motioned her inside.

''What's going on?'' Lydia asked. ''Good grief, if I hear one more debate about the merits of sterling versus silver plate I think I'm going to tear my hair out. Are you all right?''

Natalie grabbed her sister and gave her a hug. ''I'm fine. I'm not going to marry Edward.'' She said it as easily as she might have commented on the weather.

Lydia gasped. ''What?''

''I've decided I can't marry Edward. I—I just called him and canceled the wedding.''

Lydia lowered herself to sit on the toilet, her mouth agape. ''When did you decide to do this?''

Natalie shrugged. ''Just a few minutes ago. It hit me all at once. I can't marry him. This whole shower is for nothing.''

"So are you going to hide out in the powder room until everyone goes home and Mrs. Jennings goes to bed? Or are you planning to make your big announcement before you leave?"

Natalie shook her head. "I called Chase. He'll be here in a few minutes."

"Chase Donnelly? You're leaving here with him?"

"If I can get out in one piece. I need you to go back into the parlor and keep everyone occupied. Especially Mother Jennings. I don't want to face her. Not yet." Natalie glanced at her watch again. "He should be here any minute. Go ahead. I'll be fine.

Lydia giggled. "I can't believe you, Nat. You're running out on your wedding and taking up with a man you barely know." She threw her arms around Natalie's neck. "Oh, I'm so proud of you."

Natalie returned her sister's hug, then opened the powder room door. "Go ahead. I'll call you tomorrow."

Lydia slipped out and Natalie waited a few minutes before she opened the small window above the toilet. She pushed out the storm window, then crawled up on the toilet and boosted herself into the opening. But either she had overestimated the size of the window or underestimated the size of her hips. Once she got halfway out, she could go no farther.

"Natalie? Are you in there?" Mother Jennings's

voice echoed in the hall and Natalie winced as she heard the powder room door open.

"Good God, Natalie, what are you doing?"

Natalie froze, wishing herself through the window and floundering in the bushes below. Anywhere but where she was. But there would be no quick escape, no easy way out. Natalie felt Mrs. Jennings tugging on her legs and she slowly slid back into the room.

"Explain yourself," Mrs. Jennings demanded. "What kind of behavior is this?"

Natalie straightened her suit jacket and tugged her skirt down from around her hips, then headed for the door, carefully avoiding Mother Jennings's considerable bulk. "I think you should call Edward," Natalie suggested. "He can explain."

"Explain? Explain what?"

"I—I just broke our engagement. I can't marry your son."

Mother Jennings followed her into the hallway, her florid face mottled with anger. "My dear, you can't be serious! The wedding is all planned. It's just a week away. The guests, the gifts, my reputation...!"

Natalie turned and faced her, her hands braced on her hips. "We'll call the guests and send back the gifts. I just can't do this."

Mrs. Jennings grabbed Natalie's elbow, her fingers biting into her flesh so hard that Natalie's eyes began to water. "Listen here. You will not embarrass this family. And you will not humiliate my son."

"I'm *thinking* of your son! I don't love Edward. I never have and I'm not sure I ever could. He's a very good man and he'll make someone a nice, dependable husband. But Edward and I don't belong together."

"You *will* marry my son," Mother Jennings threatened, "and I'll hear no more excuses."

Natalie was sure that Mrs. Jennings was about to slap her across the face, but she was saved by the sound of the doorbell. With a low growl, the older woman released Natalie's arm, pasted a tight smile on her face and hurried to the door. Her expression clouded with confusion when she saw Chase standing on the other side. "Who are you?"

"I'm here to pick up Natalie." Chase caught sight of her, then pushed past Mrs. Jennings and grabbed Natalie's hand. "Are you all right?"

Natalie nodded. "I'm ready to go now."

Chase led her to the door, keeping a careful eye on the older woman, who appeared ready to explode. "She looks mad," he murmured, bending close to Natalie's ear. "Who is she?"

"Edward's mother," Natalie whispered back. "Come on, let's get out of here."

He reached out and cupped her cheek in his palm. "Sweetheart, I'll take you wherever you want to go."

As he pulled the door shut behind him, Natalie

heard Mother Jennings screech, "Sweetheart? Sweetheart? Did he call you sweetheart? Come back here, you impertinent little hussy!"

Then Natalie heard Chase's laugh, warm and rich and filled with delight, and she knew everything would be all right. As long as Chase was beside her, there was nothing she couldn't conquer.

Chapter Five

THE TIRES OF the Speedster squealed as Chase pulled away from the curb. He glanced over at Natalie, whose face was suddenly pale. Then he slid his hand across the back of her seat and slowly began to massage her neck. "Take a few deep breaths," he said. "You'll feel better in a minute. What happened in there?"

She did as she was told, her gaze fixed on the road ahead. When she finally spoke, her voice trembled. "I—I just called him up and told him I wasn't going to marry him. I've never done anything like that in my life!"

Chase yanked the wheel to the right and slammed on the brakes, the car skidding to a stop. He reached over and turned Natalie toward him, forcing her eyes to meet his. "You're not engaged anymore?"

Mutely she shook her head, her eyes wide with disbelief.

With a low growl, Chase pulled her into his arms and kissed her long and hard. Natalie wrapped her arms around his neck and, after the initial surprise, returned his kiss in full measure, her lips growing soft and pliant against his.

God, it felt good to lose himself in the sweet taste

of her. For the past week, he'd thought of nothing else, though he'd been determined to put what they'd shared in the past. He'd even made plans to leave Boston, to take the *Summer Day* and sail her somewhere far away from memories of Natalie Hillyard.

Chase cupped her face in his hands, then slowly trailed kisses across her cheeks and over her eyes. Her lashes fluttered and she looked up at him and smiled. "Thank you for coming to my rescue."

"Anytime, anywhere, sweetheart."

Natalie blushed. "I like that, when you call me sweetheart."

Chase leaned back in his seat and braced his hands on the wheel. "Well, sweetheart, where should we go? This is your escape, so you need to tell me the plan."

Natalie blinked. "I—I'm not sure I have a plan. I guess I'm homeless. I can't live at the Birch Street house anymore. And my sister has a tiny studio apartment. I suppose I should find a hotel room somewhere."

Chase put the car in gear and glanced over his shoulder before pulling out into the street. "First we'll go back to the house and pick up a few of your things."

"I don't want to go back there," Natalie said, shaking her head.

Chase grabbed her hand and pressed her wrist to his lips. "It'll be all right. I'll go in with you."

The next few blocks passed in silence, then she suddenly turned to him, her expression creased with worry. "What do you think will happen?"

"Happen?"

"When Edward gets back. Do you think he'll be angry? He just hung up on me."

"What do you mean?"

"He didn't even put up a fight. He didn't tell me that he loved me. He wasn't even really upset. He just hung up."

"Any man who lets you go so easily doesn't deserve you."

"I didn't want to hurt him, Chase. None of this is his fault. Do you think he'll be able to forgive me...someday?"

Chase wished there was a way to calm her fears, to erase the regret that he knew she would feel. She'd been with Edward for most of her adult life, and whether they had loved each other or not, they had certainly shared some affection between them, an attachment strong enough to warrant marriage plans.

Chase cursed silently. This was all that he ever wanted—Natalie beside him, her fiancé a part of her past. But would she come to regret her decision? Would he be able to make her happy for the rest of her life? He wouldn't know unless he tried. And damn if he wouldn't try his very best.

"I think that, given time, Edward will realize you only wanted to find happiness."

"I am happy," Natalie said. "And scared. And relieved."

Five minutes later, they pulled up in front of the Birch Street house. Chase helped Natalie out of the car, then held tight to her hand as they walked up to the porch. But she stopped before they reached the front door and shook her head. "I don't want to go in there. Can't we just leave it like it is? I can buy new clothes."

Chase pulled her against him and kissed the top of her head, inhaling the sweet scent of her hair. "Why don't you wait out here and I'll gather up your things? It will only take a minute." She nodded and Chase took the keys from her hand and unlocked the door.

He found a suitcase under her bed and tipped her dresser drawers into it. Clothes from the closet followed, along with the contents of the bathroom's medicine chest. He wasn't sure what else to take, grabbing shoes from the rack and stuffing them into an overnight bag. When he'd packed all he could carry, he headed back down the stairs.

He found Natalie standing in the doorway, her gaze slowly taking in every detail of the foyer from just beyond the threshold. "I never liked this house," she murmured. "It always felt so cold and empty. So pretentious. I don't think it would have ever felt like a home."

"Come on," Chase said. "Let's get out of here. I'm taking you home."

"Home?"

"To my house in Sand Harbor. You can stay with me until you figure out what you want to do."

She placed her hand on his shoulder. "There's one more thing." Chase watched as she twisted the huge diamond ring off her finger. Then she handed it to him. "Would you put this on the table beneath the mirror? Edward always drops his keys there. He'll be sure to find it. Maybe he can take it back, or sell it...or give it to someone else."

Chase set the suitcases on the floor and did as she asked. He had accomplished what he had set out to do. He'd stolen Natalie Hillyard away from her fiancé. The diamond glinted in the light from the doorway as if to remind him of his part in this drama.

He drew a deep breath, then turned back to Natalie. "Ready?"

She took one last look around, then nodded. "I guess there's no going back now."

"No going back now," he murmured.

WITH EVERY MILE that passed, Natalie's life in the Birch Street house seemed to fade into the distance. The afternoon was warm and sunny, and Chase had put the top down on the Porsche. Natalie stared at the countryside as it flew by, her hair whipping at her face, the wind cold on her cheeks.

She felt free, unburdened, as if her life with Edward had never existed. She had put her faith in destiny and it had brought her to a crossroads. In the past, she had always chosen the safe route, traveling slowly and cautiously. But something had happened in that powder room at the Jenningses' house. A new road had appeared on the horizon and she had decided to follow it.

Natalie glanced over at Chase. She wasn't sure what would happen between them, but she wanted to find out. He'd promised her nothing except unbridled passion and unquestioned love. For now, that was enough. The rest would follow. After all, he was her destiny, wasn't he?

Sand Harbor was not far from Redmond, but Natalie felt as though she'd traveled miles and miles. Chase maneuvered the car through narrow streets of picturesque cottages surrounded by picket fences. Then, without warning, he pulled the car over and switched off the ignition.

"This is it," he said. He jumped out of the car and opened her door, then went to grab her bags from the trunk. "I'm not sure how it looks inside. My cleaning lady hasn't been here for a while so you'll have to ignore the dust."

Natalie stopped on the narrow cobblestone walk and took a long look at Chase's house. It wasn't close to what she would have expected for a Donnelly. The entire house could have fit into a small corner of the mansion on Birch Street.

The Cape Cod cottage was sided in beautiful weathered wood, gray with age. A wide porch spanned the width of the facade, the blue trim creating a pretty contrast. And a garden on either side of the front steps lay ready to plant with spring flowers. The house was only a few blocks from the sea, and she could smell the salt tang in the air.

It was the house she'd always imagined in her dreams of happy endings. "It's perfect," Natalie said.

Chase pushed the key into the lock, then stepped aside to let her pass. "I like it. I don't have much need for anything bigger." He followed her inside, her bags in his arms, then kicked the door shut with his foot.

She slowly took in all the details of the charming interior—the comfortable furniture, the threadbare rugs...the huge bed that lay just beyond the bedroom door. Natalie finally turned to look at him, a hesitant smile on her lips. "I—I can't believe I broke the engagement."

"You're not engaged anymore," Chase murmured.

"No, I'm not engaged."

He met her gaze and held it for a long moment. Then, without blinking, he dropped her bags on the floor and crossed the room in three long strides.

Natalie met him halfway, throwing herself into his arms and meeting his mouth with all the desire they had denied for too long. The contact was instantly electric, stunning her with its intensity. He picked her up off her feet and held her tightly, then let her body slide down along his until her toes touched the floor.

Without breaking the kiss, Chase fumbled to push her jacket off. She twisted beneath his hands and tugged at the cuffs, then tossed it on the floor. Frantic fingers worked at buttons and zippers as Chase and Natalie tore at each other's clothes. Moments later, she was left in only her silk panties and camisole, Chase in his jeans, the top button undone.

She had frightened herself with this overwhelming desire that seemed to engulf her the instant his lips touched hers. He held such power over her, breaking down her inhibitions until nothing stood between them. With Chase, she had no past. Everything seemed as if she were experiencing it for the first time.

"I—I'm not very good at this," Natalie said, a tremor in her voice.

Chase stepped back and stared down into her eyes, running his fingers through her hair. Then he kissed her softly and smiled. "You just haven't been with the right man."

"Are you the right man?"

Playfully, Chase grabbed her around the waist, bunching the silk of her camisole in his fists. He tugged her closer until her hips met his, the hard ridge of his arousal rubbing against her stomach through the silk and denim barriers. A devilish grin curled his lips. "Sweetheart, from now on, I'm the only man."

A giggle bubbled up from Natalie's throat and she pressed her face against his naked chest, a warm blush burning her skin. His heart thudded strong and even beneath her cheek. "Then how do we start?"

"First we get rid of the rest of these clothes."

"Here?" she asked, glancing around the room.

"We'll start here." His fingers slipped beneath the straps of her silk camisole and tugged them over her shoulders. Natalie felt the fabric drift down her breasts. Instinctively, she drew her arms up to keep herself covered, but Chase grabbed her wrists to stop her. Gently, he lowered her arms, refusing to accept her reticence. The camisole slid over her hips and puddled on the floor at her feet.

"Now it's your turn," he said, taking a step back.

Natalie took a deep breath and tried to calm her racing heart. What if she did something wrong? She had never been a very active participant in this particular activity. Nor had she ever made love in broad daylight or outside the confines of a bedroom.

She reached for the waistband of his jeans and with shaking hands worked at the zipper. Her fingers brushed along his hard shaft and she heard him moan. Impatient, he pushed the denim over his hips, kicking off his shoes and socks along with the jeans.

He had a beautiful body, so lean and hard, with muscles rippling beneath taut, tan skin. His boxers rode low on his narrow hips, and Natalie's eyes followed the soft line of sun-burnished hair from his collarbone to beneath the waistband, drawing her attention to the blatant evidence of his desire.

Emboldened, she touched him, lightly stroking him through the soft fabric. There was power in what she did, for his breath quickened and he tipped his head back, a mixture of pleasure and pain crossing his handsome features.

Suddenly, he sucked in a sharp breath and grabbed her wrist to stop her. Chase drew her hand up along his chest, then placed a kiss on her palm, an unspoken signal that it was his turn to torment her. With exquisite tenderness, he explored her body with his mouth. Her head swam and her limbs went boneless with every new spot he discovered. And then his mouth was gone and she was in his arms as he carried her toward the bedroom.

She wanted to stop him, to tell him that she wasn't ready. But her body had betrayed her. She wanted something more, something she couldn't describe. It was so close, twisting at her core in unbearable anticipation. And she knew only he could satisfy her now.

They tumbled onto the bed, a mess of rumpled sheets and crushed pillows, the faint scent of his aftershave in the air. He pulled her up against him and slid his hand along her stomach until he reached the lace of her panties.

Natalie knew her release was there, beneath his touch, and she arched up, choosing to follow her instincts, her body craving more. His fingers found her moist core and he began to caress her. Desire twisted inside of her and she cried out as the tension became too much to bear. His name crossed her lips, over and over in a soft plea.

And then Natalie's breath caught in her throat and her body went still. Suddenly, she was there—breaking, falling, drowning as wave after wave of pure pleasure coursed through her every nerve, every vein. It wasn't supposed to feel so incredibly good, so unbearably right. But it did and it only left her craving more.

When her heart had calmed and her breath had stilled, she pushed herself up on her knees and looked down at him, at his beautiful body stretched out in the tangled sheets. She reached out and ran her palm along his chest, taking delight in the fact that she could do so without hesitation. At this moment, he belonged entirely to her. And she wanted him, body and soul. "Make love to me," she whispered.

He groaned, then pulled her over on top of him. Soft flesh met hard desire and Chase quickly removed the final barriers between them. He brought her thighs up along his hips and Natalie felt him beneath her, ripe and ready, his silken shaft probing at her entrance.

She had always known that this was the way it should be, so intense and so uninhibited, carnal pleasure the only thing that mattered. There was nothing she wouldn't do, no act too intimate. With her hand, she guided him inside of her, sinking down on top of him until she ached.

They moved together, slowly at first. But passion overwhelmed them both and restraint was far beyond their grasp. Before long, they were both near the edge, frantic with need, rocking against each other, striving for fulfillment. He called out her name, a plea for release, and she met him there, in a single, soul-shattering moment, a moment she had never known before.

Later, they made love again, this time slowly and gently, and to Natalie it was new all over again. She hadn't known how good it could be between a man and a woman, because she had never known Chase. He had uncovered a different side of her nature, a passion hidden within her. A passion that would be his and his alone.

CHASE WATCHED NATALIE from the bed, tucking his arm under his head for a better view. She had pulled a polo shirt from his dresser and tugged it over her head, covering her slender body above the delicious curves of her backside.

She wandered around the bedroom, staring at the photos on the wall—sunsets, sailboat scenes, memories of his many trips around the world. "You've been to so many places," she murmured. "I've never traveled much."

He smiled as she bent, enjoying the tantalizing view. There were many places he wanted to take her, in the bedroom and in the world. "Then we'll have to change that. When you go into work on Monday I think you should arrange for a few weeks off. I want to take you on a vacation."

"But I couldn't," Natalie said. "I—"

"Why not? The day I came into the office, John told me that you never take time off. He told me that you and Edward didn't even plan to take a honeymoon."

"Edward hates..." She paused, a flush coloring her cheeks. "I mean, he hated vacations. He wasn't the type to relax."

"Well, I am. Where would you like to go? Tahiti, the Canaries? How about the Greek Isles?"

Natalie smiled winsomely, then crawled back into bed with him. She snuggled up against his body and threw her leg over his hips. "Why don't we stay right here? Two weeks together in bed. There are so many places I've yet to explore."

Chase growled and nuzzled her neck. "That sounds good to me. When do we take off?"

Suddenly, she sat up. "I'm famished. I don't think I've eaten in days. Can you cook?"

"Can *I* cook?"

Natalie pushed up on top of him and straddled his hips, brushing her pale hair out of her eyes. "I guess you should know that I can't cook. As a wedding present, Mother Jennings was going to hire a housekeeper for me. So, unless you cook, we might not be eating very well."

Chase spanned her waist with his hands, then gently moved her until she could feel his growing erection beneath the sheets. Her eyes went wide and she sent him a lazy smile. "Right now, I'm not thinking about food," he murmured.

With a playful shove, she slipped off of him, then walked to his desk, tucked in a cozy alcove near the window. "I need some paper, I'll make a grocery list."

He groaned and rolled over on his side, the sheet slipping off his hips. "We can send out, Nat. Come back to bed."

"No, I want to cook dinner. It will be another new experience for me." She rummaged through the stacks of files and papers on his desk, then paused and picked up a copy of Donnelly Enterprises' corporate newsletter. "Did you read this issue?" she asked, showing him the cover.

"I read every issue," he grumbled. "Come back to bed."

She opened the newsletter and pointed to a huge picture in the center spread. "Here I am. I don't really like this photo. I thought it made me look too...feminine. Not very businesslike."

Chase pushed up in bed, staring across the room at the photograph of Natalie. "Can I see that?" He held out his hand and she shrugged, then crossed the room and gave him the newsletter. Flipping through the pages, he felt an odd worry niggling at the back of his brain.

"That's the most recent one," Natalie said. "It came out two or three weeks ago."

"I read this issue," he murmured. "And I remember reading the article about you."

She sat down on the edge of the bed and rested her chin on his shoulder, her gaze fixed on the open page. "That's strange that you read it and then you..." The words died in her throat and the color drained from her flushed cheeks.

"I read it," Chase said. "I saw your picture but it didn't really register...at the time." He drew in a deep breath, the worry coming into focus. "Or maybe it did." His jaw grew tight. "And then a few nights later, I dreamed about you."

Natalie pushed off the bed, her gaze still fixed on the photo. "Then—then it wasn't really destiny. You didn't dream of the woman you were going to marry. You dreamed of the woman you had just seen in the company newsletter."

Chase didn't know what to say. The instant he saw the picture, he had come to the very same conclusion. Nana Tonya had planted a seed in his mind and he had dreamed of a woman. But was she really the woman he was destined to marry? "It was you in the dream, Nat. Not someone else. That's all that really matters." He meant to ease her fears, but even he could hear the doubt in his voice.

She shook her head, her hair tumbling around her face in unruly waves. Slowly, she backed away from the bed. "No, that's not right. This was supposed to be fate. You made me believe it."

Chase slipped from the bed, grabbing the sheet to wrap around his waist. "So what if it wasn't? We're together. We're happy. And I love you."

"Do you?" she challenged. "Or do you just think you do? Have you managed to *convince* yourself that you love me because of some silly illusion your grandmother put in your head? You can't tell me that this doesn't cause a little doubt, can you?"

Chase reached out and took her hand. "All right, maybe it has thrown me off. But forget about the dream, about my grandmother's prediction. Think about us, together. Think about what we share. Who we are."

Closing her eyes, she yanked her fingers from his and pressed her palms together beneath her chin. Then she met his gaze squarely. "I knew who I was. And I knew exactly what I wanted, until you came along and convinced me differently. Why couldn't you have left well enough alone?"

"Dammit, Nat, this shouldn't make a difference."

"Look at me and tell me that you believe that. That you aren't thinking that maybe this whole destiny thing is a load of crap."

He couldn't tell her that; he couldn't lie to her. He'd believed it as surely as she had, even more so. He'd allowed it to color his judgment, to override his common sense. He'd been carried away on a dream that really wasn't a dream at all. And now reality was crashing in all around them and he didn't know how to stop it. "We just need time," Chase murmured. "Time to think."

"This was all a mistake. Maybe I *was* supposed to marry Edward all along."

Chase swore out loud. "You can't believe that, Natalie. Not after what we just shared."

"But how do you know?" Her voice trembled with emotion and Chase saw tears well in her eyes. "You can't be sure. No more than I can." With a weak sob, she bent and hurriedly picked up her clothes, scattered about the floor. "I—I have to get out of here. I have to find a quiet place to sort this all out."

Chase reached out for her, but she evaded his hand. "Natalie, you don't have to leave. This is something we need to work out together."

"I believed you," she cried. "I really believed that we were destined for each other, even though I never believed in fate before. And now I find out that this was all a mistake. How could I have been so gullible?"

"This was not a mistake!"

She pulled her jacket on over her badly buttoned silk blouse, then snatched her shoes from the floor. "I didn't think," she said, pressing her palms to her temples. "Something strange happened to me when we met and I just...went crazy. I'm not this person. I'm not someone who acts on impulse, someone who jumps into bed at the slightest whim. I—I'm not...a passionate person."

Chase followed her to the door, reaching out to grab her by the arm. "Don't leave. We can talk this out."

She pulled out of his grasp and flung the door open. "I can't talk right now. I have to think." Without looking back, she stumbled down the front porch steps and headed toward the waterfront.

"Natalie, wait! I'll get dressed and come with you."

She didn't look back. "I need to be alone."

Chase closed his eyes and tipped his head back. What the hell had happened here? Everything had finally been settled between them, and now this! Sure, he'd seen her before. But did that really mean that his dream had been a mistake? He couldn't deny the momentary sliver of doubt he'd felt upon seeing her photo. But that was far overpowered by the love he felt for Natalie.

They belonged together, didn't they? He'd never experienced such intense attraction, such overwhelming desire until he'd met her. She'd become a part of his future, and he'd known since the moment he stepped into the elevator that he would someday marry her.

But how much of that certainty had been based on his grandmother's prediction and his subsequent dream? And how much was grounded in reality? Had Natalie always been there, deep in his subconscious, just waiting to pop up in a dream? Chase leaned back against the weathered clapboard siding of his house and pressed the heel of his hand to his forehead, his eyes still pinched shut.

"Is that a sheet you're wearing?"

Chase's eyes snapped open, and to his shock, he found his grandmother staring up at him from the bottom of the porch steps. "Nana Tonya! What are you doing here?"

"I am preventing you from being arrested for indecent exposure, perhaps?"

Glancing down, Chase saw that the sheet had slipped precariously low on his hips. With a sheepish smile, he tugged it back up. "Sorry. I was..."

"In bed? In the middle of the day?"

"Don't ask questions. I shouldn't have to explain my sex life to my grandmother." He pushed open the front door. "Besides, you're the one who has some explaining to do."

"Me?"

"Why don't we go inside? You can tell me why you're here. And I don't want to hear that you've had another one of your visions."

Nana stepped into the living room, then tugged off her gloves impatiently. "I am here because you invited me to have dinner with you. And I arrive and find that you have been—" she shook her head "—doing the wild thing, is that how you say it?"

Chase couldn't help but laugh, not just at her comment, but at the charming humor that her accent added. "You better not say a word, Nana. This was all your fault."

"Your sex life is my fault? Now this is news to me."

"The dream," Chase said. "Remember your vision? Well, it came true. That very night, the night of your birthday party, I dreamed of a beautiful woman. And the next day, I came face-to-face with her."

Nana Tonya pressed her palm against her heart. "This is true? You have met the woman you are going to marry?"

"I thought I did. Hell, I even had a hand in breaking up her engagement to another man. But then, right before you got here, things got a little messed up. Destiny isn't all it's cracked up to be."

Nana took a step forward and craned her neck to see into the bedroom. "She is still here?"

"No. She went out for a walk. You see, we discovered that she didn't just appear in my dream. I'd seen her before. At least, a picture of her, in the company newsletter."

"And this is a problem? Why?"

"Because it means that fate didn't have a hand in my dream."

Nana waved her hand and clucked her tongue. "But you love her, don't you?"

He had impulsively said the words to Natalie before, and had just as quickly doubted their truth moments ago. But he had never examined the real depth of his feelings. After a moment's reflection, he had his answer. "Yes, I do love her. I fell in love with her the moment I saw her."

His grandmother stepped toward him and poked her finger into his chest. "Then what is all this doubt? You love the woman and I would assume she has feelings for you. Why are you standing here talking to your Nana Tonya when you should be out looking for her?"

Chase stared down at her, shaking his head in bemusement. Nana Tonya had an uncanny knack for cutting right to the chase. He planted a kiss on top of her head, then patted her cheek. "I think that's exactly what I'll do."

Chapter Six

SHE HAD ASKED FOR TIME—time to think, to sort out the jumble of emotions that had tossed her life into chaos. Chase had found her that day, sitting on a park bench overlooking the harbor, and they had talked. But in the end, she still couldn't bring herself to believe that nothing had changed between them. So, he'd driven her—and her luggage—to her sister's.

Couldn't he see that everything had changed? She had placed her trust in fate, in the dream that they truly belonged together. She'd ignored her common sense and logic, two characteristics that she'd come to depend on during her lifetime. Natalie Hillyard did not take risks. She did not act impetuously or irrationally. And she certainly didn't fall in love with a man she barely knew.

Natalie stared out her office window, watching the twinkling lights of the city night through a dreary drizzle. This was where her impetuousness had led. She didn't have Edward; she didn't want Chase. She was all alone again, abandoned exactly as she'd been twenty years ago, as far away as ever from finding the security and the family that she'd always longed for.

She'd found it, for a short time, with Edward—only she hadn't loved him. And then she'd found it again with Chase—only she hadn't trusted him.

Natalie closed her tired eyes and rubbed her forehead, trying to massage away the tension. She had hoped to occupy her mind with work, but her thoughts constantly returned to Chase, to that flicker of doubt she'd seen in his eyes, to his uneasy attempts to calm her fears. If he wasn't sure, then how could she be?

Sighing in frustration, Natalie pushed away from her desk and crossed her office to retrieve her coat from behind the door. Though she didn't want to go back to Lydia's tiny apartment, to her sister's curious looks and sympathetic comments, she couldn't stay in the office any longer. She flipped off her light, then made her way through the darkened lobby to the elevator.

"You work very hard."

Natalie jumped in surprise, her hand flying to her chest. She glanced around the reception area, her gaze stopping on an elderly woman who sat primly in one of the guest chairs. She slowly stood, leaning heavily on her cane, then held out her hand.

"I am sorry to have startled you," she said, her soft voice lilting with an unfamiliar accent. "But I needed to speak to you."

Natalie glanced around the office. The door had been locked, the security guard vigilant. How had this woman gotten in at such a late hour? "I'm on my way home. If you have business with the company, you can make an appointment during business hours."

"I came here to see you, Miss Hillyard."

"Miss Hillyard?" Natalie frowned. "How did you know my name?"

"I'm Antonia Donnelly," she replied. "Nana Tonya?"

Natalie gasped. Antonia Donnelly was the majority stockholder in Donnelly Enterprises, the matriarch of the Donnelly clan. And Nana Tonya was Chase's Gypsy grandmother. Natalie hadn't realized until this moment that they were one and the same. "Mrs. Donnelly, it's a pleasure to meet you," she said, taking her hand. "What can I do for you?"

"I hoped that we would have a chance to talk. I have my car downstairs. May I offer you a ride home?"

"Of course." Natalie walked beside the older woman to the elevator, then stood silently as they rode down to the street level. "I'm staying with my sister. She lives near Boston College. It's not far."

"This elevator," Antonia said softly, looking around. "This is where you met Chase, isn't it?"

Natalie glanced at her, shocked by her psychic powers. Antonia chuckled and waved her hand. "Do not look at me like that. Chase told me all about it. There is only one other elevator, so I had a fifty-fifty chance."

"He told me you have these...visions."

"Hmm," she said, nodding. "I told him he would dream of the woman he would marry, and he dreamed of you. And now you are unhappy."

"He'd already seen my picture. That's why he dreamed of me. It wasn't anything magical at all."

Antonia shrugged. "That is of no consequence. He still dreamed of you. My vision was correct. I'm rarely wrong, you know."

"Rarely?" Natalie asked.

The woman reached out and patted Natalie's arm. "Presidential elections and pro football. I can't seem to get a fix on those. But I am quite good with the ponies, my grandson tells me."

The elevator doors opened and they walked out into the brightly lit lobby. The security guard nodded as they passed, wishing Antonia a good night with easy familiarity. Outside, her driver waited, umbrella at the ready, to escort them to the car parked at the curb.

"Come," Antonia said. "I will take you wherever you want to go. But first, we will have tea."

Natalie crawled in the back seat of the car after Antonia, then settled herself, brushing the rain off her coat. The car pulled into traffic as Antonia tugged off her gloves. "I was quite anxious to speak with you. After my vision, I have been curious."

"Mrs. Donnelly, I really don't—"

"Believe in my visions? Chase told me that. But I still felt it was important to speak with you. I was watering my houseplants this afternoon and contemplating a very sad looking African violet when I saw you. You were asleep on a sofa bed in a tiny apartment."

"I—I am staying at my—"

Antonia stopped her again with another wave of her hand. "I know. You are staying with your sister. Her name is...Lydia. An art student?"

"But how did you—"

"Chase told me."

Natalie leaned back against the plush leather seat. Was she really to believe in Antonia Donnelly's powers? Or should she merely humor an old woman who listened very closely to every bit of information her grandson offered? "When I called off my wedding yesterday, I became homeless," Natalie explained. "I need to look for an apartment of my own."

"You should be living with my grandson," Antonia said, slapping her gloves against her palm. "You would be happy with him. I can see it already."

"Another prediction?" Natalie asked.

"No," she replied. "I simply know my grandson and how he feels about you. He would make you happy—this, I know. And you would have very pretty babies together. I would like to be a great-grandmama."

Natalie shifted uneasily. "I don't think Chase and I are really meant for each other. We're so different."

"This is good!" she cried. "My husband and I were very different. And we loved each other deeply. Being the same is not always good. Different is better."

"Is that why you came here?" Natalie asked. "To try to convince me to go back to Chase?"

"I came here to convince you that it would be foolish to ignore your feelings for him." Antonia leaned forward. "Winston, take us to that drive-through restaurant that I like, the one with the big dinosaur out front. We'll have a nice cup of tea and some cookies. Would you like that, dear?"

Natalie sighed and nodded. A few minutes later, they were sipping tea from plastic cups and munching on dinosaur cookies in the parking lot of a fast-food restaurant. Antonia chattered on about Chase, relating story after story from his childhood until Natalie felt as if she'd known him for years.

Antonia didn't make another attempt to convince Natalie of the truth of her vision, nor did she urge Natalie to return to Chase. Instead, she enumerated the qualities that would make her grandson a good husband.

The last time Natalie had talked to Chase, he had promised to give her some time to think, and she planned to take all the time she needed to sort out her confusion. Had he sent his grandmother, instead, to plead his case? Though Natalie wanted to believe he might do such a thing, she got the feeling that Nana Tonya had come of her own accord.

When they finally arrived in front of Lydia's building, Antonia reached out and took Natalie's hand. "It does not matter how you come to love," she said. "It only matters that you love at all."

Natalie bent closer and gave Antonia a kiss on the cheek. For a moment, the woman went still and then she blinked. "Tonight you will dream of your wedding day," she murmured.

Stunned by Antonia's odd behavior, Natalie mumbled her goodbyes and then hurried out of the car. She ran toward the lobby of Lydia's building, then turned around and watched as the car drove off. A cold shiver skittered down her spine and she tugged her collar up against the rain before she headed inside.

Later that night, she couldn't sleep for fear of what awaited her on the other side of consciousness. She lay on Lydia's sofa bed, fighting off her exhaustion by doing complex multiplication problems in her head. And when she finally drifted off, sometime before dawn, she dreamed of her wedding.

Dressed in white, she slowly walked down the aisle. Through a haze, she saw Edward waiting for her, and nearby, his mother and father watched. But as she walked toward him, a wind whipped through the open windows of the church, clearing away the fog. Swirling around her, the breeze caught her veil, lifting it from her head to float above her like a cloud. She tried to catch it, jumping up until the tulle brushed her fingers. But it was just out of her reach.

She couldn't get married without a veil. She couldn't...she couldn't....

Natalie woke up breathless, staring up at the ceiling with unblinking eyes. Her heart twisted and she moaned softly as a shiver of apprehension coursed through her. Antonia Donnelly had been right—she'd dreamed of her wedding. But Natalie hadn't dreamed of Chase, she'd dreamed of Edward.

Edward...the man she'd been destined to marry all along. Her breath caught in her throat. How had she managed to mess up her life so thoroughly? And why had she allowed a man like Chase to push her off course?

Natalie rolled over and punched her pillow. Tomorrow she would set everything to rights. Tomorrow, she'd get her life back on track.

"I WAS UNDER A LOT of pressure. After all, nothing in my experience prepared me for the...social obligations, the responsibilities. But I'm hoping that you'll be able to forgive my behavior. My lapse in judgment."

Natalie calmly folded her hands on her desk, then looked at Edward and his mother. She had never expected that Edward would accept her invitation to talk, much less bring his mother along. But the pair had been waiting in her office when she arrived on Wednesday morning.

She'd had a stilted conversation with Edward late Tuesday night after he'd arrived back home at the

Birch Street house, and they'd agreed to get together later in the week to clear up the return of the wedding and shower gifts. In a small corner of her mind, she hoped that he might find a way to forgive her.

Mrs. Jennings cleared her throat. "I certainly am not going to ask you what prompted this sudden change in your behavior, though I have my suspicions."

Natalie knew Edward's mother was referring to Chase, and she wondered how much of Sunday's events had been relayed to Edward. After all that had happened, the last thing she wanted to explain was her crazy attraction to a wholly unsuitable man. A momentary lapse, that's what it had been. And that she'd actually believed their short relationship was destiny—well, that was too embarrassing to think about.

She had put Chase and their crazy affair in perspective—and in the past. And now, thanks to Edward and Mrs. Jennings, she'd be able to get on with her life.

"I really don't want to elaborate on my behavior," Natalie said. "Except to say that I'm terribly sorry if I caused either one of you any pain. I was faithful to you while we were engaged, Edward."

"Then the damage is not irreparable," Mrs. Jennings said, watching her shrewdly.

"But your friends and family, your reputation," Natalie murmured. "I can't possibly—"

"We haven't told anyone yet," Edward said.

Natalie gasped, staring at her fiancé. He looked so calm, so indifferent, effectively hiding his feelings behind a stony facade. He was a handsome man, although he rarely smiled. "You haven't officially called off the wedding yet?" she asked. Then she winced. "Oh, dear, I suppose I'm responsible for doing that, aren't I?"

Edward straightened in his chair. "I've decided to forgive you, Natalie. We all have our moments of doubt. And I know I can be...disinterested at times."

Natalie swallowed hard, astonished by Edward's admission. "Yes, you can."

"And I'd like to apologize for that. I hope to change. And I don't blame you for finding...solace in the arms of another man."

"Edward, it was more than just—"

"We don't need to hear the details," Mrs. Jennings said, sighing dramatically. "I'm sure we all know what happened. And it doesn't matter."

"We've both made mistakes," Edward said. "We can put that in the past."

"Then you can forgive me?"

"Yes," Edward said, pushing himself to his feet. "I'll expect you at the church on Saturday, Natalie. Please don't be late."

Natalie stared at him, aghast. "The church? You want to go through with the wedding?" Was he serious? Could he really forgive her so easily?

"That is why you asked to speak to me, isn't it?

You wanted to salvage our wedding plans. Well, I've agreed. You made a mistake, I've forgiven you and we can go on as if nothing happened."

"No, I—" She stopped short. If he was willing to begin again, she should at least consider his offer. "I had hoped we might..." She paused. "I never expected..." She took a deep breath. "I'll have to think about this. I'm grateful to you for your forgiveness, but—"

"Where the hell is her office?" The shout echoed through the hallway outside of Natalie's door. She recognized the voice immediately and it sent a shiver of apprehension down her spine. Chase. She'd known that sooner or later he'd get tired of waiting. She just hadn't expected to confront him in the presence of Edward and his mother.

John Donnelly's voice joined the fray outside and then her door burst open. Natalie's heart leaped at the sight of Chase, his vivid green eyes, his thick hair combed by his fingers. He looked like he had that day they'd spent in bed—only now he had clothes on. Slowly, she stood and their gazes met.

"I've been waiting for you to call," he said, a frown creasing his forehead. "Dammit, Nat, it's been three days! Do you have any idea how worried I've been?"

Natalie glanced at Edward and his mother, and Chase realized that they weren't alone in her office. "What are they doing here?"

"We were just discussing the wedding," Natalie said.

Chase's jaw tightened. "What wedding?"

Natalie cleared her throat and gathered her resolve. "Edward, Mrs. Jennings, thank you for coming and for your forgiveness. But right now, I need to speak with Chase alone. If you'll excuse us?"

They both stood, then walked past Chase to the door, Mrs. Jennings shooting him a venomous glare and Edward merely sniffing in disgust. Chase looked like he was ready to punch Edward in the nose, but he managed to control himself.

When mother and son had finally taken their leave, Chase turned back to Natalie. "That was him? That was the man you were going to marry, that pompous, self-righteous bluenose? God, Natalie, what did you ever see in a guy like that?"

Natalie tipped her chin up defensively. "Edward and I care for each other. We're more suited than you and I are."

"That's not true," Chase replied.

She drew a long breath, gathering her resolve. "Edward has forgiven me for my...I don't know what to call it. A fling? It turns out that he takes partial blame for my insecurities. And now that we've straightened things out, we can go on with our lives as if nothing happened."

"But something did happen, Natalie. We fell in love."

"No. We shared a brief infatuation. And that was only because I thought we were destined to be together."

"I still believe we are, Natalie. I want you to marry me."

"I—I can't. I'm going to marry Edward as I planned."

Chase cursed, then shoved one of her office chairs aside as he stalked toward her desk. He placed his palms on the smooth wood surface and stared deeply into her eyes. "Tell me this is all a silly joke, Nat. Tell me you're not serious about going back to Edward."

Her gaze dropped to her hands, folded in front of her. "Your grandmother came to see me last night. We had a very nice talk. And when she dropped me off at Lydia's, she told me I would dream about my wedding that night. And I did. As clear as could be, I saw my wedding. And do you know who was waiting for me at the end of the aisle?" She paused, then looked up at him. "Edward."

Chase laughed harshly. "Why do you believe that vision and not mine?" he asked.

Natalie took a deep breath and let it out slowly. "Because my dream made more sense than yours."

Chase studied her for a long time, his gaze probing hers. "It's not about dreams and visions and destiny, is it? It all comes down to one thing. You're afraid."

"I don't know what you mean."

"You're afraid to love me. That's why you're willing to settle for a loveless marriage with Jennings. You're afraid that if you love, you'll be abandoned, the same way you were abandoned by your parents."

Again Natalie tipped her chin up. "That's ridiculous."

He shook his head slowly. "No, it's not. It's all very simple, Nat. You won't let yourself love me because you're afraid I might leave you."

She bit her lip, the truth of his words slowly sinking in. "I—I'm going back to Edward. I'm going to marry him. And nothing you say is going to change my mind."

He sighed in frustration, then bent his head. Natalie reached out to touch his cheek, but he backed away, anger flooding his handsome features. "Don't," he warned. "I can't accept this."

"Don't you see, Chase? None of this was ever meant to happen. We had a wonderful time, but that wasn't really me you were with. That was someone pretending to be irresponsible and impetuous."

Chase shook his head. "That's not true, Natalie. When we were in each other's arms, making love, I was making love to you. The real you. The warm, witty, wonderful woman that I met that first day in the elevator. I don't give a damn about the dream and I can live with your fears. The plain and simple fact is that I love you. And I want to marry you. We can work this out, I promise."

"We don't know each other, Chase."

"I know enough to know that I can't live without you."

"Yes, you can. And I can live without you." Natalie slowly circled the desk and walked to the door. She pulled it open. "I've made up my mind, Chase. Nothing you can say will change it. I'd like you to leave."

He pushed away from the desk and faced her. "Don't do this to us, Nat."

"Please," she said, her voice barely a whisper. "This is what I want."

He raked his hands through his hair and cursed softly, then started toward her. She thought he was going to walk out without another word. But as he passed, his arm snaked around her waist and he yanked her up against his body. In the blink of an eye, his mouth was on hers, hard and demanding, filled with all the frustration she knew he felt.

Her knees went soft and desire welled up from her core, setting her nerves on fire. She returned his kiss, wrapping her arms around his neck as his tongue plundered her mouth. And then, as suddenly as he had drawn her into his arms, he pushed her away. Natalie looked up into eyes now as cold as ice.

"Remember this moment, sweetheart. Remember

how I make you feel. And when you're lying next to your husband in bed, a passionless shadow of the woman you could have been, maybe you'll realize that you made a mistake."

He turned and walked out of her office, out of her life.

Chapter Seven

NATALIE HAD FALLEN ASLEEP to the sound of rain, and when she woke up to the blare of her clock radio, it was still raining.

"Well, that nor'easter we told you about yesterday is here!" the DJ crowed. "Our weather gurus tell us that as much as three inches of rain has fallen in the greater Boston area, and it looks like we'll be getting some more because this baby is sticking around for a while. For now, all I can do is keep singin' in the rain here on Boston's number one rock 'n' roll station! Hey, if you can't stand my voice, how about a little Eric Clapton and 'Let It Rain.'"

She rubbed her eyes, slapped at the radio to shut it off, then stared up at the ornate ceiling of her bedroom in the Birch Street house. Rain on her wedding day. Though she didn't believe in omens, she was at least hoping that the weather would provide a suitable start to her married life.

Of course, Mother Jennings would be beside herself. How dare the weather put a damper on her son's big day? After everything the woman had been through in the last week, Natalie wouldn't be surprised if the storm sent her future mother-in-law right over the edge. That's all she had talked about at the rehearsal dinner last night, and Natalie was certain it would be the topic of endless breakfast conversation at the Jenningses' mansion. No doubt Edward's mother would find a way to blame it all on Natalie.

She glanced over at the clock on the bedside table. It was only 7:00 a.m. The hairdresser was coming at ten, and Lydia would be by to help her dress before noon. The two sisters would drive to the church together in a chauffeured limousine and arrive at precisely 12:50 p.m.

Natalie groaned and pulled the covers up to her chin. She wondered what would happen if she decided to arrive at 12:55 or even 1:00. Suddenly, she didn't feel like playing by the rules. In fact, she was beginning to hate all the rules— *Smile, dear. Be sure you talk to every guest. Thank-you notes must be sent within a week. Chin up, you're a Jennings now.*

Perhaps she should call Lydia and ask her to bring along her purple hair dye. What would Mrs. Jennings say to a nice streak of color beneath Natalie's veil? What would the guests say? She closed her eyes and smiled.

Chase would love it. He seemed to delight when she showed the smallest hint of impetuous behavior. She could jump naked into a vat of purple dye and he'd jump in beside her. In Natalie's mind an image of Chase flashed—of him lying in his bed, long limbed and leanly muscled. A tiny thrill shot through her and her breath caught in her throat.

It had been wonderful between them. Though she had tried to put the memories of their lovemaking aside, it was no use. They would be with her all the days of her marriage to Edward. But Natalie couldn't believe she was the only woman who had started married life carrying a torch for another man. Over time, the memories would fade.

She had made the right decision. Maybe she was afraid to love, but that didn't mean she couldn't have a happy marriage. Edward was a stable and dependable man—and he had been more attentive to her needs over the past few days. And he took his responsibilities seriously. She would never have to worry about him walking out on her.

Could she say the same for Chase? A man who lived his life footloose and fancy-free? He'd met her in an elevator and pursued her until she broke her engagement to another man. What would stop him from repeating the same impulsive behavior again—only this time with a more beautiful and available woman? Love was all fine and good, but she couldn't trust it.

Snuggling under the covers, she closed her eyes and tried to catch another hour of sleep. But thoughts of Chase refused to leave her head. She saw him behind the wheel of his car, wind blowing through his thick, dark hair. She saw him on his boat, in front of his house, and over and over again, in his bed, the sheets twisted around his naked body.

Cursing, Natalie sat up and shook the images

from her mind. Then she scrambled out of bed and grabbed a silk dressing gown from the chair. She would need to find something else to occupy her thoughts. She'd write thank-you notes, a task guaranteed to numb her brain.

As she hurried down the stairs, the doorbell rang. Natalie stopped, her hand clutching the banister. She said a silent prayer, hoping that Mother Jennings hadn't decided on an unannounced visit. Perhaps Lydia had decided to come early. Or maybe another wedding gift was being delivered.

With a sigh, Natalie opened the door. Standing on the other side was the last person she expected to see on her wedding day. "Chase." The breath left her body and her heart stopped beating.

His hair was wet from the driving rain and moisture gleamed on the smooth planes and angles of his face. She wanted to reach out and brush the tiny droplets from his thick lashes, but she clenched her fists at her side.

For a long time they stared at each other silently, but she saw the emotion in his eyes, emotion he didn't attempt to hide. "What are you doing here?" she finally asked.

"I brought you a wedding gift." His voice was low and warm, the voice she'd heard over and over again in her dreams, the same voice that had called out her name at the height of his passion.

He held up a beautifully wrapped package, small enough to fit in the palm of his hand. Numbly, she took it from him and forced an appreciative smile. "That's very kind. You—you didn't have to do that."

"I wanted to. And I wanted the chance to tell you that I don't regret what happened between us."

"I don't either," Natalie said.

He reached out to touch her, then pulled his hand back, cursing beneath his breath. "All I want is for you to be happy."

She stared down at the gift, toying at the satin ribbon with trembling fingers. "What about you?"

Chase shrugged. "I'll survive. I've decided to take a trip. My boat is in the water and I'm going to leave once the weather clears."

The finality of their parting suddenly hit her. He'd be gone, out of reach, so far away that the connection between them would be irrevocably broken. "Where will you go?"

"I don't have a plan. I'll just see where the wind takes me."

She glanced up at him. "I guess this is goodbye, then."

He nodded, his gaze fixed on her face, studying her intently. She could see the indecision in his eyes and she wasn't sure that he could bring himself to turn and walk away. Lord knows, she couldn't. Every instinct told her to step into his arms and hold on tight. But she'd made her decision and she couldn't go back.

"You're sure about this?" he asked, giving her one last chance.

Natalie nodded, biting on her lip to keep the wrong words from tumbling out.

Chase shrugged again and then smiled at her one last time before he turned and walked down the front steps. Natalie clutched the edge of the door with a white-knuckled hand, fighting the urge to call him back. She watched as he got into his car and started the engine, kept watching as he drove away and disappeared into the rain. He never looked back.

She stood in the doorway for a long time, waiting for him to return, the damp wind buffeting her icy skin. When she couldn't stand the cold any longer, she stepped back and shut the door. As the latch clicked, she felt a door close deep in her heart, putting an end to all they had shared.

Natalie wandered over to the stairs, then sat down on the bottom step, Chase's gift still clutched in her hand. Without thinking, she tugged at the satin ribbon and tore off the pretty paper. Inside the box, she found a small leather case, and inside that, a delicate antique compass, so small she could hold it in her fist.

She turned the compass over, wondering why Chase had chosen such an odd gift. And then she knew. Engraved on the back were the words she'd come to depend on in their short time together.

Anytime. Anywhere.

Tears pushed at the corners of her eyes and she

pressed the gift to her heart. She found solace in the knowledge that he'd always be there, just beyond the horizon, waiting for her to call his name. Their connection would never be broken, not by marriage or time or endless seas. He would always have a special place in her heart, for he was the only man she would ever love.

"NATALIE, it's almost time to go. With this rain, we're going to have to leave a little earlier."

Natalie glanced over her shoulder at Lydia, then turned back to stare at her reflection in the mirror above her dresser. The rain drummed on the windowpanes, incessant and numbing. "Don't worry. They won't start the wedding without the bride."

She carefully straightened her veil, then ran her fingers along the shawl collar of her gown. She could feel the compass, cool and smooth, where she'd tucked it between her breasts. *Something old,* she thought to herself, plucking at the netting that cascaded over her shoulders.

Yards and yards of silk shantung rustled around her legs, and she could barely breathe in the tight bodice of her wedding dress. But she didn't want to breathe. She didn't want to think. All she wanted was to get this day over with and get on with her life.

A wedding was supposed to be the beginning of a dream, but to her, it seemed like the end, the last page in a beautiful love story. She pressed her hand to her gown, touching the compass. In some strange way, Chase's gift gave her comfort, the courage to live with the choices she had made.

"Natalie?"

She slowly turned and faced her sister, a melancholy smile touching her lips. "You look so pretty, Lydia. Like a princess. Remember when we were little, after Mom and Dad died? We used to lie in bed and pretend that we were both princesses, kidnapped from the palace as little babies and forced to live as orphans."

"Waiting for the day that the king and queen would find us and rescue us," Lydia continued. "There would be a big celebration in the kingdom and we would wear beautiful gowns and diamond tiaras."

"And we would both marry handsome princes and live happily ever after."

Lydia fell silent, her eyes searching Natalie's as if she were trying to read her thoughts. She drew a deep breath and then let it out. "Are you sure about this, Nat? It's not too late to back out."

"Why does everyone keep asking me if I'm sure? First Chase and now you. I made my decision and that's all there is to it."

Lydia arched her eyebrow. "Chase? You've seen him?"

"He stopped by earlier this morning to drop off a gift. It's all right. Everything's fine. He understands."

"Then maybe he can explain it to me," Lydia grumbled.

Natalie pasted a bright smile on her face and made a slow turn. "How do I look?"

Lydia bit her lip, tears welling in her eyes. "Like a princess." She brushed at her cheeks, then laughed. "We'd better go before I dissolve into puddles. The driver is waiting downstairs."

"You go," Natalie said, her voice calm and even.

A frown settled on Lydia's face. "What do you mean?"

"Go ahead. I'm not quite ready yet. I'll take my own car."

"Natalie, you can't drive yourself to your own wedding. Not in this weather."

Natalie reached out and took Lydia's hand. "I'll be all right. Just go ahead and keep the guests—and the groom's mother—from getting restless. I need a few more minutes to myself."

"Do you think he'll come?" Lydia asked.

"Who?" Natalie knew exactly who Lydia meant, but she couldn't bring herself to acknowledge the hope that her sister's words brought. Maybe he would come. Maybe it would be like her childhood dreams—a prince on a white horse riding to her rescue.

"Is that why you want to wait? Do you think he'll come back?"

Natalie shook her head. Wanting it would not make it happen. They had said their goodbyes.

"He's gone. For good. And he won't be back. I just need some time alone."

Reluctantly, Lydia nodded, then walked out of the room. Natalie turned to the mirror, staring at her reflection, at the stranger that looked back at her. She wasn't sure how long she stood there; she didn't really care. She waited until she could wait no longer. Then she turned and walked out of the room.

The driving rain had turned into a deluge; sheets of water fell from the gray sky, buffeted by gusty winds. Thunder rumbled in the distance and a flash of lightning split the sky. Natalie grabbed an umbrella and scooped up the skirt of her gown in her arms, then hurried to her car, parked under the port cochere. Rain spattered the silk and wilted her veil and she cursed her decision to forgo the limousine.

Wedging herself and her gown behind the wheel was much harder than she'd ever imagined. By the time she reached the church, she'd be a mass of wrinkles. And she could already feel her hair beginning to droop. So this wouldn't be the perfect day. But then, she didn't expect a perfect marriage, either.

She swung the car out of the drive, fighting her veil and the voluminous skirt that made finding the brake and accelerator close to impossible. The church was only ten blocks away, but the streets were unrecognizable through the rain that washed over her windshield. The wipers slapped an irritating rhythm, but were useless against the downpour.

Natalie felt the car drift and realized that she'd hit a huge puddle. Water flew up hitting the underside with a dull thud. She traveled only a few yards farther before the engine died.

Leaning back, she closed her eyes. "Maybe this is destiny," she murmured, listening to the rain drum on the hood of the car. "Maybe I'm not meant to get to the church." She shook her head, then reached for the ignition. "If I'm not meant to marry Edward, the car won't start."

The engine roared to life, and Natalie slowly maneuvered through the water. The next intersection was blocked by more flooding and she was forced to take a detour. As she drove on, nearly every street was blocked by water or police cars or drivers with stalled engines. She was running out of options and wondered if she'd ever find her way to the church.

"If the next intersection is closed, then I'm going to turn back. This is a sign. I'm not supposed to marry Edward." But the next intersection wasn't blocked and she turned toward the church, her heart pounding in time to the wipers.

A few moments later, the church appeared, the steeple stark against the pewter sky. It seemed as though the rain was beginning to abate. Natalie pulled the car into a spot directly in front of the doors. Through the foggy windows, she could see Edward and his mother standing in the entryway. They waved to her, but neither ventured beyond the threshold.

Suddenly, the skies opened up and water poured from the heavens. There would be no way to make it into the church without getting completely drenched in the process. Natalie gripped the steering wheel and bent her head. "Why is this happening? What am I supposed to do?"

Cursing, she grabbed her umbrella. If destiny was going to play a hand in her wedding day, then it better get off its butt and give her a sign. "If I'm not meant to marry Edward, may lightning strike the steeple of this church." She waited and listened as thunder rumbled, but lightning didn't bolt from the sky.

Gathering up her skirt, she shoved at the car door and popped open her umbrella. Natalie ran toward the entrance, dodging puddles and squinting against the downpour. By the time she reached Edward and his mother, her hem was soaked and her feet squished inside of her shoes.

"You're fifteen minutes late," Edward said, his jaw tight. "What were you thinking?"

Mother Jennings's hands plucked at Natalie's gown. "My God, you're a mess. The pictures will be ruined. I'm humiliated. Look at you!"

Natalie shook out her skirt, then nodded to the organist, who loitered on the stairs to the choir loft. "I'm fine," she called. "We can start now."

With a sound of disgust, Mother Jennings grabbed Edward's arm and hustled him toward the sanctuary.

She quickly took her place in the front pew, then turned to look back down the aisle.

Lydia appeared moments later, their bouquets clutched in her hands, her face lined with worry. "Are you all right? Good grief, Nat, I thought you were gone for good. Edward was ready to send the guests home, and Mother Jennings looked like she was about to throttle me."

"I'm fine," Natalie said, taking her flowers. The processional sounded from inside the church and she took a deep breath and nodded to her sister. "Go ahead. It's all right. Really."

Reluctantly, Lydia stepped through the door, glancing over her shoulder once more to be certain that Natalie was planning to follow.

When Lydia was the proper distance ahead, Natalie pasted a smile on her face and began the long march toward her future. The guests stood as she entered, and she saw Edward at the end of the aisle, a perturbed expression on his face.

Her shoes still squished beneath her waterlogged skirts, and a strand of wet hair hung over her eyes, tickling her nose. She felt like the main attraction at a bizarre circus, what with water dripping down her face, undoubtedly causing her mascara to run. A giggle burst from her throat, surprising guests on either side of the aisle. Before long, she could barely contain herself, forcing back laughter at her ridiculous situation.

Halfway up the aisle, Natalie stopped, unable to

take another step. She looked at Edward and then at Mother Jennings, and then took a slow survey of the guests. Her life, her future, suddenly became crystal clear. "Oh, to hell with it," she muttered, wiping her wet nose with the sleeve of her dress. "What am I afraid of?"

A low murmur grew around her as the procession continued but she didn't. Lydia stopped and turned around, confused by the commotion. She sent Natalie an encouraging look, but Natalie shook her head and shrugged.

A tiny smile curled Lydia's lips. "Go!" she shouted.

Mother Jennings stepped forward, fanning her face with her program. She started toward Natalie. Natalie looked at her sister once more, laughed, then scooped up her skirts and spun around, tossing her bouquet aside.

Her feet nearly flew as she ran down the aisle. The murmur of the guests became an uproar, and she heard Edward and Mother Jennings shout her name. Shoving open the front doors of the church, she hurried down the steps, praying that she hadn't locked the keys in the car.

She'd nearly reached the street when she looked up and saw Chase's Porsche parked next to her vehicle. Natalie froze, rain pouring down on her, drenching her to the skin. Then the passenger door opened and Chase leaned across the seat. She bent down and looked at him.

"Need a ride?" he asked, a smile twitching the corners of his mouth.

"Yes, I think I do."

Natalie stuffed herself and her wedding gown into the Porsche, battling the yards of silk and tulle that stood between them. Finally, she pushed her veil aside and found him staring at her, a bemused expression on his face. She sighed. "You came for me."

Chase chuckled, then bent closer and brushed a kiss on her moist lips. "Anytime. Anywhere."

A STIFF BREEZE FLUTTERED the sails of the *Summer Day* as the boat sliced through the choppy water. Sand Harbor grew smaller on the horizon and Chase checked the compass, then steered the boat toward the southeast and the Cape Cod Canal. The rain had stopped somewhere between the church and the marina. Sun filled the sky and the air had warmed to a balmy temperature, though the weatherman was predicting scattered storms for the next few days.

In Chase's mind, there had never been a more glorious spring afternoon. His gaze came back to the bow of the boat where Natalie stood, her wedding dress blowing and billowing around her body, her veil obscuring her face. She held tight to the jib stay and stared out at the rough waters of Cape Cod Bay as the spray shot up from the prow.

He wanted to go to her, to draw her into his arms and tell her that she'd made the right decision. But she would have to discover that on her own, in her own time. He didn't know how long it would take for all her fears and insecurities to vanish, but he was willing to wait. He loved her and there would never be another woman for him.

Chase watched her for a long time, recalling the dream that had brought them together just a few weeks ago. And then, as if part of that dream, Natalie turned around and smiled at him, brushing at her flyaway veil with her hand. "Where are we going?" she called over the sound of the water rushing past the hull.

"Wherever the wind takes us!" he replied. "We'll stick close to shore in case the weather kicks up again. And we'll spend the evening somewhere along Buzzards Bay."

She nodded, then smiled. The sun streaming over his shoulder bathed her in light. He'd never seen anything more beautiful. His Natalie, his beautiful, sweet Natalie. They'd come to the boat right from the church, Chase anxious to get her out on the water where she couldn't change her mind—and where Edward couldn't find her.

The boat hit a wave and spray shot up over the prow, falling on her head. She waved at him playfully, then laughed. He watched in delight as she reached up and pulled off her veil, and with a shout, tossed it overboard. The net caught the breeze and floated like a cloud. They watched it drift in the spill of wind from the sail before it dropped to the surface of the water.

"Just like my dream," she called with a laugh. "The wind and the veil. That was in my wedding dream."

Natalie moved toward him, her shoeless feet peeking out from beneath her gown. Then she stopped and grabbed hold of the shroud, balancing herself against the sway of the boat. Slowly, she reached behind her and unzipped her dress, sending him a tantalizing smile. Her dream had come true and now his had come to life. Chase could only stare as she stepped out of her gown and kicked it over the side of the boat.

She was left in lacy scraps of underwear—a pretty bra and panties, a garter belt and white stockings. With deliberate care, she undid the garters and slid the stockings over her ankles. Chase groaned, but he couldn't look away, transfixed by desire. His knuckles turned white as he clutched the wheel of the boat.

One by one, the stockings fluttered over the side, followed by the garter belt. Chase felt himself growing hard. She took a few more steps toward him, and with a soft curse, he flipped on the autopilot, letting the boat steer itself. In three quick steps he was standing below her, his hands out to help her into the cockpit.

With a coy look, she tumbled into his arms, all soft flesh and sweet curves. He kissed her long and deep, their tongues tangling, bodies melding, her skin cool against his palms. She shivered and he pulled back and looked into her eyes.

"Cold?"

"Freezing," Natalie murmured. "But you can warm me up."

Chase kissed the tip of her nose. "What am I going to do with you? Such a wanton woman. You threw all your clothes overboard."

Natalie's eyes grew wide. "You do have something for me to wear, don't you?"

He shook his head. "Nope. Besides, I like what you have on. The perfect wardrobe for a first mate."

"Chase! I can't sail to paradise without any clothes."

"Is that where we're going, then? Paradise?"

She wriggled in his arms, then reached down and pulled something from between her breasts. It was his compass—her compass. Natalie held it up to him and he took it from her fingers. "I guess you did come prepared."

She pressed against him and he gathered her closer, wrapping his jacket and his arms around her. "I want to live life," she said. "I want every day to be an adventure. I don't want to be frightened of what's waiting beyond the horizon. And I don't want to settle for anything less than true love."

"What about your career?"

"I was thinking that I'd be happy never to walk into that building again."

Chase chuckled. "And I was thinking that maybe I should settle down. I've got an office at Donnelly Enterprises. Maybe I should learn to use it."

Natalie looked up at him and placed her palm on his cheek. "We don't have to decide right now. Let's just keep sailing. Let's find an island where we can be alone, where we can run naked on the beach and make love in the sand."

"A place with a tiny, whitewashed church where we can get married."

"Paradise," she said.

Chase smiled and kissed her. He wanted nothing more than this—the woman he loved standing next to him, the wind at his back and the endless horizon in front of them. Wherever they roamed, they would always have each other. For he had made a dream come true and he held paradise in his arms.

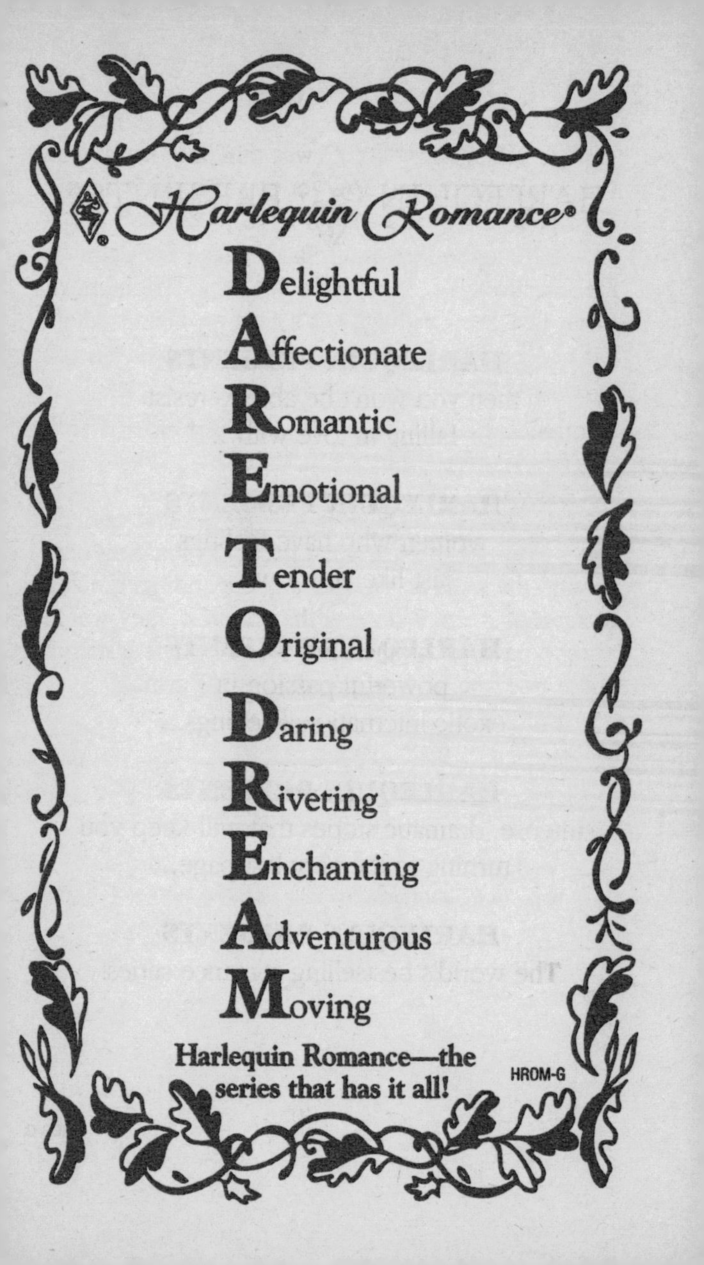
Harlequin Romance®
Delightful
Affectionate
Romantic
Emotional
Tender
Original
Daring
Riveting
Enchanting
Adventurous
Moving
Harlequin Romance—the
series that has it all!
HROM-G

HARLEQUIN
PRESENTS®

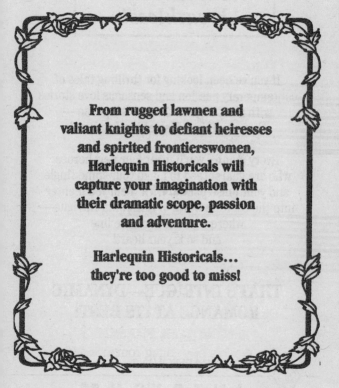

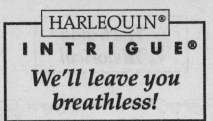